THE GREEN ISLE
OF THE GREAT DEEP

For Old Hector
and others like him
who were friendly
to many a Highland boy,
this phantasy.

The Green Isle
of the Great Deep

by
Neil M. Gunn

SOUVENIR PRESS

First published by Faber and Faber Ltd.
This edition copyright © 1975 by
Souvenir Press and John W. M. Gunn
and published 1975 by Souvenir Press Ltd,
95 Mortimer Street, London W1N 8HP
and simultaneously in Canada by
J. M. Dent & Sons (Canada) Ltd,
Ontario, Canada
Reprinted 1977, 1983
Reissued 1991

ISBN 0 285 62202 1

Printed in Great Britain by
The Guernsey Press Co. Ltd, Guernsey, Channel Islands.

CONTENTS

Contents

I

THE NIGHT BEFORE

Turning from the fire over which she had hung the big iron kettle, Agnes set the air of the kitchen into swirls. "Where was he going but to the River with that young boy Art. You would think a man of his years would have more sense."

Red Dougal laughed as he scooped up the water from the basin and washed the dried blood stains from his elbow.

"I wonder now," he said, with large innocence, "what they could be wanting at the River?"

"Wanting at the River?" she repeated. "What but the poaching that will be the death of me?" and the teacups rattled on a table staggered into position. "That River has been a nightmare in this house as long as I can remember and that's near forty years."

"I'm surprised at you letting them go," said Red Dougal.

"It's no joking matter," retorted Agnes, "and if the cow had died on him it would have been the price of him, and may Himself forgive me for saying that."

"Well, it was near enough to touch and go," admitted Red Dougal with a fair air of solemnity. "I have seen a small turnip in a beast's throat before now, but that one was stuck tight as a wad in a cartridge. I thought she was off with it."

"And off with it she would have been," replied Agnes, hurrying to him with a towel, "if you hadn't happened to be passing. We owe the cow's life to you, Dougal, and——"

"Whisht!" said Dougal, listening.

"Oh, it's that boy Art again," replied Agnes, who had no time to waste on such nonsense. "Hamish told me that they

7

The Night Before

were near at the River before he overtook them. The boy will be grieving now that he didn't get there!"

Red Dougal let his laughter go. He was a big hearty man, well up in the forties. As Old Hector and young Art came in, he paused in his rubbing to peer at them.

"It's getting dark in here," said the old man mildly.

"It might have been darker," said Agnes to the teapot.

Red Dougal could not contain himself. Art clung close to Old Hector and his face was pale in the gloom of the kitchen which was already beginning to dance the ghost dance of the slow peat flames.

Agnes stooped, brought the peats closer together, and set the flames to a more sprightly measure. Her face shone in the glow and Art saw that it was earnest. The tongs rattled as she dropped them.

"I think," said Old Hector to Art, "that we might have a little more light on the subject," and he took the funnel off the lamp.

"We have had plenty light on the subject," said Agnes to the dishes which she slid together on the dresser.

"Poof, woman," said Old Hector out of his whiskers, which he scratched lightly; "isn't the cow now herself again and shouldn't we be grateful to Dougal here? It's not every day he is passing our house."

"That's true," she replied cryptically, and added nothing, for after all Old Hector was her father. But Red Dougal laughed once more.

Soon the kitchen was bright in the lamp-light, the table laid, the eggs boiled, and the brown teapot ready. "Sit in," said Agnes.

But Old Hector had scarcely finished his grace before meat when the door rattled and in Morag came like a flame out of the night. When she saw Art she stopped and said "Oh!" on the breath that went from her.

"Did you think you had lost him?" asked Old Hector, smiling. "Come in, now, and take a cup with us."

The Night Before

"No, no, thank you," said Morag, and she turned to her small brother Art who was only eight past. "Where on earth have you been?"

"You may well ask them that," said Agnes.

"Art and myself," explained Old Hector, "just took a walk down the Little Glen to see what the grass might be like for the wintering of the sheep."

"Huch!" snorted Agnes.

Morag's brown hair shook and her teeth gleamed with mirth in her mouth. She was seventeen gay years at that moment and her mirth was infectious. "We thought he was lost again," she said. "You'll catch it when you get home!"

"He will not, then," said Old Hector, "for I told Hamish to tell your mother he was here. Didn't you meet Hamish on the way?"

"No," said Morag. "I—I—was looking up—up the hillside," and she looked confused.

Agnes glanced at her sharply. So Morag quickly started to get the story out of them.

She had hardly succeeded when a neighbour, Willie Macpherson, stared in. He was a sallow earnest man and when he asked, "Is the cow all right?" everybody began laughing except Agnes.

The news concerning Old Hector's little red cow must have spread rapidly for soon there were no less than five men, two women, and four boys in the kitchen, each from a different house. When Tom-the-shepherd, a dark good-looking young man, put his head round the door, Agnes at once said drily, "Yes, the cow is all right," and this evidence of humour in her eased the kitchen to a roar.

With the table tidied away and the fire going well, folk sat where they could, the boys on the floor. For no-one thought of returning home with the good news that the cow was well. Those at home would understand, for bad news travels quickly.

9

The Night Before

At first Art was troubled by the dark allusions men solemnly made about a young boy's going wrong early, but Old Hector was equal to them, and soon Art began to feel a shy importance in the doings of that afternoon. For Old Hector and himself had in truth set off for the River, the fabled River which Art had never yet reached. Art had not really thought of Old Hector and himself as two going to the River to poach salmon. His old friend had merely at last given in to his entreaties to be taken to see the wonderful River, the River where his own brother Donul and Hamish (Old Hector's grandson) and other men, young and not so young, going back into far distant times, had run the knife-edge of gamekeeper and river-watcher in many a wild adventure, full of night and danger, not to mention the old desperate fears of eviction.

So altogether the kitchen was charged with sallies of good-humour, and the quicker and neater the retort the swifter the laughter. Agnes had only to open her mouth and it was enough. She was over forty and had now got the follies of men within four walls and could deal with them. Old Hector's only unmarried child, she kept house for him, her mother being dead. Her feeling of responsibility for the good conduct of all those near to her increased with the years.

It was an evening for stories and songs, but Red Dougal could be relied on always to introduce some controversial topic, for he was that kind of man. Now he shook his head. "Ah well, woman," he said to Agnes, "it's good to live in a land where fun can have its play and not be put in a concentration camp."

"No-one was talking of a concentration camp," said Agnes. But now no-one laughed.

"It was an eye-opener," said Red Dougal to Tom-the-shepherd, "that last paper you gave me. Do you think it can be true?"

"It seems to be true enough," answered Tom, "though scarcely human, I admit."

The Night Before

"The world's in a queer state," said the sallow man, Willie, solemnly. "A queer state. I'll say that."

"You're saying a lot," replied Dougal, who could never resist countering Willie. "But that's not the point. It's not the brutalities I was thinking of. We've had enough brutalities in this land of our own in the times of the evictions, as Hector here knows. That's not what I was thinking of."

"What then?" challenged Willie. "I'd like to know what's worse than brutality?"

They all looked at Red Dougal. "You can ask Tom, there. He's better up in it than me, for it's him that gets the paper every week from the young fellow who was here in his little tent."

They all looked at Tom. But Tom hesitated. "Tell it yourself," he said to Red Dougal.

"Is it about the mind?" asked Old Hector quietly.

"It is," said Red Dougal. "It's about how they break the mind."

There was silence, and a strange reluctance came upon anyone to speak.

"Surely," said a woman simply, "it can't be true?"

"Isn't it written in the paper?" said Willie.

"I know," murmured the woman.

"If it is true," said Agnes, "God will call them to a terrible judgment for it."

The use of God's name held the silence profoundly, and Agnes could not have used it had she not been deeply stirred that night already.

"The trouble seems to be," said Red Dougal, "that, for some reason, He does not always interfere when wrong-doing is going on. What do you say, Hector?"

"His ways are beyond us," answered Old Hector simply.

"They are beyond more than us then," said Red Dougal, who was getting restive. "The prison camps are bad enough and the tortures. Indeed, I thought that beyond that human nature could not go. But it seems it can."

Each had a word to say, and presently one or two of the more ghastly stories were being retold, with a curious emphasis now and then on some detail that had specially haunted the mind. In this way a story became extremely vivid. If the victim was a professor or man of learning (they had great respect for learning) they could see the poor man staggering under his burdens, and they could see him at last trying to lift the big stone up—but the stone was too heavy for him—yet he nearly did it—nearly—and then the stone fell on him, fell back on him, and crushed his chest.

At the sound of his crushing chest, the women groaned.

But that was not the worst of it. That could be understood, in pity and in red anger.

It was this business of breaking the mind itself that was beyond them. "For the awful thing seems to be," explained Tom, who was expected to explain, because he had read most about it, "that when they have finished with you, you are different. In the old days they could torture a man, and the man might be broken, but when he came round a bit he was still himself, he could still hate them. Under torture, for example, they could make him sign a paper saying he no longer believed in his religion. But when they brought him to the fire to be burned, he could recant. He could hold his hand in the flames and say, 'This unworthy hand', as one great churchman did, as you know. But not now. He would not recant now."

"And why couldn't he?" cried Red Dougal.

"They say not," replied Tom.

"The bloody rascals!" said Red Dougal, and Agnes did not reprimand him.

"It makes you wonder," said a neighbour, "what the world may be coming to. It makes you think. It does."

They all thought for a bit, but could make little of it. A

horrifying ghost story could be understood, for at least with the mind's eye one saw the ghost and all that happened. This was the unseen horror behind the ghost. This left a man without words in his mouth or substance in his mind.

Willie, in his dry factual way, began to tell a horrible story of what was done to a little boy who refused to betray his parents. And though the women hated this story above all, they listened to every inflection in Willie's voice, hating the dry man's way he had of giving the facts, but listening as if life depended on it. For the women hated this story because of what was done to the little boy, while the men specially hated it because of the betrayal at its core. "They could," said Willie, "take a little boy like Art there——"

"If they could catch him!" exploded Red Dougal.

At that there was some welcome laughter, for not so long before Art had won in memorable style the race for boys under nine at the Clachdrum Games. They looked with special favour on him now, and his mouth, which had been a little open with the intensity of listening, closed, and a warm confusion spread over his face.

"As I was saying——" continued Willie.

"We know all that," interrupted Red Dougal. "What I want to know is—is this." But for once in his life the words would not come readily and he turned on Old Hector. "You're very quiet to-night."

"I do not know what to make of it," replied Old Hector. "The mind is all we have finally. If they take that from us—if they change that—then we will not be ourselves, and all meaning goes from us, here—and hereafter."

The word "hereafter" hung in the air and gave to the talk a new and piercing significance.

Red Dougal shifted on his seat defiantly when someone suggested that surely therefore it could hardly be. "But it is," he cried. "It happens. That's what we're talking about."

"What seems to happen," said Tom, "is that your mind is

not taken from you. It's that certain beliefs are knocked out of it and others put in their place. You are still yourself—but you're different."

"But how can you be yourself—if you're different?" asked Willie.

"We all change," said a quiet voice.

"No," said Old Hector slowly, "not in the things that matter. If we change in them——" He stopped.

They all grew silent. Never before at a ceilidh in Old Hector's house had there been such uncertainty, for never before had such conceptions of the unclean come so close to the thresholds of their minds. There was something of horror, with a weird feeling of vomit against it near the throat, a queasy blind feeling that knew it could say nothing without saying too much in wild and violent denunciations.

Art's face was pale in the lamplight and his dark eyes glittered as they looked up from the floor.

The talk went on sporadically and Willie had his say in full, but at last Tom got up, for he had a long way to go to the next township. As Tom left, others arose and folk stood for a little talking on their feet. Then Morag turned to Agnes: "They'll be wondering what on earth has come over us. We'll have to run!" Old Hector went with them hospitably to the door.

"To-morrow," whispered Art to him.

Then they were out in the night. Morag caught Art by the hand. "Isn't it dark?" she said. "Watch your feet."

"Watch your own," said Art as she stumbled.

She laughed softly and pressed his hand. Morag was the only girl he liked, particularly when no-one was seeing. All the same, he did not answer her hand-pressure, he just accepted it.

Morag was now like one rushing away to where it was always warm and friendly. Art understood this only too well. Yet he would like to ask a few questions about—about the terrible things, even though it was dark.

The Night Before

"Do you know what I would do if they were after me?" he asked in a low voice.

"You would run," said Morag, "so that they wouldn't see you for the speed."

"Don't be silly," said Art, "for no-one ever ran as fast as that. Did they?"

"Why not?" said Morag, whose own spirit seemed to fly ahead even faster.

"Sometimes—you know—inside me," confessed Art, "I feel myself going just as fast nearly as lightning. Queer, isn't it?"

"It is," said Morag. "Sometimes I feel I could jump over the moon."

Art gave a small laugh. "There's no moon in it anyway."

"There's always a moon somewhere," said Morag.

After a moment, Art said: "It's a queer world, isn't it? In some places things couldn't be worse."

"And in some places they couldn't be better."

"Do you think this a good place?"

"I do," said Morag.

"Do you think it's the best place in all the four brown quarters of the globe?"

"I do."

"So do I. I'm not even frightened of the dark now."

Just then a tall figure loomed. Morag clutched Art's hand, but Art was too stricken even to scream.

"Aren't you home yet?" It was Tom-the-shepherd!

"What a fright you gave us!" panted Morag. "Oh dear me!"

"*You* might be frightened, but I bet you Art wasn't," said Tom. "Were you, Art, eh?" And he ruffled the boy's silent head. "Come on. I'll see you as far as the corner."

Tom talked away, and Morag answered him sometimes, and soon they were at the corner.

"I've got something to say to you, Morag, about yon business." He turned to Art. "You just wait one minute. Only a minute." And he drew Morag back round the corner.

The Night Before

Art waited, hearing the murmur of their voices. Surely Tom might have told him if he could tell it to Morag! It was not one secret message he had run between them. But soon even their murmur stopped, as if they had gone away. He was alone in the dark night, and struggled against the cry that wanted to come up into his throat. But he would not let it come. He would not let Tom know that he couldn't keep a cry down.

Then Morag's feet came rushing, rushing and stumbling as if she had landed from the other side of the moon. "Oh, Art!" she cried and she caught him in her arms.

II

AT THE RIVER

As they came at last on top of the green ridge, they paused.

"That's the River," said Old Hector in a voice that spoke from long ago. The smile ran into the thicket of his whiskers. Then his face, high in the air, took on a look that might once have fallen from a weathered eagle.

Young Art looked at the River, too, but somehow it was not so big as he had expected it to be, nor so wonderful. It was new, certainly, and ran through strange country, but it was not marvellous. It was not the River of his dreams which he had desired so long and so ardently to see.

Thus in silence they stood for a little time.

"What do you think of it?" asked Old Hector, an ancient merriment stirring in his voice.

Art did not answer.

"Eh?" said Old Hector, looking down at him.

"I thought," murmured Art, "it might have been bigger."

At the River

"Bigger?"

Art, sorry to disappoint his friend, felt a little shy, so he withdrew his hand from the rough palm and explained: "It was Donul made me think it was big . . . as big. . . ."

"There is no limit to that bigness." Old Hector nodded in understanding. "But come, let us go down to the Hazel Pool."

As he took a step forward a large piece of paper hit his right heel and flew between his legs. Art dived after it.

"Strange," muttered Old Hector, pausing to look behind.

"I know what it is," cried Art, holding up the printed sheet with its horrid illustration of human cruelty on top. "It's about yon concentrated camps which men are put into and tortured in the paper of Tom-the-shepherd."

"Is it?" said Old Hector. "Can you see anyone about anywhere?"

"Not one," said Art. "This must just have come on the wind."

"That will be it." Old Hector nodded. "It will have come bit by bit."

Observing, however, how closely his old friend continued to spy out the surrounding country, Art began to look around more carefully himself.

"Do you think," he asked in low tones, "it's a good sign or a bad?"

"If things go by contraries, as they say, it should be good," replied Old Hector.

"I'll bury it whatever," said Art, and he put the paper under a grey stone.

This small incident heightened the mood of wonder he had been in about the fabled River, and as they descended the hummocky brae, he kept all his wits about him, glancing from one place to another, and stuck close by Old Hector, for though the River might not be vast in its scope, it was still the River, the place where adventurous things had happened and anything might hide.

At the River

As they entered the sheltered Hazel Wood, he stuck still closer by Old Hector, who, however, because of his height was able to pull down a branch on whose very tip grew a cluster of nine nuts. As he held on to the branch he told Art to pluck the cluster. This Art readily did, but even as the cluster crushed in his small hands the nuts slid out of their sheaths and lo! there were the nine of them, red and green at the sharp end but browner than honey at the blunt.

His eyes glistened as they glanced up and his old friend nodded: "Put them in your pocket."

Art very quickly did that, and then in an instant his sharp eyes beheld many clusters aloft in the sun in an airy life of their own.

"They're a bit high for us, that lot," said Old Hector.

"Wait you!" said Art, and straightway he started climbing.

Old Hector stood under him, telling him at one and the same time where to put his foot and how to be careful. Art's excitement now was more than he had looked for. Indeed it mounted with each foot, for no trees grew round his home, and the only wood he had ever been in before stood below the ruins of the Clash, the wood where his elder brother Donul and himself had gone to poach rabbits. And one did not climb trees when poaching rabbits: one hid under them.

"Am I getting high now?" asked Art, able for the first time in his life to look down on Old Hector's bushy countenance.

"You are that," answered Old Hector, "but mind yourself. Go easy."

"I'll do that," said Art.

But it was not so easy to go easy as all that, because the branch was rapidly getting thin and beginning to sway. His heart moved up and a small trembling came upon the muscles above his knees. The clusters looked nearly as far away as ever in that high airy world where sun and wind played together. He gulped down his fear and lifted his right foot. The foot got

At the River

a hold and, gripping the branch hard, he heaved himself up
and, not waiting to think, made the left foot pass the right
into another slender fork, and heaved himself up again. The
branch swayed and he paused to hold on.

"I don't think you'll manage it," cried Old Hector. "You
better come down."

This advice helped Art, and carefully now, his belly to the
branch, he groped aloft with his right foot. Up slowly slid his
belly. Down slowly slid the branch until its tip, which contained the greatest cluster of all, came in contact with another
tree and curved back and over.

Art hung on, a little sick with excitement now, eyeing the
cluster, so near and yet so terribly distant. He could have wept
for it to come to him.

"There's one just by your right ear and another under your
chin," called Old Hector.

Holding his breath, Art turned his head slowly, and all at
once saw the Hazel Pool away below him; and the ground
below him. Everything was below him and he was high above.
His hands gripped the branch tightly and would not let go.
Slowly the trees began to sway and move around and he
closed his eyes. A great urge came on him to cry out to Old
Hector, but no more than the smallest whimper came
through.

"It's all right," shouted Old Hector. "If you fall I'll catch
you."

When Art had waited for a little time he made his right
hand slowly let go its hold and feel for the leaves under his
chin.

"Out a little . . . yet," called Old Hector.

Art's hand closed over a cluster and he opened his eyes.

When in this way he had found two more clusters, Old Hector called to him strongly to come down.

But Art, lifting his eyes, saw the great cluster, full of colour
and brightness, and it laughed at him. There must be thirteen

At the River

nuts in it if there was one, and each as bright as the head of a tiny singing bird sitting in its nest. Over from him and up, they clung in merriment together.

It was too much for Art. Donul always did say that a thing laughed at you when you couldn't catch it. It ran off or flew away, mocking as it went.

"Are you there?" he called to Old Hector.

"I am. Come down now!"

Art reached upward along the branch and got a new hold with his hands. Slowly his feet followed, and then, with a mighty effort, up scraped his breast. As the branch swayed down the tip curled over. Art reached out a hand. He was short yet. Old Hector shouted very strongly. Up and out slid Art, and, as the cluster nodded in amusement, he made one grab at it—and missed, and lost his balance, and, clinging to his slender hold, went crashing down.

As Old Hector caught him, there was a crack like a pistol shot, and they both sat heavily on the ground.

"Are you all right?" asked Old Hector anxiously.

After Art had looked over what used to be himself, he muttered, "I think so." All of him was there—with the branch added. On the tip of the branch was the great cluster.

"Look! look!" and he scrambled forth.

"It's surely the king of all clusters, that one," nodded Old Hector, as he combed the leaves from his beard.

"Is it?" said Art, and paused. But he could not see the cluster properly. Wiping some water from his eyes, he caught his friend's glance. "It was the wind—up yonder," he explained.

"I can well believe that," agreed Old Hector comically, "for you knocked the wind clean out of myself."

At that, Art, now beside himself a little, laughed until the wood rang. He could not count the nuts in the cluster for laughing, but at last he managed.

"Surely not thirteen?" replied Old Hector.

At the River

"Count them yourself, then," cried Art eagerly, dragging the branch with him.

With Art's help, Old Hector agreed that the total number was thirteen. He shook his head.

"What is it?" asked Art.

"They look to me like the nuts of knowledge themselves."

"That's what I thought," said Art, realising the truth of it in a flash, "when I saw them looking at me up yonder," and he was astonished.

"It's a beautiful cluster."

"Isn't it?" said Art. "And do you think," he added, "that they were meant for the salmon of wisdom?"

"Who knows?" answered Old Hector. "But if they weren't, what other cluster would be?"

"There couldn't be another," Art agreed, and his mouth remained open for a little while. Then very carefully he removed each nut from the cluster and finally put the whole thirteen in the pocket which his sister Morag had made for him. It was a secret pocket, which his knife could not fall out of when he fell himself. He looked about him at the wonder of this wood. "I'll climb a bigger tree than that yet." Then he withdrew the branch out of Old Hector's way—and realised that it was broken. "It's broken," he said in a small, guilty voice.

"So I notice," observed Old Hector, who had been casting his eye along it. "Have you your knife on you?"

When Art had produced the knife which he had once got in a present from his eldest brother Duncan, Old Hector opened its big blade and began slicing off the twigs from the main stem. In no time, he had a stout five-foot wand, trimmed and neat.

"What's it for?" asked Art.

"You'll see in a minute," replied Old Hector. "Follow me."

And Art followed him to the edge of the Hazel Pool.

At the River

If he had thought the River small, his mind now began to change. For the Hazel Pool was not only long and far across, but of a depth more fearsome than the sea at the jetty, because on its bottom were dark boulders with darker shadows, and out in one place was a darkness you couldn't see through at all.

"Yes," replied Old Hector, "it will drown you easy enough, so keep well back." He stood on a ledge of rock above the water and slowly scanned the pool. Then he went to another point and scanned again.

"Can you see anything?" asked Art.

"Not a thing," replied Old Hector. "The light is bad."

Art could not understand how the light was bad, there was so much of it.

But Old Hector muttered again that the light was bad, and then, lifting his eyes, he scanned all the hollows and ridges within sight.

"Are you expecting anyone?" whispered Art.

"I hope not," said Old Hector.

Art realized that he did not care for the Hazel Pool very much. It was like a place that any moment might be some other place. "Will we be going home now?" he asked.

"In a minute." But it was hardly to Art he was speaking. Stepping down to the pool's edge, he put one foot on a stone that was two inches under water. "You watch," he said as he leaned outward with the stick in his right hand.

Gripping one of the loose folds of Old Hector's trousers, Art watched. The stick went out and down until its point disappeared under the near edge of a tilted flagstone. Then Old Hector gave it one sharp thrust. At once there was a whirling darkness below—coming up—and right on the surface the whirl boiled, spitting drops upon the air, together with a silver and a blue gleam. In an instant, the turmoil was gone.

Pointing, Old Hector said: "See him!"

And Art saw the living salmon swimming rapidly up the

At the River

off side—before he disappeared into the blackness of that place where the glitter on the water was brightest.

But Art was watching now, and in a few moments he cried: "Look!" And there was the salmon circling round the shallow bottom of the pool.

"You have the good eyes on you," muttered Old Hector. "Watch him. I've lost him again."

But Art hadn't lost him. "Look!" he cried, pointing.

"Don't move," said Old Hector. "Can you see him yet?"

But Art now had lost him—but no—but yes—but no— "He's coming back," whispered Art. "Look at him! look! look! . . . he's under the flag."

"Out he'll have to go in that case," said Old Hector.

And out the salmon went at even greater speed than before.

Hardly knowing whether he was on his toes or off them, Art followed the salmon to the shadow of a boulder higher up on their own side. Old Hector asked him if he was sure.

"As sure as death," answered Art.

"That's sure enough," nodded Old Hector, who thereupon took a large hook out of his pocket, again scanning the hollows and ridges as he did so. When the hook had been tied to the slender end of the stick, Old Hector had one more look around then carefully proceeded upward, Art at his hip.

After reconnoitring the spot, Old Hector drew back and nodded. "He's there!" he whispered and his eyes were all light together.

"Let me see," whispered Art.

And when through four feet of water Art discerned the dim outline of half the fish sticking out from the boulder, he nodded, unable to whisper.

"If I can," said Old Hector, "I'll throw him in over the ledge we're on, but keep you well back. There's a deep hole just below you there, where the stream hits the rock."

Old Hector looked as if he might talk now to Art of many things and times of long ago. In the moment that could wait, all of life could be told. A strange and silent smile, such as Art had never before seen, glimmered on his face, and in that moment Art entered into his heritage and he loved Old Hector and the presences of all those who had been here before, alive or dead. The creases gathered on one side of Old Hector's face in a fabulous wink. Life is good, too! Then he smiled to Art, looking at him alone, and Art could not speak.

Instead, he looked at the deep hole below him.

"How deep is it?" he asked softly.

"So deep," murmured Old Hector, "that we could only come out through the bottom."

"Where?"

"In the Green Isle of the Great Deep." And, lifting his fingers in a silent hush, Old Hector turned to his task.

Nothing could stop Art looking now, and hard by Old Hector's haunch, he followed the bright hook as it went down . . . down . . . down out of sight under the dim shape of the salmon.

Old Hector steadied himself, and Art, leaning over the water, watched, for his eyes had to be ready now.

As Old Hector struck, he had to sway backward to offset the great pull of the fish. It was a twenty-pound cock fish, and as he heaved he half turned and his stern hit Art. In that moment of exquisite balance, while the fish was hurtling through the air, Old Hector's stern was wildly grabbed at by Art.

The stern gave; Art fumbled his hold; and as he went headlong backwards into the river, he let out a wild scream.

There was an immense splash as Old Hector's body was launched above him.

Down went Art, the water gulping into him, choking him, choking him . . . until at last the smother of sleep had him and his arms fell away wanly, below, in the deep undercurrent where the stream hit the rock. And there Old Hector joined him.

III

THE GREEN ISLE

"I don't know the place at all," said Old Hector, "though I seem to remember it, too. The sea looks a bit bluer than the sea at home at this time of the year. Are you quite dry?"

"I'm fine," said Art in a small voice, for the place was altogether strange to him.

"The grass is as green as I have ever seen. And look! there are some cows up there. We should be coming to a house soon. Are you hungry?"

"I'm not that hungry," said Art. "See! There's a man yonder." And he held still closer to Old Hector.

"He'll be herding likely," nodded Old Hector. "It must be fertile land, this. Indeed it looks the finest country ever I have seen. And I can remember being on the Black Isle once, in behind Conon in Easter Ross, where the fine farms slope to the sea, and you see the mountains far away beyond the gleaming firth. I thought it very beautiful yonder in the autumn, but it hardly touches this."

"Look! he's coming down," whispered Art.

"That's fine. We should know where we are soon."

They watched the man as he strolled down onto the road in front of them.

"It's a fine day," Old Hector greeted him, smiling politely.

The man gave them a queer quizzical look as if he were thinking on the surface of his face.

"We are strangers here," continued Old Hector, "as you can see. We belong to the Clachdrum country and I was wondering if you would be so kind as to tell us the way to it."

The Green Isle

When the man's eyes had run over them, he said, "You will continue along this road for three days, and then you will come to the Seat on the Rock, and you will report yourselves there."

"Thank you very much," replied Old Hector. "Maybe we are a long way from Clachdrum then?"

"You are," said the man.

"Would you at least tell me, if you please, what the name of this land is?"

The man's eyelids flickered. "It is called The Green Isle."

"Thank you," said Old Hector, with a polite nod to cover the jump of his heart. "It looks very fertile country. You have some fine cows up there."

"I am the Coastwatcher here," said the man.

"Oh indeed," said Old Hector. "You will forgive me for not recognising the uniform. Have you many wrecks hereabout?"

"None," said the Coastwatcher. "But folk arrive in many ways."

"I see," said Old Hector vaguely. "Well, I suppose we may as well be going on." But still he lingered. "It will take three days, you say, to reach the—the place?"

"Three days and nights to reach the Seat on the Rock. And each night you will stay at an Inn. You will follow this road and not leave it, nor eat what you may see."

"How will we know the Inn?"

"It is in a town which you will always reach at evening and the road takes you there."

"I see," said Old Hector. "Will I mention that you told me to call?"

"I have already taken a note of your arrival." The last look he gave them was over his shoulder, but it still stopped short of the shallow laugh as he moved away.

"He seems a merry fellow," remarked Old Hector to the air in front, as Art and himself walked on.

There was silence for a time.

The Green Isle

"I did not like that man," whispered Art, with a backward glance. "Did you?"

"I thought by his voice at first that he came from Gairloch, but they are kind folk in Gairloch," answered Old Hector, "even if some of them are narrow."

"I thought," said Art, keeping what fear he could from his voice, "that he was laughing at us."

"I don't know that he knew he meant it," said Old Hector. Then he looked down at Art and smiled. "Do you know what I think he was laughing at?"

"What?"

"At my whiskers."

Art ventured a small smile himself then. "Maybe it was," he said hopefully. "Do you think it would be?"

"Why wouldn't it? I have the feeling that nobody has whiskers on him in this land."

"I was thinking that myself," said Art. "Are there no ones with whiskers in Gairloch?"

Old Hector gave a quiet chuckle. "There are," he said, and to Art he looked again as he used to look.

"Was that a good one?"

"Fair to middling," said Old Hector, and Art gave a little hop.

The country now began to open out, for they had come over the sea-ledge, and presently they paused to look at what they saw before them. And indeed it was a picture. A broad, slowly-uprising valley, with fields of grain having the sunny yellow in them that gold has missed; parks of green trees, glistening with red and yellow points that must surely be singing birds; a village of houses and each house white as sleep in the afternoon; cool green acres everywhere with sometimes a purple haze; paths winding up the slopes and figures moving on them; and, passing through all, the road that caught a pale gleam as it topped the ridge far away and disappeared with the sky.

Art looked up at Old Hector, whose face was like the face

The Green Isle

of a fisherman holding the tiller in times that need cool judgment. "Do you know this place?" he asked.

"No," answered Old Hector, "it is strange to me, but we'll hold on."

Art took a good grip of his hand, and after a while he asked, "What are they?"

"They are clusters of grapes," answered Old Hector. "I once saw them in a shop in Inverness."

"Are they good to eat?"

"They say they are, but I have never tasted them."

"There's a woman coming down there with a basket."

But the woman did not come onto the road; instead, she stopped a few paces up, her eyes opening wide.

"It's a fine day," called Old Hector politely.

She lowered the basket to the ground and stood still and erect in order to take them in. Then she laughed. She was a young woman and her laugh was bright and shallow.

Old Hector held on his way.

"Who do you think she was?" whispered Art.

"I think," said Old Hector, "that she was the sister of that Coastwatcher."

Soon they discovered that the glistening spots on the trees were not singing birds but apples and oranges. And they looked more happy and tempting in the clear air than any clusters of nuts. When they passed under a tree which hung over a grassy bank and Art looked up, the juice of the orange soaked into its glowing colour in a way that brought water from under his tongue.

"I could climb that tree easy," he said. When suddenly he saw a man's face behind the tree, he lowered his own and walked on with Old Hector.

Men and women were busy in the village, carrying the baskets of fruit to a space standing back from the square and marked out by poles, up which vines grew before they flattened and spread their branches in a cool green ceiling, from which flecks of light filtered through and danced over bare arms and faces and fruit.

As they packed the fruit in lattice-crates, the talk and cries, with a chattering of laughter, got mixed with the dancing specks. The skin of their arms and faces glowed as in firelight.

Suddenly all the specks stood still, the gabble and the laughter ceased, and the eyes steadied on the advancing strangers, as if a stream had stopped flowing.

As they passed there was a ripple of laughter, and in no time the speckled stream was more noisily flowing than ever.

Feeling the laughter in his back, Art was attacked by an urgent desire to cry.

"Keep your heart up," Old Hector rallied him. "They don't mean any harm."

"P-perhaps," stuttered Art, "they k-know no better."

"You're the best fellow for a joke in a whole day's march," nodded Old Hector.

Art was somewhat cheered at that, for he was always surprised to find he had made a joke. Often he had only to repeat what he had heard some old person say and it was enough.

"Is it a g-good one?" he asked.

"One of the very best," nodded Old Hector, laughing in his nostrils. "We'll keep our own end up whatever."

Singing now reached them, thin and clear. Children's voices from a wide building with a great flat roof. They decided it must be the school. Art felt more frightened than he had yet been, and Old Hector had to quicken his step.

"I know what they were singing," said Art, when they were well past.

"What was it?"

"It was about the farmer's wife who cut off the tails of the blind mice with a carving knife."

"Was it?"

"It was. We got it in school."

"It's an odd song to be singing in a place like this,"

murmured Old Hector thoughtfully. There was a moment when the clear bright voices had seemed to him innocent as the voices of angels.

As they were going out of the village they saw coming towards them a man who, though the oldest they had yet encountered, had not even a moustache on him. His face, however, was grave, and that was a welcome change.

"It's a fine day that's in it," said Old Hector with his friendliest courtesy.

The man stood and looked at Old Hector, and his thought worked just below the skin of his face.

"Every day is fine here," he said.

"I'm thinking," replied Old Hector, gathering his scattered wits, "it's not much use us looking for Clachdrum in that case!"

The stranger did not smile.

"We were told," proceeded Old Hector, and Art felt his hand working in its stress, "that we were to report at the Seat on the Rock. Will it be far in front of us yet?"

"You will reach it on the third day."

"We were in such a hurry," said Old Hector, "that we forgot to take anything with us."

"Each night you will come to a town and you will stay in the Inn."

"But we have nothing with us to pay for our keep?"

"You have enough."

"Thank you," said Old Hector, in the silence. "We are much obliged to you."

The man stood still, following them with his eyes until they had gone past.

Art was frightened to look back. "I would like to go home," he said.

Old Hector comforted him, saying that this was an adventure and that all life, from its beginning to its end, was an adventure.

"I'm thirsty," said Art.

"And there's a well."

The Green Isle

The well was so crystal clear that Art could not see the water except where it was running out. But when he had drunk, he felt cool.

Old Hector wiped the water from his beard and sat down. "It's good water, that," he said. "Very good."

"It's a pity," said Art, "you didn't ask him if we could take an apple."

"Are you very hungry?"

"I am," said Art. "I could be doing with something." And, putting his hand thoughtlessly into his pocket, he found the nuts. Proud he was when Old Hector complimented him, and he ran around looking for a stone, but not a stone could he find. Then he remembered his teeth. But though he kept shifting the nut into new positions with his tongue, he could not crack it.

"Have you your knife?" asked Old Hector.

"I have," said Art, and in a sudden fear gripped at the secret pocket. The knife was still there, and—"More nuts!"

They both remained still.

"The nuts of knowledge," added Art in a hushed voice.

"Let us leave them yet a while," said Old Hector. He took one of the other nuts and, cutting off its very tip, disclosed a thin line into which he pushed the point of the blade, levering it from side to side as he did so. The shell split in neat halves, and he offered the kernel to Art.

The kernel he brought forth for himself he sliced into small pieces, for his teeth, he said, were not too good.

When they had thus eaten six of the nuts they drank again.

"Are you feeling any better?"

"Not much," answered Art.

As they moved on, Old Hector saw the shells lying on the road, so he returned and picked them up and shoved them into the roots of the grass.

They discussed this act, which neither of them had ever done before, as they continued on their way.

The Green Isle

When at last they came to the crest, they saw another valley, broader and longer than the last, and far in the distance they saw a small white town, and remote beyond that the line of the horizon. The light was surely fading slightly, for now it was as if in all space there was only endless distance.

Old Hector began to tell Art a story, and the story was about a man who went on an adventure, and no matter what happened to him he refused to give in. The dangers he encountered were so fearsome and terrible that, by contrast, this adventure they were on was something to look forward to.

But Art did not look forward to it, and when at last in the half light they saw the town only a mile or two ahead, he stopped. He was terrified to go to the Inn.

Old Hector's reasoning now had no effect except a bad one, for the clearer the reason the worse Art got.

"Hush!" said Old Hector, following the boy as he ran up a little path by an orchard. The workers were all gone from the land and it was quiet. In a hollow at the top or back of the orchard was a great pile of straw. Art felt safe now, for he knew it was real straw by its smell.

"Look at that tree," he said as they sat down to rest. It was a big tree and wide-branching, and the apples that grew on it were ruddy and gold in the evening light. The more Old Hector looked, the quieter the tree became, until its stillness held the beauty that being pure was strangely ominous, and into his mind came the words: *The tree of knowledge of good and evil.*

Presently he heard Art's low voice: "What land do you think this is?"

"The Coastwatcher called it the Green Isle."

"Do you think," asked Art, "it might be the Green Isle of the Great Deep?"

"How could it be? because the Green Isle of the Great Deep is Paradise."

But as he gazed on the tree, Old Hector was sorely troubled.

IV

THE VOICE IN THE ORCHARD

When Old Hector began to come to in the morning, his hand hunted for the straw that had gone down his neck. This was so familiar an act that when his eyes fully opened he was the more astonished. Indeed his hand remained in his neck as he gazed at the tree, for now in the dawn he saw the apples and the gold and heard the singing. Never had so lovely a dawn come upon him in all time, and more than once in his youth a grey dawn over a moor had brought eternity's small shiver to the outer and the inner skin.

For a little while he was so caught up that to sit in silence was fulfilment for ever; but as his hand came away, time seeped into the opening it had left and he looked slowly about him. Memory and time being one, he missed Art.

Yes, the little fellow was gone. He looked at the tree, and he looked at the golden sky, and he hearkened to the spaces between the singing birds, and he caught a lush ploppy sound. On all fours, he peered round the wall of straw.

Art was sitting with a bunch of purple grapes in his lap and the chewed cores of two apples by his side. His mouth, fully extended, was just big enough to take in a grape whole, and, when it closed, a faint smash was followed by such a swallowed glunk that his eyes closed also and water ran from them as if the juice had overflowed. Then his jaws worked fully and richly; and hardly had the last swallow gone when the next grape was coming up. He spat out nothing.

Old Hector's own throat made a dry swallow and Art looked swiftly round. Colour ran over his face until it was nearly as red as his lips; his eyes glistened in the mixture of shame and challenge that brings life to being everywhere.

33

The Voice in the Orchard

"What's this you're at?" breathed Old Hector.

"I'm only eating," answered Art, with a small cock to his head, his eyes watching. Then, whatever he saw, he said, "Try one."

Old Hector shook his head and took the berry from Art's eager hand. As Old Hector opened his mouth, Art's opened in sympathy and closed as Old Hector's closed. Then Art watched, and when he heard the great glunk and saw the tears, he laughed, and laid the bunch between them, and, thrusting his hand under the straw, brought forth an apple which he presented to his old friend, saying, "It doesn't matter if your teeth are not good: try it."

Then Art had some fun, for try as he would the apple bobbed against Old Hector's mouth and among his whiskers in an elusive manner.

"Put your teeth in it," Art encouraged him, "like this," and quickly drawing another apple forth, he had a chunk of it in his mouth in no time.

At last there was a breaking sound, and Old Hector began to munch. And because he was surprised at the ease with which he munched, Art nodded, saying, "Didn't I tell you!"

Art himself, however, went back to the grapes; and when Old Hector had finished his apple, he went back to the grapes also.

As Art produced another bunch, Old Hector said, "God bless me!" And Art laughed, for he had been so afraid when gathering the fruit that he had been reckless.

"I thought," he said, "we might as well be killed for a sheep as a lamb."

And then Old Hector laughed in that lovely morning.

When they had hidden the seven apple cores under the straw, Old Hector got up and looked about him. "I think," he said, "we could give the town a miss if we kept to the hillside."

"I was thinking that myself," said Art.

There was no-one about, and wandering by the orchards and

The Voice in the Orchard

below the terraces of vines, they found this new land very beautiful. The birds were still singing, and Art, now full of an abounding energy, raced here and there to try to steal a proper glimpse of them. Often he called to Old Hector in a quick undertone, but by the time his friend came up the bird would be gone.

They were sorry to have to go down onto the road again, but men and women could be seen wandering out into the fields, and as they presently paused to look back at the town, they beheld a small company leaving it.

"Who will they be?" asked Art.

"They will be those who slept at the Inn," answered Old Hector, and he was thoughtful.

"We won't let them catch up on us, will we?"

"Not if we can help it."

Silence fell on them, and into it crept the uneasiness for which there was no word. When they met a grave man, Old Hector said in a pleasant voice, "It's a fine morning," and walked past him. The man stood looking after them.

"Who do you think he'll be?" asked Art.

"I think he's one sent to see that we keep on the right way."

But Art was not so frightened as he was yesterday. And he could not help recalling the fruit.

"To tell the truth," said Old Hector, "I feel as if it was making me younger."

"Do you? That's funny."

"How so?"

"Because it's making me feel bigger."

Old Hector looked at him. "One thing is certain," he said, "and that is that you're a brave little fellow."

Art looked back over his shoulder. "I don't mind much," he said, "supposing they are coming."

"Why should we?"

"What's it to us?" said Art. "Where do you think we'll sleep to-night?"

The Voice in the Orchard

"At the Inn," said Old Hector.

"No," said Art. "Why?"

"Because we must," answered Old Hector. "You heard what the Coastwatcher said. If we don't do the right thing it might go against us."

"Where?"

"At the Seat on the Rock."

"I don't want to go to that place," cried Art suddenly.

"We'll have to go there," said Old Hector quietly. "It's ordained."

"I don't care, su-supposing it is," said Art.

"Hush," said Old Hector. "Besides, once we're there, then you'll have all the food you want."

"I will not," said Art obstinately.

But after a time he quietened and even began to think that this new world was a better place than it had been yesterday. Old Hector stopped wishing anyone a good day.

Once a four-wheeled vehicle, drawn by two chestnut horses, came up behind and went bounding past. They discussed it at length, from the horses to what was inside the crates. Art said he knew what was inside the crates all right!

When they came to the crest, they saw a greater valley, vaster distances, and a town that was bigger than the last. But Old Hector's vision steadied on the remote horizon. Beyond it must be the Seat on the Rock.

For a while he walked in silence, lost in thought.

Art was caught up into this silence, too, for something in the bright extended air was at once beautiful and sad. It may have been just the great distance, as though brightness must be in small compass for the eye to quicken.

However it was, nothing was said between them, and only when Art felt he was on a pilgrimage did queerness come at him. He glanced back and saw the group that had left the Inn. They kept together and yet were strung out on the road, and their heads looked as if they were hooded.

The Voice in the Orchard

In a few yards the crest hid them from his view, and he wanted to run.

He explained his desire to Old Hector, who, awaking to meaning, quickened his stride. Art trotted and felt a little better.

"We won't let them gain on us, will we?"

In front and behind, the upper and the nether millstone. "Not if we can help it," answered Old Hector.

But the long day passed and they were still on the road, the town near at hand and the pilgrims behind.

"I'm not going to the Inn," said Art, stopping suddenly.

"Won't you come with Old Hector?"

"No," answered Art and he began to cry.

"Hush," said Old Hector.

Art ran up by the side of an orchard and Old Hector went after him.

Upon the straw above the orchard, Old Hector had to sit down, and now he was so weary with his thought that he stared through it.

Presently Art's face came glimmering in the dusk and Old Hector looked upon the grapes.

The dawn was lovelier than the dawn before, or so it appeared to them as they set out, for they had eaten more this time than the last.

They avoided the town, and in the early hours even the road was fresh as a road on a moor. They were happier together than they had yet been, for indeed Old Hector could not see any great harm in their sleeping out and so saving labour to the folk of the Inn, and as for the fruit, they would have had to eat something anyway. So strangely refreshing was the fruit, too, that as they went on an odd pleasant fantasy was born in them, and they imagined that if they could thus continue to journey they might in time find a way to the place that would lead them by a long curve round to another place, and so to the place beyond that, after which it might be fairly plain sailing back to the starting place where the peewits made their home in freedom—in Clachdrum.

But the crest came at last, and the valley, and a town far on its other side, and each distance seemed greater than any before, and more inexorable.

Of all this, however, Old Hector saw little, for his eyes were held by a mountain that rose beyond the town and against the sky. This mountain looked exactly like the great magic mountain of Sutherland that is named Ben Laoghal, and pronounced Ben Loyal by many. He counted its peaks and they were seven. But, as he looked, the shining light that had come into his eyes slowly died. That was not Ben Laoghal: it was the Seat on the Rock. And now he knew why Ben Laoghal had always appeared as a towering of ramparts and battlements.

About a mile from the approaches to the town, Art left the road and Old Hector did not catch him until, amid the green peace and the flecked shadows, they stopped to listen, and from far behind heard the shuffling of the feet of the swollen body of the pilgrimage. In the dusk the straw piled its pale gold.

Art was a nimble climber now and when he gave a low cry, Old Hector went round the corner. "Catch!" said Art's voice above him, and one after another four oranges dropped down.

They hadn't had an orange yet, and they were thirsty. The fragrance bathed the senses in a sweet cloud. The first gush into the mouth set the eyes in a swimming dream. The pith dissolved and slid away. The second orange followed the first without interruption. But if Art was smaller he was quicker, and before Old Hector started saying "Ha-a-a", Art had a third orange in his hand, for he had brought two down on his person.

"I would not have believed it possible——" began Old Hector, squeezing his beard, but Art was gone.

With a mighty grape cluster in each hand, Art staggered back. For though the apple was good beyond all belief, and the orange beyond all credibility, Art preferred the grape. He had, however, two apples on him.

So they made festival that night, for Old Hector felt it might be their last together, and he began telling Art a story. When the story stopped having words, Old Hector fell asleep, one second after Art.

But it had to happen as Old Hector knew, and it happened as he awoke in the dawn. Art was gone. The stillness was on the orchard, save for a small shiver of leaves in an apple tree. From that tree Art dropped. A voice called from the edge of the orchard and Art stood.

The man came, and came on. When the man stopped, Art ran. Old Hector arose.

"I sent him," said Old Hector, "for the fruit."

The darkness of the man's eyes made his face pale. He stood straight and quiet, slim and well built, a man perhaps in his early thirties, and he looked at them but did not speak.

"We thought," said Old Hector, "that with so many pilgrims there might be no room at the Inn."

"There is always room at the Inn," said the man.

No more excuses could live in that dawn so pure in its beauty, and what was ominous became finer than a thin wire.

"Follow me," said the man. And they followed him without a word.

V

THE SEAT ON THE ROCK

As the man walked before them, Old Hector could not help seeing what was obviously the bulge of apples in his pocket, and this comforted him a little, for it showed it must be quite natural in this land to pluck the fruit off the trees. Indeed, if it wasn't natural here, where would it be?

The Seat on the Rock

When the man had come to the off corner of that orchard he did not turn down to the town, but instead followed a little path below the vine terraces until presently he entered a hollow that was like a corrie; and there was a cottage, with cattle grazing on the slopes. They were small dun cattle, with short blue horns white-tipped, a full neck, and when they lifted their heads they looked like stags. Two deerhounds came towards the man with slow speed.

"Hush," whispered Old Hector, "they won't touch you." The man kept the dogs in, and as they approached the cottage a woman appeared in the door. At sight of her, Art's heart turned over in him, for he thought she was Peigi Maclean who was betrothed to his brother Duncan. He had only seen her face once, in the crowd at the Games before he had won the race for boys under nine. Peigi's face had looked at him then in a dark intimacy and smiled. This face did not smile, though it looked.

"It's a fine morning, ma'm," said Old Hector politely.

She glanced at the man.

"I found them above the orchard," he said to her in a level voice, "and I thought I'd take them the short-cut to the Seat." He seemed uneasy.

"But didn't they sleep at the Inn?"

"No, ma'm," answered Old Hector. "The little fellow here was a bit afraid of it and we slept out."

Her dark eyes dropped from Old Hector's face to Art's. Art lowered his forehead.

"How long have you been doing that?" and she gazed at Old Hector.

"Only for three nights. We are used to the open country and we have lost no time."

"But—have you had no food?"

"To tell the truth, ma'm, we did have a little at night and in the morning. We ate the fruit."

"The fruit!" It was hardly more than a whisper.

The Seat on the Rock

"I am sorry if we have done wrong," said Old Hector, breaking the silence. "But does not everyone eat the fruit?"

"No-one eats the fruit," she said.

Old Hector looked at her as she glanced swiftly at the man. She had dark eyes, dark hair, and a comely face. In height she was a little above the average for women, and her body had fine pliant lines. But though he saw this, he saw also that in some way she was different from the other inhabitants of the Green Isle. She thought below the surface of her face. She was almost human, in the way that he himself had always known human beings. Last night, in a fancy of his mind, the others on the Green Isle had seemed to him like clean empty shells on a strange seashore.

He followed her glance to the man's face. He, too, was dark, with glowing brown eyes. His expression now was netted in a certain intolerance, a human expression. And Old Hector thought of him at once as the woman's husband. He had known many a man like him, labouring under some hidden pressure.

"I thought," said Old Hector, "that it's fruit we would have been given at the Inn, we saw them gathering so much of it."

"You thought wrongly," said the man. "And it may be as well for you not to labour the point. I'll show you the way to the Seat."

"Did you have anything to eat this morning?" asked the woman.

"No, ma'm," answered Old Hector quietly. "But it doesn't matter."

"Then you'll come in and have something."

"I think they should go," said the man.

"Aren't they going in any case?" answered the woman. "They'll get plenty of the right food there," and she looked straight at her husband.

"It'll make no difference, I suppose, in that case," he answered drily. "But you know it is not our business to feed the stranger."

The Seat on the Rock

"I know that," she said succinctly.

But Old Hector begged to be excused, for he would not trouble anyone.

"It's no trouble," she said. "Come in. The porridge is ready anyway."

She had dished out two platefuls when her husband called "Mary!" from outside. Excusing herself, she told them, with a smile, to eat up. It was a quick, slightly flurried, but beautiful smile. Then she went.

Though fruit can be surprising it was not, strictly speaking, to Old Hector, a food. Porridge was, especially in the morning. If the milk was good, man could ask no more. Old Hector put his bonnet on his knees and, lifting his hand to his forehead, said grace. The air in the cottage caught the stillness before the pin drops. Then he began to eat.

Art tried a spoonful and their eyes met. Old Hector nodded. "The milk of the old black Highland cattle," he said.

"But they are not black," whispered Art.

"They never were," said Old Hector.

And then they said no more.

The horn spoons being soft, they were able to scrape their plates quietly. Old Hector shoved his plate a few inches from him and inverted the empty bowl over the horn spoon as he always did at home. Art did not do this at home, but he did it now, and felt the better for it.

The woman came in and they arose.

"I do not know how we can thank you," began Old Hector.

"I'll show you your way," she said, and she smiled again, and led them out of the house. The man was rounding up the cattle.

She pointed to the path that would take them beyond the town where the road started to wind up to the Seat.

When from a little distance they looked back, she was still standing by the gable-end; then she turned into the house.

"What did you think of her?" asked Art.

The Seat on the Rock

Old Hector was silent.

"I liked her myself," said Art, "and she's the first one."

After a time, Old Hector said, "We needn't mention to any-one that we were there."

Art looked at him. "Why?"

"I don't know," said Old Hector. "But we needn't mention it."

Art nodded, and with the help of the porridge began to ask a great many more questions, and in this way the ground was soon covered, though his old friend seemed deeply preoccupied.

But when they came to the road and Art saw the full length and height of the seven peaks of the embattled Seat, he was silent and his feet began to drag.

Old Hector spoke to him then, and, when he was finished, Art was committed.

People were in front of them and people behind, and people coming from the Seat as well. There were heavy waggons going slowly up and light waggons coming quickly down. There were so many things to see on this road that Art had more than enough to do looking at them all.

One thing he could not help noticing, however, was the difference between those who were going up and those who were coming down, as great a difference as had been between the two of themselves and the Coastwatcher.

The encompassing wall was smooth rock of a livid greenish hue and so high that it made him dizzy to look at it. Then they were through the great arched gateway and on a street. The houses were taller than houses he had seen in a picture of a street in Edinburgh below the Castle Rock, and they had the greenish hue of the encompassing wall. High up, this hue caught a glisten that was like a glisten of speed, and the street curved in this speed yet did not move.

There were many streets, but each street curved upward. Men and women went into doors and came out of them, busy as the curves of the street; and even inside a shop they were

43

busy, never standing still but doing something and moving always.

When they came to a point of intersection, Old Hector took the street to the left because it looked quieter. Along this street they could hear themselves again and felt less confused, for, like a leaf that falls slightly away from the forming heart of a cabbage, it was less abrupt in its aspiration.

From this street to another quiet street, they went curving on. Street after street that, but for crossings, might all have been the one street. Never had Art walked on hard pavements before, and when excitement and weariness produced a dizziness in his head, the streets began to move at a rapid pace, then to rush past him in vast curving walls, a livid light high up on them where they whizzed out of sight.

Art leaned his head against Old Hector, who patted him comfortingly.

A grave man paused and spoke. Old Hector thanked him without a smile, and in what seemed no time they were back on the main way.

Soon they were passing through a gateway into a great forecourt where people were continuously coming and going. On its far side was a door in a building so massive that it did not need to look down to command silence. Towards that door, having Art by the hand, Old Hector asked the feet that had taken him on many an adventure to take him, as well as they could, on this, the last.

Never, surely, had space before been so vast within a building. In the distance folk looked small and moved as soundless shadows move. This sea of space had bays and headlands and the rock everywhere was perpendicular and smooth, but here the outside livid green was transformed into a pallor of green that glowed, as the inner cabbage leaf glows in the sun. Above closed doors long words were cut in the stone, but quietly so that they were not seen until stared at.

The bays were full of human traffic, and towards one of

The Seat on the Rock

them a young man, after looking for that second which seemed a long time into Old Hector's face, led the way.

There were officials behind the counter and the young man remained, watching and listening, while Old Hector answered questions about himself which were written down in a massive book.

Then Art's turn came, and when Old Hector was asked the name, the ghost of an old smile came to his face and he said, "We just call him Young Art."

But the official did not smile. "Is he your grandson?"

"No, sir," answered Old Hector Macdonald. "He's no relation of mine. He's a neighbour's boy, and the name is Art Macrae."

The official regarded him in a curious searching way and then wrote. "How did he come to be in your company?" he asked, as he looked up again.

Then Old Hector was confused. "He's just a friend of mine," he said at last.

The faces of other officials now regarded the confusion that spread so guiltily, for Old Hector had had a swift memory of the Hazel Pool and the poaching.

"For anything that may have been done between us," he added, "he was not to blame. I would like to make that quite clear."

A piercing silence fell away to more questions concerning Art, and the answers were recorded.

When the census was concluded, the young man, who had been narrowly interested, beckoned and a young woman came up to take Art away. For one blinding moment Art thought that she was his sister Morag. But as she looked at him, he saw that she was not, so that in an instant she was more terrible than all other women.

"Come," she said, with the authority of a schoolmistress.

Art clove to Old Hector.

"Come," she repeated.

The Seat on the Rock

"I will not," muttered Art.

Then she put her hand on him, and Earth was let loose.

Those who had but newly arrived were appalled at the freedom of Art's lungs and the kicking power of his legs, as though condemnation must now fall at a stroke; but the officials showed no anger, only a deeper interest than ever.

"Did you stay at the Inn?" asked the ledger official.

But Old Hector was busy trying to pacify Art and did not answer.

The question was repeated and the great book reopened.

"Go with the lady," whispered Old Hector strongly.

"I will not," cried Art, hanging on.

"He's not anxious to go," said Old Hector, trying to smile. But the great book waited.

So Old Hector gave his explanation of how it came about that, in their ignorance, they had not stayed at the Inn, but had slept together in a cock of straw.

The piercing silence caught a more piercing glint.

"What did you eat?"

"Won't you go when Old Hector tells you?"

"No," answered Art.

The silence waited.

"There was only the fruit yonder," answered Old Hector.

When the appalled silence could contain itself no longer, Art was ordered to be removed, and the whole of that great hall registered the fight he put up. Never, surely, had the country of Clachdrum declared itself so fully, or so far into space, as Art was borne away.

Then a great weariness descended on Old Hector, and the young man, seeing this, nodded within himself and led the way to the door which Old Hector was yet to know well, even to understanding the terrible meaning of the two long words above its lintel.

VI

IN THE REST-HOUSE

In the evening of the same day the young man was outside the door when Old Hector came forth.

Like one walking in his sleep, knowing he was so walking, but caring no more, Old Hector went with him.

He was so weary that he was beyond distress and heard things finely and remotely.

"Feeling a bit tired?"

"I am," murmured Old Hector.

"But it was not what you expected?"

"It was not."

"He soon put you at your ease?"

Old Hector looked dreamily in front of him. "What was that?" he asked.

The young man smiled. "Even I did not think he would be so long with you." And he looked secretly elated.

His hair was black and so smooth that it glistened. His thin mouth was sensitive, his cheekbones distinct, and his skin slightly olive. His name was Merk.

Old Hector was led into a vestibule where voices were raised freely, then along a corridor. Merk showed him a hall where young men and women were noisy and full of laughter, though here and there many stood silent. There were rooms in which the human hosts sat or moved about. Then he found himself at an endless table and his porridge and milk appeared before him. He lowered his head, and as he said grace there was a ripple of laughter. He opened his eyes and tried the food.

The milk was thinner than the skim milk of Friesian cattle, and the porridge fainted on his palate for lack of salt. He did his best, for he wished to be polite, but half-way through the mess he gave up.

"You'll have to excuse me," he said to Merk, now standing beside him again. "Hunger is not on me."

Merk's eyes understood and Old Hector arose and followed him.

There was a sound everywhere of hissing waters and Old Hector stood before a basin that had the green of the sea over sand. Therein he washed himself, for though he was tired, yet he was irked by the knots of fruit juice in his whiskers, and when Merk handed him a white towel he rubbed his face and his beard slowly but profusely.

In an inner oblong chamber there were bunks such as Old Hector had seen on an East Coast drifter, only they were exposed in a pleasant airiness and clean as beds in an Inverness hotel.

"This is your one."

"Thank you." Old Hector gladly sat down and took off his boots.

But now his exhaustion had reached the point beyond tiredness, and he glanced at his guide who was talking to the young man opposite him, for the two bunks were in the bow of the chamber with Old Hector's on the starboard side. There seemed no commandment upon him to undress further for the moment, so, swinging in his stockinged feet, he lay extended, beard jutting upward, closed his eyes, and breathed the breath out of him in a long quiet sigh.

Presently, he became conscious of their voices, talking in a way it was difficult to follow. Merk's voice was bright and insinuating: "I know it was a risk on my part, taking him direct to the Questioner, but I was sure he was the old genuine by the way the features reacted in the smile and the eyes glowed. It's altogether a curious expression. . . ."

Old Hector's mind wandered from the twining sounds of the low voices to the face of the man who had talked to him so

In the Rest-House

long that day. So extraordinary an excursion the man had made with him that he would never forget his face . . . it was still looking at him, with its steady greenish-grey eyes and clear features, infinitely patient, going from one point to another.

If anyone had told Old Hector that he would have remembered his past, as he had remembered it before this man, he would have said it was impossible. But after he had got over the hurdle of wrong-doing, such as smuggling, things came fairly easy. For the astonishing thing was that never for an instant was there in that face a suggestion of condemnation; only of interest. Upon Old Hector, whose worry had been his sins (for in his mind the Seat had, of course, been the Judgment Seat), there then came an inward urge to confess, and in this way the man led him through his life. But the man was not particularly interested in his sins. Indeed at times it seemed to Old Hector that he was more interested in his happinesses, and frequently during those hours he had Old Hector smiling. Sometimes Old Hector found it extremely difficult to tell why he had liked someone or hadn't liked another; or why this adventure or that mood stirred him strangely. But the man helped him until, now and then, he had stood beyond the tiredness and the puzzlement, speaking whatever came into his mouth in simple clear words, like a man in a trance. . . .

The voices of the two young men penetrated his mind again. By moving his head very slightly he could see them. They were in the heat of an argument and thrust long curious words at each other. It was not necessary to listen to the words, their faces were so alive. The dark one, Merk, who had been his guide, was lively and sly in his thrusts. He called the other Axle. Axle's hair was brown as sand, a strong growth. The bones in his face were prominent and stubborn and he looked like one who could be dour and merciless. He was plainly not too sure of Merk now, and Merk knew he had the better of him.

"I have only been in the Rooms a week," Axle was saying.

In the Rest-House

"I am no more than an assistant myself," replied Merk, driving in his sly thrust.

"I only speak of what I know. And at least I know what could be done with the use of drugs and hypnotism—even if we were only at the beginning of knowing. Anyhow, we would have found not the least difficulty in dealing with this case."

"How would you have dealt with it?" asked Merk.

"Obviously the peasant type. There's no more to it than that. You can act on them in groups. All this need for analysis of the sentiment that underlies such a perfect sample, as you call it, is just waste of time. The sentiment is purely primal or animal. They are conservative in their habits as animals are. They'll stick to their ways of life or plots of ground with a blind animal violence. Fear is a more potent force in their lives than any other. Use fear. Defeat their violence with a greater violence. And in the end you will get them to accept your new conditions with gratitude. We proved it."

"The trouble is," said Merk, "that man has always 'proved' it—and then has had to 'prove' it again. Why?"

Axle looked into the eager young face with its smile.

A vague but profound disquiet made Old Hector stir.

"I must be off," said Merk, turning to glance at the old man. When Old Hector opened his eyes again he saw Axle looking after the youthful Merk with a slight uneasiness.

VII

RELATIONSHIP

The following evening, Axle was combing his brown hair on the edge of his bunk, when he saw Old Hector approaching.

The mouth of the old man was slightly open, the lips lax.

50

Relationship

The skin tension had become puckered and loose. The eyes were hazed and bewildered. It was as if the façade of the face, the appearance of wisdom, had crumpled, revealing a vague stupidity beneath. The disordered whiskers conferred on the whole the somewhat fantastic effect of a rifled nest. A gleam of understanding shone deep in Axle's eyes.

"Well," he said, "you have got back?"

Old Hector turned his face towards the sound and stared for a little while. Then he breathed a vague "Ah" and nodded, feeling at the same time for the edge of his bed on which he sat down.

Axle continued to watch him, his eyes travelling over the whole figure, now sitting in complete stillness, shoulders bent, hands on knees, eyes staring at nothing. The patient and enduring peasant!

How old the conception! How much had been written about it by intellectual man! How much idealism had been poured into this static blankness! Extraordinary!

Axle saw it all—the myth created by the intellectual who, incomplete in himself, needs "something".

He became excited by the sureness of his analysis and began making clear notes in his mind for a possible thesis, that, in due course, might command attention in the proper quarter. World figures came to memory from East to West, with Tolstoy midway; from the beginnings of human time, with——

He became aware that Merk was standing beside him.

"Something exciting?" asked Merk.

"Oh, nothing," answered Axle. "Trying to remember a note or two from an analysis."

Merk saw that Axle did not quite trust him, and smiled. He appreciated, too, the way in which Axle could wipe all expression from his face. The skin hardened around the eyes; the cheekbones grew smooth.

Merk glanced at Old Hector and remained silent for a little time. Then he went and put a hand on Old Hector's shoulder and tried to wake the old man.

Relationship

"Eh?"

"It's about Art," said Merk.

"Wha'?"

"It's about Art."

"Is it?" said Old Hector, staring like a rain-pitted boulder.

"Yes. He has disappeared."

"Ah."

"Do you understand?" Merk brought his mouth to Old Hector's ear. "Art has gone."

"Eh? What?" And after a little time, "Where?"

"We don't know."

"You don't know," repeated Old Hector. "Ah." And he nodded vaguely.

Axle said, "They have exhausted too quickly the little that was there!"

"He has been hit pretty hard somewhere," Merk admitted. "I wonder just where?"

"All over, I should say."

"No," said Merk. "I see you don't understand our methods yet."

"You think not?" Axle raised his brows in half-mocking disbelief.

But Merk was watching Old Hector, who presently sighed deeply and, after recognizing himself uncertainly, stooped to his boots. The effort, however, was too great and he might have fallen to the floor if Merk had not come to his aid.

Merk took off his boots and helped swing the old legs onto the bed. With a muttered "Thank you" and the automatic ghost of a dead smile the old man lay on his back, his mouth falling open as his eyes closed, his breath coming in chesty gusts.

"What happened to the boy?" Axle asked.

"He has simply disappeared since this morning. No trace of him. It is quite incredible."

"But someone was bound to have seen him."

Relationship

"No. He has just vanished. Nothing like it has ever happened before. You see, there was nowhere he could possibly go, unless he had the power of walking through stone walls."

"And at least he had not developed such four-dimensional magic."

"You may smile—but there it is. And what is magic but that for which you have not yet discovered the laws?"

"Tell me," asked Axle, "can you, here, *picture* the four-dimensional curved space-time continuum?"

"It always was a difficulty, wasn't it?" remarked Merk lightly. "Though pure mathematicians did have elusive glimpses of it, just as, in poetry, others spoke of revisiting the glimpses of the moon."

"Are you trying to make fun of me?"

"Surely not," said Merk, his eyes opening wide. "For the moment I would give anything to know what happened to little Art. If only I could think it out." And he glanced at Old Hector.

"You were banking on the boy as a hostage?"

"You mean?"

"Many would have stood up to physical torture for a prolonged time who broke down quickly when their families became involved."

Merk nodded. "Only here we are primarily concerned not with adjusting the psyche of the newcomer to the new conditions—which would have been a simple task—but with getting at the elements of his particular kind of psyche in the interests of research."

"Do you mean you have not done it before on ten thousand peasants?"

"We are always doing it. Just as your scientists were forever researching into matter. Or your biologists hunting for missing links. You must credit us with the capacity to recognize a missing link when we see one."

53

Relationship

"You could be more explicit," remarked Axle drily. "Anyway, you don't seem to have impressed the old fellow very much with your tale of the vanished boy."

"That," answered Merk, who had only been giving half his attention to Axle, "is what has astonished me."

"Why? What relationship between them did you suspect?"

As Merk concentrated on the eyes of Axle, Old Hector groaned.

Old Hector groaned from deep in his chest and his head moved from side to side on the pillow, in a gesture of revulsion, utter revulsion. He was seeing the man's face again.

Merk and Axle might chatter away about how exhaustion could be induced by the right degree of damp heat, by a nicely adjusted insomnia, by electric shocks, by personal anxiety-stresses and in other ingenious ways, but for Old Hector nothing could have been more exhausting than the finding of words by voluntary effort in which to answer the Questioner. When he broke down and shook his head, the Questioner would frame his question in another and simpler way and so the tentative answers would begin again. Sometimes Old Hector felt himself so involved that the only way out was by means of words, almost of any words, any sounds.

The Questioner carefully explained to Old Hector why he asked all these questions, and though Old Hector might be too weary to follow him rationally, yet he was left with the feeling that in some way he was assisting at the salvation of Clachdrum. The more he could explain, the easier it would be for those who came after him. As the burden of this came on him fully, his anxiety became almost unbearable.

It was at this point that his story, his picture, reached young Art.

Relationship between them? . . . And there was the face, watching him, the eyes, the clear eyes, clear as glass.

That guilty confusion came again, because if there was one person he would protect from his own aged follies, it would be

54

the little boy who had run to him with so many of his troubles and hopes.

The questions came at him again, at first phrased in a way that he could make nothing of. He shook his head. But the questions about their possible relationship became clearer . . . they became so clear that Old Hector's body closed slowly upon itself like a fist, and he stared into those greenish-grey eyes in which there was no feeling, only an incredible intelligence.

Half an hour after that Old Hector had stumbled from the room and found his way, he did not know how, to the Resthouse.

VIII

AMONG THE RASPBERRY CANES

Where the rough grazing began beyond the crofts at home, there was an old wooden gate across the cart track to the peat banks. Here the sheep used to gather on a sunny day, and sometimes Old Hector, passing through the gate, would hear an urgent buzz of flies as if innumerable bluebottles were whizzing in invisible arcs through the air. Often he had tried to see the flies, but their speed must have been too great and he had always failed.

At first when he awoke he thought he was standing by this gate, and a peace, exquisite in its surprise, possessed him. The buzzing had lost its urgency or anger and was now at a great distance; seemed indeed to have fallen asleep to its own hum. But as he listened more carefully he came fully awake and looked about him.

The face of Axle asleep in his bunk, and other faces down both sides, were quiet as the faces of the dead. Everywhere there was stillness in the grey morning light, and silence—

Among the Raspberry Canes

save for the hum that, listening, he fancied was the sound of the fine wheels of the brains that never slept. A far sound under the tower, the whizzing of the invisible wheels of thought; the light in the eyes and the intelligence that never ceased.

He stretched himself out on his back and his arms fell straight by his sides. His breath came in a faint moan and his eyes closed. But the face was whole again and the skin less pitted.

As Axle, dressed, looked at him he hesitated until he saw the movement of breath in the chest.

When breakfast was at its height, Old Hector sat up and put on his boots, then slowly went to his place at table and ate his insipid porridge.

Leaving the dining-hall, he followed the passage to the main entrance, but instead of turning right towards the Atomic Psychology room, he turned left with the natural air of a man who had to do this. Two looked at him, but Old Hector's eyes were dreamily set and he passed out of the building. At the arched gate leading to the streets a grave man said: "Where are you going?"

"I am going," answered Old Hector, "to give them a hand with the crops. It looks like being a good day for it." And there appeared on his face the ghostly smile.

The man stared after him, then nodded to himself in understanding. After the change, men—particularly old men—often acted in an automatic way, like the imbecile. From the look of the face it was possible to estimate the degree of the break which had produced the change.

Old Hector held to his way down the curving street like one going about his appointed business. Neither hesitation in his step nor cunning in his eye arrested the inquiring glance. "Yes, indeed," he answered a man and passed out under the arch in the wall.

When he had gone on a little way, he turned left off the road as naturally as he would have turned up to the moor to

Among the Raspberry Canes

bring home the little red cow. Following the track that ran above the orchards and the grain fields, he was interested in the work that was going on, with the expression on his face of a vaguely remembered dream. He was in no hurry and he kept going.

But when he came by the edge of the corrie and saw the cottage where Art and himself had last eaten together, he paused, and slowly passed his open hand up over his forehead, and, after a time, his mouth which had fallen apart closed of itself.

Looking around, he saw in a shallow fold of the ground above him the upper part of a thicket of raspberry canes, the berries red against the green leaves. They were fresh and attractive, with the glancing innocence of youth, the merry challenge of wild youth. A memory of their wet mornings stirred on his lips and he went up with the intention of resting among them, for now suddenly he felt tired.

Threading his way through the thicket for the open space that would be found in the heart of it, he came on the body of young Art.

The body did not look ravaged but as if it had died in its sleep. The eyes were shut and the lips, stained with fruit juice, were open, showing the fine white tips of the teeth. It lay on its side with the left hand protruding beyond the head and the right arm fallen over the abdomen, the fist curving like the frond of a slain bracken shoot. In its death stillness it had a great fragility.

Old Hector could not move and his eyes, crawling of their own accord round the body, saw two chewed apple cores, bright orange rinds, a smear of raspberry seeds, and a half-eaten cluster of grapes. Slowly he came to his knees and, leaning forward on his hands, brought his right ear to the delicate mouth.

The faint but regular thresh of the breath was a playing of music that he could hardly hear enough of, and as he turned

Among the Raspberry Canes

over and settled on his seat, the smile sank deep into his eyes. It was God that was good, too!

Well, let come what might, he was here now, with growing things about him and the boy asleep. He would have had a night of it, the little fellow, all alone, with fear before him in the darkness and fear at his back. No wonder he was exhausted and lying there water-wan as a dead fawn.

In this life or any other a man can do no more than one thing at a time, and, drawing the half-cluster of grapes to him, Old Hector picked one off and put it in his mouth. It drenched his palate and went down in a gulp. In the morning the eyes of nightmare are veiled, and what is too sweet in the grape can be cleansed by the wild raspberry. Moments live in their own right like sleep or content, and it would be a pity to disturb the boy. They were safe enough here.

And then suddenly he doubled over a small knot in his gut. The knot untied and he breathed again, but like one waiting or hearkening. The knot came again, bigger, and he doubled over his knees. The knot at once swelled and grew tighter and he lay over on his side, smothering the groan of agony, lest he waken the little fellow. But soon his gut was a nest of knots, with edges on them sharp as flints, and, root as he might at the raspberry canes, their pressure was not eased. As they began to cut like knives, he clawed at the earth and bit the grass.

Art awoke and sat up and his face opened in terror. The cry was out of him before he knew and Old Hector rolled over, looking up in welcome. Pressing knuckles into his stomach with great force, he said, "Hush. It's all right." There was sweat on his forehead and Art's eyes were large in fascinated fear.

Hearkening inwardly again, Old Hector drew himself on to his seat with the care of one who is made of fine glass. Shakily he wiped his forehead. "Must have been the raspberries," he whispered with a nod. "Did you eat many?"

"I did," answered Art.

Among the Raspberry Canes

"Did you?" said Old Hector; and then, gripping himself, "Never mind me," he rolled over in a new spasm.

In his anxiety, Art began to whimper only, which was plucky of him, for he wanted to run away, crying out.

But Old Hector managed a few words to him in between times, and when Art realized that his friend was suffering from no more than a pain in the belly from eating raspberries he was able to assure him that he himself had suffered no pain and to add, "Maybe it was a bad one you got."

"Maybe it was," answered Old Hector carefully.

"Maybe," said Art, "it was one with a worm in it."

Old Hector nodded. "You have it now," he said.

"I'm thinking that," agreed Art. "It could be a worm easily."

There was a rumble. "The worm is getting broken up, I think," said Old Hector hopefully, as he felt the knots give way slightly.

"If he gets broken up and killed then he couldn't kill you, could he?" asked Art.

"He could not," said Old Hector.

Art nodded and waited. Old Hector's fists knotted, his eyes closed, and a groan came through his whiskers. A mighty rumble followed.

"There can't be much left of him now," said Art encouragingly.

"It should be working down towards the tail-end of him indeed," agreed Old Hector, wiping his brow.

But the contest took much longer than they expected, and by the end of it Old Hector was exhausted, yet, in the sweet absence of the awful pain, almost happy. He withdrew for a little time and when he came back he was smiling.

"And tell me—how on earth did you manage to get away?"

"I just went," answered Art.

"That was the simplest way certainly."

"You see," said Art, "there were some children forming up and as the lot of us was passing that lot I stepped into it because

59

Among the Raspberry Canes

I was coming last in my lot and no-one noticed me because they never thought I would do it because you see who was to think? I didn't think but I just did it because I didn't want to be with the one that took me away and she didn't see me because she was looking over at him that was forming the other lot, the man who was doing it. Do you see?"

"I see," said Old Hector.

"So then you see the man said to us to march after him and he led the way and we marched after him and no-one could run away because ones were standing everywhere, and I marched too and I was in the last. And do you know where we went?"

"Where?"

"Away out and then down the street and the man now walked about the middle of us and he was keeping his eye on the long line sometimes, and then we got outside the town, and then we were going on and going on, and then some of the carts came down behind us and do you know what happened —you would never guess?"

"No."

"Didn't two of the empty crates fall off one cart and go rattling on the road right beside the man and he stopped and looked and everyone stopped and looked and do you know what I did?"

"What?"

"I slipped off the road up and away and no-one ever saw me and I was out of sight in no time. Do you think that was clever of me?"

"It was about as clever as I have ever heard."

"Do you think so?"

"I am certain of it."

"Are you?"

"I am. And what happened then?"

"Then," said Art, filling with confidence now that he had found his old friend again, "I crawled into a place and hid for a while. And after that I hid in another place. I took good care no-one would catch me. Where do you think the man was taking them?"

"Where but to a school?"

"That's what I thought," nodded Art, "myself. I didn't want to go there whatever."

"Hush, we'd better not speak so loud or someone will be hearing us. Where did you spend the night?"

"The night," said Art, "came on me."

"It would," agreed Old Hector.

"I didn't know where to go and then I saw—I saw yon house—remember—where the woman gave us the porridge?"

"Well do I remember that house. She was a kind woman."

"That's what I was thinking," said Art. "It was a long way off—and the night was coming—and then I saw the dogs. And I—I—was frightened of the dogs. Anyone would be frightened of them, wouldn't they?"

"They would."

Art nodded and a distant look came into his eyes. Old Hector saw the shadow around them and read their story of fear and weeping in the night.

"Then I lost my way, and I did not know where I was, and it was dark."

"And when you cried out, no-one came to find you?"

"No-one," muttered Art, and his eyes grew very bright.

Old Hector nodded. "You were a brave little fellow if ever there was one and that's certain."

"I'm not crying," said Art. "It's just that——"

"Hush!" said Old Hector, at the same time putting his palm on Art's shoulder and pressing him down.

The voices of two men approached.

". . . I said what was the use of getting up in the dark, but when the daylight came I had a look around, just to satisfy her." It was the voice of the man who had caught them in the orchard.

"And you found nothing?"

"No. And yet I did find something. I found an apple lying on the path."

"An apple?" said the second man, and he stopped.

"Yes. On a spot where no picker could have dropped it."

The silence held for quite a while.

"Can you think of anyone who could have dropped it?" asked the second man in a low searching voice.

"Not just there. I hadn't been that way myself. . . . I didn't mention it to Mary. Women get fancies. The boy left a strong impression on her."

"Lord, we cannot be too careful!"

"I know. The effect of the fruit grows. I notice it on myself."

"Hush, for heaven's sake! Tell me again—what was it exactly she said she heard?"

"She said she heard the sound of a child crying in the night."

The second man could not help a soft chuckle of amazement. "If our fancies grow at that rate. . . ." They moved off and his voice faded beyond the raspberry canes.

IX

ART ESCAPES A SECOND TIME

So great was Old Hector's weakness after his terrible pains that at last he could hardly crawl over a small ridge. When he had done it, he lay on his face, but Art nudged him. Looking up, he saw the cattle. The beasts were feeding in a shallow strath beyond the corrie and neither man nor dog could be seen anywhere. The great valley, with its town and orchards and grain fields, was shut away from them, and as they crawled down a few yards the last peak of the Seat sank from sight.

Art Escapes a Second Time

They were alone in the little strath, and the sight of small birch trees touched them with a momentary wonder. It was like being at home, and when a peewit cried Art's heart all but stopped on him.

"He won't take them down to the corrie until the late afternoon," said Old Hector.

"For the milking," said Art.

After Old Hector had rested again, he said, "Keep you quiet, and we'll try them."

As they moved slowly down, all the cattle lifted their heads. Old Hector approached the nearest one on tottering legs. She was shy and wild and tossed her head away, but turned again to look. Slowly he approached, murmuring the tender Gaelic words that Art had often heard his sister Morag speak to their own cow.

Each time the beast shortened the distance she turned away, until at last Old Hector got scratching the hard forehead. The beast danced off, but took more scratching the next time. Soon he was caressing her back and haunch. Her skin twitched and she could hardly stand still. He began humming a milking croon which Art knew well and his hand travelled downward. She mooed and her eyes shone but she stood still. He nodded as he felt her udder. "Bend down," he whispered to Art, "and I'll try if I can aim your mouth."

Art bent right over and an orange fell out of his neck.

He quickly picked it up. "I forgot I had it on me," he said, "nearly. It's the last."

Old Hector regarded it as he continued to stroke the beast.

"Would you like it?" asked Art, offering it eagerly.

But Old Hector shook his head. "Have you your knife on you?"

"I have."

Old Hector sliced the top off the orange as he would the top off an egg. Then he stirred and slackened the pith with the

Art Escapes a Second Time

blade and handed the fruit to Art. "Eat the inside, but mind, don't break the skin."

"Won't you have a sook yourself?" asked Art politely.

"I'm frightened to chance it. Hurry, for she's getting restless again."

When the golden bowl was white inside, Hector renewed his humming and milked it full. Art refused the first offer, and Old Hector on his knees drained the bowl slowly. After waiting a few moments, he nodded. "That's what I needed." And he set to the milking with more heart.

The rest of the cattle were very interested in what was going on and particularly in the words of endearment and the singing. Then an odd thing happened, for as Old Hector and Art, satisfied, began to walk towards the birch wood, the cattle threw up their tails and their heels and danced around, butting the air, but the milked cow followed them quietly, mooing now and then.

At first Art was frightened by the pounding hooves, but soon he began to laugh.

It was fine to be in the birch wood after that, with small birds singing the little songs of lonely places. The milk suffused them with a gentle warmth and presently, without having thought about it, they fell sound asleep.

Art's scream woke Old Hector. The dogs! The sniffing dogs! "Get away!" cried Old Hector. "Off with you!" Art clung to him in terror, hiding his face from the lowered muzzles.

The man appeared and looked down at them.

"Good day," said Old Hector. "The little fellow is frightened of the dogs."

The man considered them gravely. "How do you come to be here?" he asked.

"It's a long story," answered Old Hector.

"Did you not go to the Seat?"

"We did. But the little fellow left it and I came after him to find him."

Art Escapes a Second Time

"How did he leave it?"

"He just left it," answered Old Hector. "That was yesterday morning. At least I think so, for I am getting a little confused with time. But I know he spent last night by himself and it was him your wife must have heard crying in the night."

"How do you know," asked the man, "that my wife heard anyone crying in the night?"

Old Hector turned his eyes away from those eyes. "Once he starts, it isn't very difficult for anyone to hear him." Then he said to Art, "It's all right now. The dogs won't touch you."

The man sat down. "Tell me," he said, "all that happened."

"I'll do that gladly," began Old Hector, who thereupon explained how they had gone to the Seat, how they had been separated, how he had heard of Art's disappearance, and how he had followed and found Art and learned his story.

"You have not told me how you know that my wife heard him crying in the night."

"I forgot that bit," answered Old Hector. And when he had told how he had found Art in the raspberry canes and had heard the passing voices, he added, "I might have called to you but I was too weak from the illness that was on me."

"Illness?"

"The little fellow," explained Old Hector, "is very fond of fruit and he had some by him and I ate it, for he was asleep and I was thirsty. I think I would have been all right if I also hadn't eaten some of the raspberries."

For the first time a smile appeared on the man's face. "You needn't blame the raspberries," he said.

"No?" said Old Hector, heartened by the smile, even though it was a little grim.

"What's the boy's name?"

"We just call him Art. But his full name——"

"Did he eat any of the porridge at the Seat?"

Old Hector repeated the question to Art, who answered, "N-no, because—because I didn't like it."

Art Escapes a Second Time

Old Hector regarded the man's humoured expression of understanding. "Tell me," he asked, "is it eating their porridge that did it?"

Nodding, the man replied, "I told you before that no-one ate the fruit. If they did, they would suffer terribly."

"I thought I was going to die," said Old Hector.

The glimmer of humour shone deep in the man's eyes. "We suffer here—but we do not die."

"Ah," said Old Hector.

"If you had gone to the Inn," said the man, breaking the silence, "you would have been specially told not to touch the fruit."

"Would we have got the same porridge there?" asked Old Hector.

"You would."

Old Hector nodded slowly. He was beginning to see light now. The fruit became a poison to the stomach only *after* one had eaten at the Inn or at the Seat. Each Inn would have its bunks to sleep in, its porridge to eat, just as had the Seat. The Inns were there to collect the travellers and set them on the way they must forever go.

Old Hector saw this, and saw also that the travellers to the Green Isle would never taste the living fruit. But for the waywardness of Art, he himself would never have tasted it, for he would most certainly have gone to the first Inn. And once a man went to the first Inn, the living fruit became the poison fruit. It was a great mystery, greater surely than the forbidden fruit in the Garden of Eden!

Saying "Wait here," the man moved off with his dogs.

"What do you think he'll do?" asked Art.

"He can't do much, I'm thinking," replied Old Hector slowly.

"I'm not going back," declared Art "I'm not! I'm not!" His voice rose passionately.

"Hush," said Old Hector. "There's nothing to harm you at the Seat. Surely not."

Art Escapes a Second Time

"There is! There is!" cried Art.

"Nonsense," said Old Hector. "What could there be?"

"I know," cried Art. "They—they break your mind." And he burrowed from the terrible thought into the earth.

Old Hector looked far into space, and his mouth fell open a little. Art, lifting his eyes in the silence, saw this distant look and it frightened him, because until that instant he did not really believe that what he himself had said might be true.

"It isn't true, is it?" he cried.

"No," said Old Hector. "You know it could not be true."

"But it is! I see it is!" cried Art.

"Now, Art," said Old Hector in the solemn tone he rarely used, "you must listen to me."

By the time the man came back the sun was nearly set. As they started for the cottage, he said, "It's too late for you to go to the Seat to-day." He looked troubled and was not inclined to speak much.

Old Hector had his own thoughts and Art now went quietly beside him. Once Old Hector's eyes rested on the man who was walking a little in front, and they caught a faint speculative gleam. For one or two queer enough things had happened. For example, after eating the porridge at the man's house, Art —who had taken no porridge at the Seat—was still able to eat the fresh fruit off the trees without harm or pain. Again, when the man had caught Art in the orchard, what had he himself had in his own pockets but apples? If no-one could eat the fresh fruit without being poisoned, why fetch apples so very early in the morning? Then there had been that curious talk of the two men by the raspberry canes.

Old Hector's mind rose to the question: *Could this man eat the fruit?*

Suddenly he decided that he could, but in the same moment he felt that this knowledge was hidden and of so terrible a nature that he would not hint of it even to the man himself.

Art Escapes a Second Time

In the old days on the blessed earth, two or three of them had been smugglers and made whisky in a turf bothy and been hunted by the men of the law. That had been bad enough. But this, *this!* Old Hector looked slowly over each shoulder, as if terror might come with wing and talon out of the invisible air. Then he composed himself.

When they came in sight of the cottage, the cattle were feeding in the hollow, but they all lifted their heads as the three passed by. One cow mooed and began walking after them, and the others, some with a playful kick in their heels, followed.

The man's brows gathered. The woman looked upon them from the front of the cottage as they approached. "It's a good evening, ma'm," said Old Hector. The cow had come beside him and he scratched her forehead.

"Is that the one that gave no milk?" the man asked her.

She did not answer, for her eyes had come to rest on little Art, who was close by Old Hector, looking at her from under his brows.

Then upon that hollow of silence in the soft gloaming fell two voices, and everything stood ominously still, including the cattle. Merk and the girl whom Art had mistaken for his sister Morag appeared before them.

"Ah," cried Merk, "here they are!" His voice was bright as silver. "We have been looking for you everywhere!" But his eyes were brighter than his voice, going from one to another and not omitting the cattle. "Where did you go?" he asked Old Hector.

"I went to find the boy because you told me he was missing."

"But how did you find him?"

"I found him lying asleep. And then this gentleman found us both in the wood up by, and brought us here with him."

As Merk's eyes turned on him, the man answered quietly: "The dogs found them. They were asleep and the dogs woke them, and I heard the boy crying."

Art Escapes a Second Time

"You are all so solemn!" said Merk with his bright penetrating smile. "But we'll have to hurry, if we're going to get through the gate before the dark. I'll explain how you found them, Robert. Thank you. And now, Mavis . . ."

But as Mavis advanced towards Art, Art backed away. "Come!" she called, stretching out her hand. Art turned and bolted.

She ran after him, but the cattle were in her way; and as Merk swiftly joined in the race, the cattle threw their heels up, tossed their heads, and swung this way and that. The man spoke to his dogs. "Robert!" called the woman in fear.

Now the receding pattern of movement in the deepening dusk was more than the eye could readily command. Merk was trying to outflank the beasts on the left. Mavis was already behind. But of Art there was no sign. The intricate pattern flowed over the upper edge of the corrie and disappeared.

The three who were watching broke into action, but the cattle kept going towards the birch wood and the dogs were merely driving them on, for that was what the dogs did at night after the milking.

Merk and Mavis came back with flushed faces and glancing eyes. The darkness was falling "We'll call for them to-morrow," cried Merk. "See you have them ready, Robert." The words sounded more like a threat than a command. Then Merk and Mavis hurried away in the direction of the Seat.

"That," said Robert in the profound silence, "was the most wonderful running of a boy I have ever seen."

"He was always clever on his feet," agreed Old Hector. "Indeed," he added, "he was the best runner for his age in all Clachdrum."

"Clachdrum!" said the woman.

"Yes, ma'm. Do you know the place?"

"I was born there," she replied.

"Are you telling me that?" And Old Hector's nod of agreeable surprise was courtly. "I am indeed pleased to meet you.

Art Escapes a Second Time

I myself was born in the Clash and my name is Hector Macdonald."

"I came from Torbeg on the other side and my name is Mary Campbell."

"I know Torbeg well," he replied. "And there are some good Campbells there yet. Indeed the Campbells and the Macdonalds were two great clans—even if they did have their differences now and then!" And he smiled. "They say the world can be a small place." He put out his hand and she took it.

"This is my husband Robert. He came from the Lowlands."

"I'm glad to meet you, sir," said Old Hector. "The Lowlands stood the poor Highlands in good stead many a day."

"Come into the house," said Mary, on a sudden rush of words, "for it's hungry you must be."

"But the boy?" said Robert. "It will soon be dark."

She met his searching look with a careless challenge.

"Never mind the boy." She turned to Old Hector. "That's one thing about the people from the south—they always did need such a lot of explanations!"

"It is sometimes that a poor man, wherever he comes from, has a mind that works slowly in comparison. For the most part in these matters I early resigned myself to do what I was told."

She suddenly laughed and it was the loveliest sound Old Hector had heard since he arrived, including that of the birds in the early morning.

She turned towards the house and Old Hector did his best to keep up with her. His exhaustion had gone so far that it was no longer unpleasant, but it left his legs uncertain.

Robert followed for a few paces, then stood still. His brows gathered darkly, for he knew the terrible danger of the reckless mood that was now invading his wife. The boy must be found.

As Old Hector entered the house, he said, "I have a confession to make to you, ma'm. It's about the cow."

"You needn't confess to me," she answered, attending to the table.

Art Escapes a Second Time

"Thank you," said Old Hector. "The fruit had played sore havoc with me and I was weak."

"What did you milk her into?"

"An orange," answered Old Hector. "The boy had one on him, so we took the pith out of it and it served well."

She laughed and stepped quickly to the window. There was no sign of Robert in the ever-increasing gloom. Old Hector saw the mocking yet anxious challenge in her face as she turned swiftly to a wall cupboard and brought out a jar of green jelly. She handed a large spoonful of it to him, saying, "Suck that slowly. It will put your stomach right." Then she went to the window again, to watch.

The jelly had a tart green flavour. Its juice cleansed his mouth, freshened his stomach, and penetrated in a slow cool surprise through all his body.

"You know about wild herbs," Old Hector complimented her.

"My grandfather, he was a Bethune of the old medical school of the Gaels," said Mary. "But he never made a jelly like this one. He never had the need," she added.

Old Hector looked at her as she took the spoon from him and turned to hide the jar in the cupboard. Then she went to the window again. He saw her smile.

"I think he's coming back," she said. "Maybe he forgot that the hounds have been trained to fetch cattle, not human beings."

It was quite dark when Robert came in against the lamplight.

"No trace of him at all?" she asked.

He glanced at her. "No."

"I hope you didn't frighten him completely," she added. "But sit in to the table."

When Robert had brought a spoonful of food to his mouth he nearly choked over the swift glance he gave Old Hector. This would poison the old man! But Old Hector's first spoon-

Art Escapes a Second Time

ful was already gone, and there was the second spoonful going up—and in—and over! Could she possibly have given him the herb jelly? Surely not! Surely she had some element of sense, of caution, left in her`

She was laughing, laughing with pleasure at what Old Hector was telling about Art. Clearly the food was doing the old man good. He was thriving on it. Robert looked at his wife as if he would read the skin on her face.

The meal over and the table cleared, Mary excused herself busily. "I'll have to see about a bed." And out she went, closing the inner door behind her.

"Where do you think the boy went?" asked Robert.

"He's in hiding," answered Old Hector. "But we'll find him. You must remember he has stayed out one night already."

"Isn't he frightened of the dark?"

"Very. But there are other things he may be more frightened of. However, leave him alone and he'll come in about."

"We must find him," said Robert. "We don't want the people from the Seat poking about here too much."

"I can understand that," said Old Hector. "I wouldn't want it myself."

"And Mary—you know what women can get like. Once they commit themselves to anything, they lose all sense of proportion. And I can see that boy has gone to her head."

"Or to her heart," said Old Hector, "which is worse."

The strain in Robert's manner eased at the correction. He looked at the old man in a satiric, amused way. "We think more of the head here than the heart," he said.

The old man nodded slowly. "I'll tell you what I was thinking," he said. "You'll be starting the harvest soon?"

"The day after to-morrow."

"You'll need extra labour?"

"Yes. But I don't order it. Everything is planned from the Seat."

72

Art Escapes a Second Time

"You have no idea who's coming?"

"None. I never ask. Everything is planned."

"It merely struck me like this," began Old Hector smoothly. "If they want me to earn my keep, I could help you with the scythe. It's the only thing I can do. And as for the boy, he's good at herding cattle. If he thought he would be coming back here, it might be easy to get him to go to the Seat then. Indeed, it would be a pleasure for both of us to go then."

The lids gathered around Robert's eyes as he stared at Old Hector. He could not ask if he had got the herb jelly: it might embarrass the old man, particularly if Mary had made the giving appear a secretive act.

"That might be a pleasant way out. But I cannot order it so."

"Would you mind if I spoke of it myself?"

Robert looked at him again.

"You see," said Old Hector, "we could have that as our plan. Find the boy and then the boy and myself will go to the Seat and get it all over and get accepted. Then we could be coming to see you, maybe even to help with the harvest."

Robert gave a faint ironic smile. "Who were you thinking of speaking to?"

"I could drop a word that same way," said Old Hector, lightly.

Robert laughed. "Business is hardly done that way here," he said.

"Maybe not, then," said Old Hector slowly and his head drooped.

"What did you expect?" asked Robert, watching him.

For a few moments Old Hector sat lost in thought. "I hardly know," he replied in a voice distant and gentle. "You expect something in your mind but you do not think it out. I awoke the other morning in the dawn by the orchard and heard the birds singing, and for a little while it was as though it had come, what I had been expecting."

73

Art Escapes a Second Time

"And I came instead?"

"You were very kind," murmured Old Hector.

"Kind! Surely you need to be kind only where things are not perfect. Where all is perfect, kindness is no more needed. Can't you see that?"

"I find questions very difficult," answered Old Hector. "It's not much schooling I had and you'll have to excuse me."

"What did you think kindness was, then?"

Old Hector's brows gathered for he felt coming upon him the awful burden of the questioning at the Seat. "I'm a little weary," he answered. "Kindness seemed natural as the singing to a bird or the taste of fruit to a boy. But I see now I never thought what it was. I am very ignorant."

"You think it would be kindness not to press a tired man too far?"

The door opened and Mary came briskly in.

"Now," she said, "I'm sure you're longing for your bed."

"I am tired, ma'm, and that's true," answered Old Hector on his feet, "but I am more than sorry to have put you to all this trouble."

"It will be a poor day for me when I cannot give a Clach-drum man a bed."

"God's blessing on you, ma'm," said Old Hector, forgetting all argument, "you have the kind heart."

"Thank you. And you can call me Mary. So come away."

Old Hector turned and shook hands with his host and began to follow her. Then he paused, uncertain, his head lifted to the night outside.

"Don't worry about the boy. He knows you're here. Like every natural boy, he'll come back to his home." Her voice was gentle.

"I could take the dogs and have a last look around," said Robert gloomily, getting to his feet.

She turned on him like a tongue of fire. "Have you no sense at all?" she cried. "Would you frighten the life out of him

74

altogether?" Then on a somewhat calmer note she went on: "I have shut the dogs up, so that they won't frighten him when he comes. And this time—when I hear him crying in the night —I won't ask you to go—I'll go myself."

Robert could not take his eyes off her.

She turned away and conducted Old Hector to the other room.

Robert stood on the middle of the kitchen floor, hearing the murmur of their voices. The talk went on for a long time in that next room. Then her laugh pealed out and the merry sound of it hit him so sharply that it sent him twice the length of the kitchen on random feet.

X

OLD HECTOR IS TAKEN BACK

But Art did not cry in the night, and as the three stood by the cottage in the early morning, Mary's face had got back its old uneasy concern.

"I'll bring the cattle down first anyway," said Robert, "and while you're at the milking, I'll take the country before me with the dogs."

"I'll come with you and search the birch wood, for he liked that wood," said Old Hector.

But though Old Hector wandered through the wood calling Art by name, he got no answer; and though Robert searched into every straw cock above the orchards, he found no trace of the boy. By the time they met below the birches, the morning was well advanced.

As they returned to the cottage they saw both Merk and Mavis talking to Mary and waiting for them. Robert's brows gathered. Mary looked secretly distressed.

Old Hector is Taken Back

"We have found no trace of him," said Robert with restraint.

"But surely he could not have gone far last night in the dark?" suggested Merk.

"That's what I said." Old Hector nodded. "I thought we would have found him close at hand for certain."

Merk looked narrowly at him. "Do you still think he must be near?"

"In my opinion he must be, yet how can I say? For what troubles me is this: he may have lost all sense of direction in the dark."

"But he would know not to climb up?"

"As one who lost himself in the dark before now, I have found up and down not very different from down and up. And when the fear is on you, you keep going. He is only eight."

"And what now?" asked Merk.

"I'll do what I can," answered Robert, "but a proper search may have to be organised. If he got over the crest beyond the birch wood and awoke there, he may have continued on, thinking he was coming here."

"You had better stay with them, Mavis," said Merk, "and help in the search. Meantime I'll get back—and you," he looked at Old Hector, "are to come with me."

"Very well," said Old Hector quietly.

As the two went up the slope, Merk was full of questions. Soon he had Old Hector describing exactly how he had come on Art and how Art said he had escaped. The simplicity of Art's escape seemed particularly to strike him, and as the two empty crates fell on the road he laughed his sharp clear laugh.

"Where exactly is the spot you found him?"

"Well, now," answered Old Hector, "I don't know this country very well and it might be difficult for me to find it." He withdrew his eyes from a thicket of raspberry canes.

"You said it was among some bushes. What kind of bushes?"

Old Hector is Taken Back

"They were not so very high, if I remember," answered Old Hector, "and yet they were high enough to hide him."

"I gather it was not in the birch wood you first found him?"

"It must have been before that because we went into the wood to rest."

"Tell me," said Merk, "were the bushes anything like that?" and he pointed to the thicket of raspberry canes.

Old Hector stared at the bushes dully. "They may have been like that."

"Let us go in and see," said Merk.

But Old Hector could not follow, could not move. He saw Merk's arrestment in the midst of the thicket, saw the head turn and beckon with a peculiar smile. Pushing before him feet that had grown heavy and weary, he entered the thicket. But Art was not there.

"Was this the spot?"

"It looks like it," answered Old Hector slowly.

"And the fruit—did you eat the fruit?"

In every spot except this spot, they had hidden the cores and the skins.

"I think the boy must have eaten some before I found him, for when I found him he was asleep."

"Did you eat?"

"I tried a berry, for I was thirsty, but it did not agree with me."

"You suffered much?"

"Enough—not to make me want to try again," and he tried to smile.

Merk watched him with his bright dark eyes. "It's a long way from here to the birch wood above the corrie on the other side of the valley?"

Old Hector was silent.

"Why did you go in that direction?"

"Who knows?" answered Old Hector. "The human mind cannot bear a great deal—not when it is old. It wanders." He added vaguely: "Perhaps I was just thinking I could help them with the harvest. It is all I can do."

The humour in his eyes grew bleak.

This expression, as if drawn off the very lees of experience, excited Merk and there could be seen in him the movement of thought about the old man's request to work at the harvest and the press of innumerable questions as well.

For it was apparently difficult for him to stop this exciting game of teasing the human mind into its strands, of combing the strands, and leaving them knotless and gleaming and smooth over one's arm or the back of a chair.

The busy main road saved them both and Old Hector breasted the incline in a slow remorseless ongoing; stood as in a waking sleep while Merk went into the bay and spoke to the ledger official; followed Merk's eager face through the door which bore in square-cut letters above it: ATOMIC PSYCHOLOGY.

Axle and the other students looked up as they entered, but Merk went straight to the Questioner, and, before he had quite started to speak, the Questioner ushered them both into a side room.

"Please sit down," said the Questioner to Old Hector, and then with Merk he went over to the window.

Old Hector glanced across at them. Merk was telling his story and the Questioner was listening with the close attention that looked through the window. Sometimes his eyes moved incuriously upon objects outside. But when presently he spoke, Merk answered in heightened tones as if he had been at once questioned and complimented.

Old Hector dropped his gaze to his knees. The face of the Questioner was so clear that the eyes, the greenish-grey eyes, were like glass. The skin beneath the soft fair hair was smooth and full. He was middle-aged and, in repose, his face took on the look of a benign idol. There was that, however, also in the face which quickened the old man's breathing and made his flesh tremulous, so that thought ebbed away.

Old Hector is Taken Back

Presently he heard the names of Mary and Robert in Merk's clear rising voice, something about "a throw-back" and Robert's being affected. He glanced up.

The Questioner had withdrawn his eyes from the window and focussed them on Merk.

"I see," he said, with the faint smile that knew what was going on inside Merk's mind.

"I may be wrong——" began Merk.

"Do you think you're wrong?"

"No——"

"Proceed," said the Questioner mildly.

Again Old Hector's ears grew dull in the warm drowning pulse of the blood. For it was clear not only that Merk suspected what was going on in the minds of Mary and Robert—and particularly of Mary—but had a plan about it. The word plan had no meaning for Old Hector, but he began to feel weak.

They were coming towards him.

"I hear you would like to give Robert a hand with his harvest," said the Questioner.

Old Hector stood up. "Yes, sir, I would."

"We can arrange for you to go with one or two others tomorrow."

"Thank you. I have always been used to the outside."

"Naturally. Now you must have something to eat. Then Merk will bring you back and we shall have a talk."

As they passed out through the entrance hall a man of medium stature entered with an air of decision that was felt by everybody.

"Who is he?" asked Old Hector as they crossed the courtyard. For he had to say something to keep his legs steady.

"The next to the Head," answered Merk.

Then Merk smiled as he saw the dim question about the Head, who might be God, in Old Hector's eyes. But he almost stopped as though an extraordinary thought was being born in his own mind. For the rest of the way he did not ask a single question.

XI

IN THE CORNFIELD

Mary came up and Robert started.

It was the old song of the scythe.

The grain fell like a small wave of the sea, piling where Robert gave it the tilt before sweeping back the bright blade.

The next scythe started behind; and then the third scythe behind that.

The harvest was in motion. When Mary laid her armful across Old Hector's band, he pushed her gently aside and tied the band with the ease of long practice. "I could keep up with him myself," he said, "and when you want to go, you can go."

"You're not tired of my company already?"

"No, ma'm," answered Old Hector. "Not yet."

Mary glanced at the twinkle and she laughed softly. "You may have another tune in your head before the harvest is over."

"It will take a fortnight surely before it's all gathered in?" he asked a little anxiously.

"If we worked hard enough we might make it less."

"You're full of fun," he said, "and it's good to be here. To think that we looked upon it as hard labour so often!"

"Did we, I wonder?"

"Ah, you're right again. We were anxious when the weather was bad; but when the sun shone on us, it was the reward of all labour."

"For girls," answered Mary, "it was often an exciting time enough."

"Was it then you met him?" asked Old Hector.

"It was," answered Mary. "Are you anxious about little Art?"

In the Cornfield

"What good would that do? They'll find him. They'll find out everything. Nothing can be hidden from them, so why should we worry? The boy will have to make his own way."

The talk could proceed only in snatches, and the work kept it sweet, the bending of the back and the gathering of armfuls and the deft movements of the hands.

When all three scythes were being whetted at the same time, Old Hector sat on the last sheaf and smiled. "It's like a field of corncrakes," he said.

Presently Mary returned to the cottage to prepare the midday meal, and when it was ready she called them.

There were three men and two young women from the town, and they were interested in Old Hector's manners and ways of talk. Their brittle laughter confused him slightly.

Then in the late afternoon an odd thing happened to him. Mary spoke to her husband and pointed to the western edge of the corrie, over which a man was coming. After a glance, Robert turned back to her—and stared over her head. The girl Mavis was coming down the eastern slope by the cottage. Robert spat lightly on the palm of one hand and continued firmly with the work.

Occasionally when he straightened himself too quickly, Old Hector experienced a slight dizziness, so he was careful to moderate his movements. But whatever it was of tension in Mary's attitude, he presently stood up and turned round in a way that induced the dizziness, and within its wavering shadows he saw the girl Mavis as Morag, Art's sister, and the man who reached them at the same moment as Tom-the-shepherd, who at home was Morag's secret sweetheart. He saw them look at each other with so curious a look that he brought his hand up across his eyes, and blinked, and as the mist passed he realised that they were strangers to each other.

Yet when Robert addressed the man as Tom, Old Hector got a slight shock, and when he heard the man's voice and

In the Cornfield

knew he had heard it before, he wondered—remembering a strange hallucination that had come on him in the night—whether he was going to be unwell. He put his hand over the back of his neck.

Art had vanished completely. That was the news.

The little group stood still in the cornfield. "This morning a watch was set on the orchards," said Mavis.

Mary looked at her, but Mavis's eyes were troubled.

Down the slope came Merk. Robert gripped his scythe, then looked at the sinking sun. It was about time to stop the day's work. "That will do," he said calmly, and the town workers departed as Merk drew near.

There was a subtle hard change in Merk's eyes as they leapt from face to face. His pleasant manner had a sharp edge. At once he said, "This can't go on. We *must* find him."

The voice was very explicit, very penetrating; the simple statement became charged with a peculiar significance. In the silence that followed, Art's disappearance caught for the first time an ominous note.

Merk turned to Tom and gave him instructions about combing the far side of the western ridge, down past the orchards to his home. He would have what helpers he needed. "And, remember, the responsibility is now on each of us," he added with narrowing eyes as Tom set out.

Merk turned to Old Hector. "You will stay here to-night—and a watch will be kept by each of you." His eyes rested on Robert. "These are my instructions—from the Seat."

No-one spoke. He looked them over as if making quite sure they understood. Then, with a smile, he turned to Mavis and together they departed.

For some time Mary, Robert and Old Hector stood in the silence.

Then Robert's satiric humour came to the surface. "It seems to be getting beyond a joke," he said. His mouth twisted and his eyes roved over the land. But a note of true wonder crept into his voice as he added, "I wonder where in heaven the boy could have gone?"

Old Hector looked out over the cornfield that lay against the near slope of the corrie to the right hand. The third man from the town had stooked the sheaves and their long rows were orderly, like a childhood memory of houses of the little folk. Little houses one could remember seeing under the moon as a child. Peaked shadows ran from them and their gold gleamed in the dusk's quietude.

Far up on the left the cattle were still grazing and the two slim hounds were investigating a grassy mound on the edge of the burn that divided the grazing from the grain. Their herding would finish when the cattle lay down and the night fell.

"It's a beautiful land," murmured Old Hector.

"Come in," said Mary quietly.

When she had put the washed dishes away and tidied the kitchen, she got her knitting needles, sat down to a sock, and began talking cheerfully of other harvests.

"The taking in of the last sheaf and the harvest home!" she murmured, looking at Old Hector.

"I can remember it as a boy," he answered, playing up to her, "but that custom passed long ago."

"Did it?" Her dark eyebrows arched. "And what had you in its place?"

"Nothing much. Indeed just nothing—though it was always fine to see the harvest gathered. With a good harvest gathered, you felt snug—you felt it could snow now!"

"And it generally did. Snow! And your brothers catching the singing birds alive under the riddle. Many a fight I had with them over that."

"I'm sure you would," agreed Old Hector.

"Yes. But tell me—have the old customs died out, then? Even Robert here must remember the harvest home—or perhaps he doesn't?"

In the Cornfield

But her husband, lost in his dark thought, did not appear to hear her.

Mary started a new row. "He was a very bashful fellow, as you can imagine," she said to Old Hector.

"Indeed I have known many a fine lad bashful then, for if there is one thing more terrible than another to a young fellow it's a good-looking girl with spirit. You talk of the boys catching linnets." He shook his head. "They were merciful in comparison."

"And they generally let the birds go," added Robert suddenly. "They had that grace."

"They let them all go except one," she said, "and that one they shoved into a cage, taking its freedom from it forever, poor thing."

"Tell me," and Robert gave the old man a curious look, "which of you was put in the cage?"

"That's a difficult one," answered Old Hector thoughtfully. "At first I certainly did not think it was me. I was so glad to have her there . . . but maybe I was only bewitched. And she didn't come from Torbeg either. But I had a grandmother who came from there."

"What was her name?" asked Mary.

"Her first name was the same as your own though we called it Mairi. But she was not a Campbell. Mairi Ross she was."

"Ross was my mother's name," answered Mary. "Shiela Ross."

"There was a Shiela," answered Old Hector, "but how many generations before me I can't remember. But would you be going as far back as that?"

"Yes."

"Would you?" said Old Hector, and he looked at her, then looked down at his hands.

But their talk became disjointed, and though Mary evoked the past and got the old man speaking, time went by them on slow feet.

In the Cornfield

At last she got up. "You must be tired," she said.

"No indeed," answered Old Hector. "I have enjoyed the evening."

"It might have been a bit brighter," she suggested, not looking at her husband. "However, perhaps you'll sleep well."

"I'm sure I will." He arose. "But what about arranging who is to watch for the boy?"

Outside a peewit called. A dog barked. At once Robert was on his feet. But Mary had her hand against him. "I'll go," she said.

"No you won't," he answered.

"I will!"

Robert looked searchingly into her eyes.

"Let her go," said Old Hector quietly.

She left them, closing the inside door behind her.

"He'll come to her," said Old Hector, "when he wouldn't to you."

Robert looked at him. "Do you think that was a real peewit's call?"

"It was fairly like it."

"They're keeping watch on us," he said. "That's what it is."

"Why should they do that?"

"We'll find out soon enough. They'll be questioning her next."

"Who? Mary?" Old Hector's voice was low and appalled.

"Who else? If they cannot find the boy soon, aren't they bound to question us?"

"But—but—you have nothing to hide. The boy—you——"

Robert laughed in his harsh way.

The door opened and Mary stood before them, her face pale, her eyes glancing.

"I think it's just the dogs," she said. "They don't like being shut in."

"Mary!"

She faced her husband's challenge with a stormy look.

85

In the Cornfield

"Did you hear anyone going about?" asked Old Hector, quietly.

"I felt there was someone," she said.

Her husband started for the door, but she stood with her back to it.

"Get out of my way!"

She refused to move, spreading her arms backward against the door. "You are not going out."

"No?"

"No. You—are not getting into trouble."

"What do you mean?"

"They may be watching." Her eyes never left his face.

"Mary—is Art there?"

"Never you mind."

There was silence—in which she faced them unflinching. "You are not going out now," she said.

"Where are the dogs?"

"Still shut up."

Robert never took his eyes off her.

They listened to the night.

"There is no hurry now," said Old Hector. "And what has to be done is just this. It would surely be foolish for either of you to get into trouble. If you did, I would hardly forgive myself. But in any case, it would serve no end. You can see that? No end at all. So leave me to deal with the boy—and with the others."

She looked at Old Hector with the bright considering eyes of one who had no interest in what he was saying.

Her husband was still watching her.

"Did you see Art, outside, just now?" he demanded.

"No." She turned her eyes upon him.

"What do you think you're trying to do?"

"It has nothing to do with you."

"Hasn't it?"

"No. And you won't see Art, either of you. And you wouldn't

find him now in the dark, even if he had come in the dark. And he didn't come in the dark."

"You saw him outside?"

"I did not see him outside."

"Mary," began Robert in a tone of deadly decision—but there was a sound of scratching at the outside door. Mary quickened. Her husband strode forward, bodily flung her aside, and pulled the inner door open. Standing in the gloom of the short passage was young Art with a hound on either side of him.

XII

ROBERT TALKS

He looked like a legendary boy, and to Old Hector it seemed he had grown two or three inches. There was a flush of colour in his face, and dark smudges from sleep or tears. His eyes rested upon each of them in turn, but with that alien look which Old Hector had seen more than once before on Earth.

"Well, boy, have you come back?" he asked, quietly but naturally.

Art half turned away.

Mary went up to him and stooped to whisper. He began to cry and she brought him in, shielding his face against her body.

Now that he had let himself go, he wept very strongly, and she comforted him, but gently, letting him have his way.

Robert turned away abruptly and saw the dogs. "What are you doing here? Get out!" Clearly they were unused to this voice, for while their eyes looked at him their bodies quivered and shrunk. They retreated before him and he shut the outside door with a bang.

Robert Talks

As Art's weeping subsided he developed a hiccup.

"So you knew all the time where he was?" Robert challenged Mary.

She murmured softly to Art, her head down.

"You knew he was outside there in the dark and told a lie about it. You saw him and denied it. Well—I'd advise you to have a better story than that—when they have you up."

She paid no attention to him, sitting there with Art beside her. Robert took a turn about the kitchen. "However, this settles the business now." His voice had a final harshness.

"Now—you're better now, aren't you?" said Mary softly to Art.

"I—I didn't—hic!——"

"Hush," said Mary. She looked up at her husband. "Is there any sense in frightening the boy?" she asked him mildly, but with a gleam in her eye. Then she turned her attention to Art again. "I know," she said. "It came over you. I don't know how you stood it so long; and Hector doesn't know, do you, Hector?"

"Indeed it's a complete marvel to me altogether," replied Old Hector.

"I—heard a noise. I thought—it was—someone."

"And you wanted to tell me? That was the right thing to do. Wasn't it, Hector?"

"It was the only thing a fellow could do in the circumstances," agreed Old Hector. "Certainly."

"There now!" said Mary. "Hector is wise and knows everything. Doesn't he?"

"He knows a good lot himself," said Old Hector. "For once he ate of the salmon of wisdom without hardly burning his fingers. And that's something."

Presently Art lifted his head and from under his brows stole a look at Robert. It was still that alien look, and Mary could hardly bear it, but she kept her arms still.

"What sort of sound did you hear?" she asked him.

Robert Talks

"Someone—walking," murmured Art.

"Did you cry at once—or did you wait?"

"I waited."

"Did you think it was a good cry he gave?" Mary asked Old Hector.

"Good? It certainly deceived me completely, and I have heard more than one peewit in my time."

"There, now!" said Mary. "And it sounded far far away, like a peewit in the hills."

"Where was he?" asked Robert, in a deliberate voice. He sat down.

Mary looked at him. "Does it matter?"

"Whatever story we tell it had better be the same story," he answered with restraint.

"But you couldn't tell—what you didn't know."

"And so all the blame would be yours? It's very thoughtful of you."

"Robert!"

"I think," said Old Hector, "that we had better know. It's the only way for us to know where we are."

Mary thought for a moment. "Very well. Only—I did not tell a lie, for I did not see him when I went out. He was not outside—he was in the barn. I spoke to him through the door."

"Has he been there—the whole time?" asked Robert.

"Yes." Her voice answering his piercing tone was cool and ready.

"How did you find him?" asked Old Hector.

"I saw him for an instant as he slipped from among the running cattle into the stream. I knew he would hide there, and while you thought I was gone to make up your bed, I went out and found him. The dogs were with me and I saw that they made friends. Art knew that he could have no better guard in the world than the dogs. They stayed with him in the barn. He is very fond of them now. Aren't you, Art?"

Robert Talks

Art nodded.

Mary looked up, white challenge in her face.

"You certainly have landed yourself now," said Robert, "head, heels, an' all."

"Well, what if I have?"

"Oh, be quiet, woman!" He got to his feet.

"Don't worry," she said. "I'll bear it. Women are used to bearing." The words were bitter in her smiling mouth.

"Rebellion, not through ignorance—sheer and designed! And I suppose you'll start by lying about it!"

"I knew," she said with deliberation, "that I shouldn't have told you."

"Have you any further plans?"

"If I have, I'll know how to keep them to myself."

He laughed. "And what do you think of this fine situation?" he asked Old Hector, as if probing him with a spike.

"My trouble," answered Old Hector, "is that I do not know enough. Maybe you forget that I am little more than a stranger here."

"Of course! A stranger in the Perfect Place! You have never seen the caverns of the Industrial Peak where the fruit is processed? Of course not! I forgot that! When they find out what's been happening here, they'll shove me back there again, to make me perfect once more. I don't know where they'll shove Mary. They might use her sympathetic mind, once they have 'cured' it, for moulding the minds of little children, like Mavis." Something gargantuan in his internal derision seemed physically to enlarge him.

"I'll not get any of you into trouble if I can help it," murmured Old Hector.

"If you can help it!" repeated Robert. "Have you been able to help it?" And he threw himself into his chair.

"It might be easier to help it if I knew more. You can always fight better for your friends when you know their need." The light in his face was bleak.

Robert Talks

"Fight!" repeated Robert, and the word swelled up like an idiotic bladder.

"If we cannot fight, we can at least give ourselves up, the boy and myself."

Art stirred and Mary murmured comfortingly to him. "Come," she said, "and I'll make a small bed for you beside Hector."

But Art did not want to go to bed. At last, however, she persuaded him and they left the room.

"You think you might help, eh? When this gets known to them—as now it must—it's not you they'll worry about. You think they haven't broken you yet. Have they tried? Have they done anything more than talk to you?"

Old Hector was silent.

"But it had to come. It was working up to it. One way or another it would have come anyway. You need let no blame rest on you," said Robert.

"Why had it to come?" asked Old Hector.

"Because she's a woman," he answered. "And a woman always fights not for a theory, not for a system, but for life. For dear life! In that fight, she'll lie and be treacherous with extreme cunning. She doesn't care about words like lying and treachery. They're our words, not hers, anyway. She just fights for dear life. She doesn't give a tinker's curse for reason. Mary there—I see it in her—I see the madness in her—Mary there is now prepared to bring down all heaven in small pieces about our feet, whatever should come of it."

"Why?"

"Why?" echoed Robert, and in his black-blown humour there was an extraordinary bitterness. "Because the fruit has brought back life into her again, just as the boy Art brought back the memory of her son—our son—who was destroyed on earth."

Old Hector's head hung in the silence.

"I shouldn't have said that," came Robert's low voice.

Robert Talks

Old Hector looked up into a face with glowing searching eyes.

"If it's about the fruit, you needn't be afraid of what you have said to me. I knew."

"You knew? Had she told you—already?"

"You know she wouldn't do that." Then quietly Old Hector told him of the various signs—the bulge of the apples in Robert's pockets, the lack of ill effects from the porridge first partaken in his cottage, the words heard outside the raspberry thicket—whereby he had silently judged that Robert and Mary could eat the fruit.

Robert blew out breath. "And we thought—the four of us, only four of us—that we could hide it forever!"

Old Hector said nothing.

Mary came in and glanced at them and withdrew again.

Old Hector stirred. "Was not the fruit always forbidden?"

"No."

"Why was it forbidden?"

"So that man would be restored to his original innocence, so that he would be without blemish, so that he would be the perfect worker, so that he would do all things he was told to do, so that perpetual order would reign everywhere." The precision in the tones was bitter.

Old Hector looked at him, troubled.

"Have you been in the history room?" asked Robert.

"No," answered Old Hector.

"One day there and all your doubts will vanish. You will understand with a new freshness the sin of disobedience. You will realise that obedience is the highest of all virtues, for in it is order, and seemliness, and an end to the burden of thought and decision. Man's curse has been the curse of disobedience. They educate you over again very profoundly in the rooms."

Old Hector stirred uneasily.

"Was there disobedience—and sin—when you used to eat the fruit?"

Robert Talks

"We ate and we gave and we laughed and we sang, and sometimes in moments of ecstasy we made verses. We lived in a state of ignorance." Then he added, "I was a bard," and laughed in self-mockery, but softly now.

"Were you happy?" asked Old Hector.

"Perfectly. A bit crowded here and there, because folk will be clannish. That started it. We had to be spaced out." His eyes gleamed.

"Who started it?"

"Those up by," answered Robert, "guided by a few who came in with the new ideas. The new ideas were very wonderful. There hadn't been enough organising, and in particular no spacing. They said that in another millennium it mightn't be convenient to extend the Green Isle any farther. The idea of a lack of living room in a thousand years haunted us more than if the lack was to be next week. It caused a tremendous amount of talk."

"Extend the Green Isle?" Old Hector looked at him.

Robert's dark eyes glowed now with an almost friendly satire. "You thought that the one place would be big enough to hold everyone, though they kept on coming for ever?"

Old Hector smiled remotely. "I've known me wonder about it—for a moment."

"Who were you to wonder? But it was very simple. The Green Isle of the Great Deep was just shoved out a bit, as needed."

Old Hector nodded at the simplicity of the solution. "It must be a big place, then?"

"Very. How big, none of us knows."

"And is everything ruled from the Seat?"

"There are many Seats."

"Are there?" Old Hector was startled.

"Yes. They are the governing centres of the great Regions. They run everything, from the coastwatcher to the industrial worker, from the orchard to the lecture room."

Robert Talks

"And who is over them all?" asked Old Hector, curiously but gravely.

"There are rumours of a Perfect Administrator, a Head. But we do not ask questions about him—for much the same reason as you did not on earth ask questions about the size of Paradise. In fact, for much the same reason as makes you hesitate even now to ask if the Perfect Administrator is God."

Old Hector regarded the light in Robert's eyes.

"No," answered Robert. "He is not God—that at least is certain. In these temporal affairs He has handed over the power to the Head. That gives Him time to meditate. And one meditation may take a thousand years, for within the meditation of God there is no time."

"Where does He abide?" asked Old Hector, quietly.

"Sometimes here, sometimes there, but no-one among the people can be sure. The western Peak in any Seat is His Peak."

Old Hector was silent for a little time. "Can no-one, then," he asked, "come before Him?"

Robert smiled as he shifted on his chair. "We understand that anyone has the right to come before God. That was one of the conditions in the new dispensation which God laid down for His people—though it is not known among the increasing many."

"Why is it not known?"

"Because the lack of such knowledge may be a convenience to those who would have to arrange such an interview."

"But *you* know—and you could ask?"

"Verily," answered Robert.

Old Hector regarded the satiric gleam gravely. "Has no-one like you ever asked?"

"Oh yes," said Robert. "You can ask. Then you are taken into a room alone with the Questioner and he asks you: *Why do you ask?*"

"I see," said Old Hector.

"So in the end you don't ask. Indeed you are left with a

knowledge of the enormity of your presumption and with a feeling of gratitude to the Questioner, who, having shown you your own secret motives, your hidden mutiny, the wickedness of your heart which would imperil God's new dispensation for the good of all, then forgives you out of his profound understanding and sends you on your way a changed man. And even when you have picked up your strength, the memory of your ordeal remains like a nightmare."

"But if God heard no man, must He not wonder?"

"From time to time He hears men, who tell Him of this perfection and of that. It is arranged."

"But surely God can see into the hearts of these men?"

"He does. But they are men who delight in the perfect Administration. They have nothing to hide."

Old Hector looked at Robert and on his face appeared a bleak smile, for there is a neatness in perfection that commands tribute.

"But in the beginning," he asked, "when they were introducing this new system, was there not trouble?"

"Very little," answered Robert. "For it started with a process of enlightenment amongst the people. The people were continuously being enlightened in many ways. They talked and they took sides. But the Perfectionists, as they were called, grew in number, and the Reactionists, those who held to the old ways, were looked down upon. For the Perfectionists had all the good arguments. The others were just the lazy who did not want any change, who did not think of the future. Yet in a thousand years the Green Isle would be too small—the thing was getting serious."

"But surely God could make the Green Isle big enough in a thousand years? Surely nothing is impossible to Him?"

"It was not so simple as that. Certain things are given, like the Green Isle and administrators who have to rule. The scientists at the Seat, they said these things were given——"

Robert Talks

"Given by whom?"

"You can say by God, if you like. But that's only a manner of speaking. Absolutely or mathematically, they were given. The rationalist philosophers at the Seat accepted them as given for all time everywhere. That being so, they were given also for God."

"I do not understand that. What God gives surely He can take away?"

"Can He? God gave the earth, and left man to work out his fate on it. If man was to work out his own fate, how could God interfere? Often you must have wondered, when great wrongs were being done to you or to your people, why God allowed it. For great wrongs were done to your people, weren't they?"

"They were," said Old Hector.

Mary came in quietly. In answer to their look, "He's asleep," she said, and glanced about for her knitting, and sat down, and it was as if all this had never ceased taking place.

"He'll have been worn out," said Old Hector, but as one lost in his own thought.

Robert glanced at the busy fingers and bent head of his wife, but she did not look up. By the soft gentleness of her appearance he was not deceived.

"Tell me," said Old Hector, in the voice of one listening to a fatal story, "what happened then. Did they use force to disperse the people?"

"To use force indicates failure," answered Robert. "The only final way to deal with an opponent is to convert him. Those who had arrived from the earth with the new ideas had not only learned that, but also had come near perfecting the methods of attaining it. Here they had scope for their new ideas beyond all earthly dreams. So they first converted the existing Administrators, which was not very difficult."

"How that?"

Robert Talks

"Because it not only seated them more surely in power but also gave them the belief that their power was at last to be exercised in achieving that perfection of management of which men always dream."

"What side did you take yourself?"

"With my head I took the side of the Perfectionists, but with the rest of me I took the other side. In such a division it is the head that wins, because the head says: This has to be done, for when it is done everything will be better than ever before."

"The power of the idea," murmured Old Hector. "When I was a young man there was a schoolmaster in our place. He was older than me, but he had much devilment in him—indeed it had gone against him when trying for his degree. As he failed in that, our little school got him. When on a night ploy together, many an hour the two of us spent in a turf bothy or on a moor crest, talking of strange things. But when he had taken a small drop, it was Plato then! The manner of your talk brought him to my mind. He was a great Greek scholar, they said."

Mary lifted her eyes and glanced across at the old man. So did Robert, with a glimmer in his dark humour.

"I suppose there would be young fellows like Merk going among you, too?" said Old Hector.

"There were," said Robert.

"He's an eager lad," said Old Hector in the silence. "One like him would be able to tell you many a thing."

"We found," said Robert, "that he not only told—he listened."

Old Hector nodded. "Did the people begin to grumble at last, then?"

"They did. But when you are committed you are loyal. Yet after a time you question. And then they started on the fruit. It was the master move."

"Did you rise against it?"

97

Robert Talks

"Did you rise against the lairds and the factors and the clergy when they told you that you had to be cleared off your own ancient lands and your homes burnt down?"

"No," said Old Hector sadly.

"Think then of us. For all we were to suffer was a new kind of feasting. Not the old fruit that grew on the trees and the vines, not the old grain we milled ourselves, but a new exciting food, made all ready for us. You can see how easy it was."

"Was the fruit on the trees forbidden?"

"If I offered you such fruit now, would you take it?" asked Robert with a mocking glance.

"But why did they bother with the fruit?"

"Because the fruit is the fruit of life," answered Robert.

"*The tree of life also in the midst of the garden,*" issued Old Hector's voice softly from the Book of Genesis.

"Take that element out of the fruit; take the will out of the mind; and you know the people who inhabit the Green Isle of the Great Deep," said Robert.

"They look like that," murmured Old Hector. "Shells on a strange shore."

There was a noise from outside the window, like the thud of a small stone or a slipping foot. Robert leapt from his chair, hearkened a moment, then swiftly strode to the door and went out.

From the kitchen they heard his footfalls, heard him call the dogs. In a little while he returned, his face pale, his eyes glittering. "They must have been listening," he said. "I could see no-one." He was breathing heavily; his eyes roved, then rested on his wife from under lowering brows.

She held his look in her open face then turned away to the dresser. He watched her rummage there. She took out one of his old shirts and at arm's length examined it. "Do you think I could cut this down?" she wondered thoughtfully. "The shirt that is on him is in rags."

XIII

THE THIRD DISAPPEARANCE

"Yes, Robert told me a little about the past, but it was only because I asked him," admitted Old Hector. He was getting desperately tired, for this continuous questioning affected him like a great weight of wool pressing ever more heavily upon him and smothering him.

"What did he tell you?" asked the Questioner.

"He told me," answered Old Hector, "that this land in the past was not run very well and then there came those who ran it in a perfect way. He had great admiration for those who came and he helped them."

"Has he still admiration for them?"

"Yes," answered Old Hector.

"Now before saying Yes you paused for an instant. Why did you do that?"

"I didn't notice I did it," answered Old Hector.

"Well, I did. And you wouldn't have paused, even for that small moment, unless something of doubt had crossed your mind. What was the small doubt?"

"I don't know. I can't think of any."

"Now you are not being frank. And unless you are frank, how can we arrive at the truth? You have a great respect for the truth. So have I. Everything must be cleared away, so that the naked truth will be seen. Only then when we know the truth can we feel free. I do not need to tell you that." The Questioner's voice was touched with an austere understanding, and it was this that penetrated deep into Old Hector's soul where the austerities of his forebears lay.

"I don't know," he answered in an automatic way that turned his face to stone and drew the light in from his eyes.

99

The Third Disappearance

It was the dour unyielding attitude of the head prepared to take punishment and to endure. How naïve the attitude of one who would hide the doubt! As if truth could be spoken only in words, revelation be given only in language! As if, until the word is spoken, one has said nothing! In silence, the Questioner read all the lineaments of the face, the lineaments gathered together in the act of repression, and remaining like an ogam script not only of the conscious but now also of the unconscious mind. Endurance and conscience; the hardening and the motive for the hardening. And when this hardening was broken, through the inducement in the mind, by questioning, of an unendurable complexity, then from the unconscious would ascend, almost crying out, that which volition had buried there. Conscience in this man was extraordinarily strong, yet it had to struggle forever with the burdens laid upon it by loyalty. The exact degree of the primitive in this loyalty was difficult to assess, and fascinating to disentangle, for in this old Highland stock it was almost instinctively active. In others it was part of a clear superimposed behaviour pattern. Here it still lived very close to the region of instinct. And perhaps here, along this line, lay the true relationship with the boy, for it extended back into that sheer warmth of human gregariousness, concerned ultimately with self-preservation rather than with sex or——

Old Hector stirred. The burden was now just heavy enough.

"While you and Robert were talking in the kitchen," the Questioner went on as if, out of delicate consideration, he would not pursue the difficulty between them, "Mary, you say, was in the other room, putting the boy to bed."

"She was," said Old Hector.

"So she took no part in the conversation?"

"She never opened her mouth," answered Old Hector.

"She just sat listening to you?"

Old Hector put his hand up over his forehead. "She never

said anything," he repeated dully, and added, "she only came in at the end."

"She cannot therefore be held responsible for having heard what Robert said to you?"

"No."

"You think a lot of her?"

"She is a fine woman."

"She would be particularly anxious to do what she could for little Art?"

"She was."

"Naturally enough. Any woman would be fond of a small boy—particularly a small boy in difficulties. She would act to him just like his mother?"

"Yes," said Old Hector.

"And would naturally be prepared to shield him against Robert and even yourself? . . . I am not blaming her," said the Questioner. "But we must understand her if we are going to find Art, who has now escaped for the third time. Otherwise it's going to be difficult to help you. There is no reason why Art should not go to school here and why you shouldn't get a job suitable to your years in an orchard or even on a place like Robert's. The boy could then call on you from time to time, and life would be pleasant for you. But—if—Art is going to behave like this, breaking all our laws, then he will have to undergo some very special treatment, and will perhaps be sent to work in the Industrial Peak in a distant Region." There was silence for a moment. "Nothing has yet gone too far. Small irregularities can be forgotten, not only in Art's case but in the case of Mary and Robert and even yourself. All can be put right—if all is known. But I must know. And you know that I must know. I have dealt with you in a spirit of understanding—for your own good; and you have helped me by making me understand what is true in men like you. And I appreciate that. Moreover, Art is a little boy who knows no better. Have not his elders responsibility towards him? You

The Third Disappearance

must think of that. Mary has been affected by him, and Robert through Mary. In the end, there is nothing we cannot find out." The Questioner paused. "Now about Mary," he said.

A small dew broke upon Old Hector's forehead.

"But won't you wash yourself?" Merk asked him two hours later.

"I don't think I'll bother," muttered Old Hector.

Merk gazed at the old man with penetrating interest. "But with a clean up you'll feel fresher."

"I'm clean enough for me," answered Old Hector, and he stood quite still like one who had lost himself on his feet.

Merk's interest grew avid. "You don't want to clean yourself?"

Old Hector, from staring stupidly before him, looked again at the translucent water, then slowly turned his back on it and began walking away.

"What's gone wrong?" asked Axle, who had just finished washing.

Merk flashed him a brilliant look and, as they began following the old man, said, "It's getting more and more complicated. The boy has vanished again!"

"How vanished?"

"I don't know yet. But I'll know later, when I have a talk with the Questioner. It's clear he has got it all out of him."

"How do you know?"

"Couldn't you see?" asked Merk with his amused but challenging smile.

"How can I know what you're getting at?" asked Axle a trifle drily.

Merk all but laughed. "Couldn't you see that he feels unclean? Which means he has given a full confession."

"I don't see that," said Axle. "When a person confesses himself he can feel he has lost a burden, he can feel clean."

Merk looked at him closely.

The Third Disappearance

"Furthermore," continued Axle, not without a touch of malicious pedantry, "I should say that, being a peasant, he was not used to washing himself overmuch and, in the tiredness that follows a state of stress, is merely reverting to type. It is possible—in fact it is something to be warned against—one can be over-subtle."

"Without that capacity for extra subtlety," replied Merk, "it might be impossible to distinguish one peasant from another, impossible to pick out one and say *this* is the particular which reveals the general. But perhaps you think that we are born with the generalised law in us, that, epistemologically, we innately know the law, and that the empirical process of first examining phenomena before arriving at the law is waste of time?"

"I say no such thing," replied Axle.

Merk had all he could do to keep his mirth within bounds. There was something so heavy and solid about Axle! What a perfect governor of a prison camp!

"In that case, then," he answered, "we are merely driven back on individual observation. The value of such observation can be assessed only by its results. May I be permitted modestly to suggest that here we have a case which the Questioner has considered worthy of unusual attention."

"And your extra subtlety in discovering it is therefore established," said Axle, with a politeness of sardonic humour.

Merk glanced about him. His enjoyment of passages with Axle often produced this delightful restlessness.

Old Hector sat still on his bunk.

"You should take off his boots," suggested Axle, as he combed his hair.

Merk, who had been contemplating doing this, laughed as quietly as he could.

When he had combed his hair, Axle turned round and regarded the old man. "You'll find," he said in a controlled

The Third Disappearance

voice, "that he'll now lie down with his boots on. Not going to bed in your boots is a civilised reaction."

Merk waited. They both waited, as if they had laid a bet on the matter.

And at last Old Hector looked at his boots. From looking at them directly he stared at them absently. His mouth fell open, his eyes blinked, his head nodded.

"The behaviour, as you will notice, has all the characteristics of the behaviour of the horse," said Axle.

The head gave a small upward jerk, the eyes opened and beheld the boots. Upon the face came an extraordinary dismay, as if the boots were living boots, and the fingers began fumbling at the laces. The fingers stopped, the whole body paused—and then pitched forward with a soft grunt on the floor.

When they had lifted him on to the bunk and stretched him out on his back, Merk tugged the clothes loose at his throat.

"Leave him alone," said Axle. "That's nothing. It's quite normal."

"I'll take off his boots anyway," said Merk.

As Merk pulled the second boot off, Old Hector opened his eyes.

"Thank you." The eyes closed.

Merk watched the curious phenomenon of a smile, which had nearly come to the surface, dying inward, like water into dry ground. What was left was moulded clay, the mouth amid its hairy growth letting the breath out like a soft snore-hole.

There was a smile on Axle's face as Merk came across to his bed.

"Well?" challenged Merk.

"You have not yet told me what's happened," answered Axle, ignoring the challenge to his smile.

Merk thought a moment. "It's rather curious," he said. "And perhaps you might help with a suggestion. The boy Art turned up last night. That was their story when I went there this morning. He turned up in the dark. They took him in,

The Third Disappearance

fed him, and put him to bed in the same room as the old man slept in. But when they got up this morning he had gone. He must have gone, it seems, before it was quite daylight."

"Which of them woke him up?" asked Axle.

"None of them."

"Do you believe that?"

"On the whole—I think—I do."

"Of course if you do, that's that."

"Is it? Why, then, did they tell the story at all? They need not have told it. Having got hold of the boy, it was their responsibility to keep him. If they were wanting to shield him, why tell the story? Why get themselves into trouble? Unless the story is true, there simply is no rhyme nor reason for telling it. Or is there?"

"Such a story might be told if they wanted to make you believe he is still in the neighbourhood—when he is not. But anyway, why trouble about it now, when, by your own analysis of the old man's uncleanness, the Questioner must know the truth and presently will tell you?"

"Because I am interested now. I should like to know, within myself, straight off."

"You mean you have interest in interest for its own sake?"

Merk looked at him with that smile which always put Axle slightly on edge. "Are you not interested, intensely interested, in any curious manifestation of the mind—for its own sake?"

"I can hardly imagine a scientist starting on an experiment without any end in view."

"If he is a physicist, he always has only one ultimate end in view: the discovery of the pattern of physical events. If he is a psychologist, the discovery of the pattern of mental events."

As Axle had declared, when he first came, for pure psychology, these words of Merk, with the smile behind them, were in the nature of a sly criticism—that just might have repercussions in high quarters, that just might have him sent to the department where psychology was applied.

"I have understood that the events were to be discovered purely in order that they might be elsewhere applied. But perhaps I have been wrong," replied Axle.

"No, you are quite right," answered Merk. "But you seem to forget that it was always convenient to classify scientific effort in two ways: pure science and applied science. We, too, have our section for applying the findings of psychology."

But then Merk smiled. "However, I must be off." Turning on his heel, with a cheerful nod, he walked down past Old Hector—and paused to look at that aged face. The eyes opened and regarded him with the distant enigmatic look which a patient might bestow on his doctor who is finally withdrawing from him. Then they closed again. The spirit had pulled down its blinds.

XIV

MARY IS CALLED

Old Hector's body was heavy upon his weak knees, and when at last they came in sight of the croft (as he now thought of Robert's home) and saw the workers in the harvest field, the scene was too much for him and he began to breathe heavily and sag to the ground.

Merk eyed him carefully. "You would like to sit down?"

"I think I would," said Old Hector.

"Very well. You can rest here and we'll go on."

But they saw the workers in the field stop their labour and look up at them. They saw Tom coming down the western slope of the corrie. For Hector it was an old scene—an old loved vision—turned ominous in a moment's dream.

"I think," he murmured, with quiet courage, "that I'll manage."

Mary is Called

Merk looked at him—and secretly smiled. For clearly the old man was desperate now. And what could the old man be desperate about if not to put them on their guard by telling them all that he himself had confessed?

He arranged his setting with premeditated care. First, he hailed Tom and spoke with him apart while Mavis and Old Hector waited. And now Old Hector could not look towards those in the cornfield, who were again working steadily, led by Robert, but stood with his head down, lifting it once or twice to gaze at the far crest with hazed eyes, like one dreaming on his feet of what guilt might find beyond the hills of defeat.

Robert and Mary stood upright, as they were hailed, and looked across.

"Mary, I want to speak to you," called Mavis.

Mary walked slowly over. Robert spat on one hand and gripped the scythe as if to start working, but paused and then laid it on the ground. As he saw Mary's attitude when Mavis spoke to her, he strode towards them, his head up, his chest bare.

"You're getting ahead with the harvest," Merk greeted him.

"Yes," answered Robert shortly.

"Any word of Art?"

"None."

"His capacity for disappearing is becoming chronic."

"We can't help that. It has nothing to do with us."

"That's just what they want to know at the Seat—if you can help. They wish to have a talk with Mary."

"With Mary!"

"Yes. A woman understands a child better than a man. In any case, it is a request. She would be advised to go now."

"Now?"

"At once."

Robert's eyes, hard and stormy under the sensitive brows, turned upon Old Hector.

Mary is Called

Even the empty hands of the old man hung in a pitiful way by his sides. But his face was up, and the eyes met Robert's and told their shameful story. They melted inward in a soft, dreadful way; and in the face, most dreadful of all, was the ghost of his old dead smile.

Mary looked at that face. The silent telling of his shame was horrible, but tell it he would, in this last strait, to warn and help them. A softness came upon her features.

Robert turned to Merk abruptly. "Won't I do instead?"

"Not—just yet. It's Mary they want."

"But—she can't go just now. There's the harvest."

"That can be arranged. Hector will take her place, and Mary can tell one of the girls here, if that is necessary, where to find things."

"But—that's hardly good enough. Surely to-morrow will do and by that time the boy may have turned up and it won't be necessary."

Merk regarded the rising of the internal tempest with extreme interest. "I don't think putting any difficulty in the way will help either Mary or yourself."

"What's it to me what you think?"

"Robert!" cried Mary. "You know I will have to go. Don't make it more difficult for me."

"But there will be no difficulty," said Mavis simply.

Robert groaned. With clenched fists, he strode back to his scythe.

"He merely thinks that the talk will distress me," explained Mary, with a frank smile. Merk looked at her for several seconds.

But she was looking at Old Hector. "Come to the house," she said to him in a friendly voice. "I'll give you something to eat. You are very tired."

Old Hector swayed on his feet. Merk caught his arm. "Come along," he said. "A short rest will do you good."

Mary called a girl from the field and they went to the house.

Mary is Called

"Your bed is all ready," said Mary cheerfully. "In you go and lie down for a little."

"He seems to get very tired," said Mavis.

"Yes. His years are still heavy on him," Mary agreed. "Now, Betsy, I'll show you where you'll get the dishes and the food. Please sit down," she said to Merk. "We won't be long."

Briskly Mary went about her business and when it was over: "Excuse me, but I'll have to get something decent to put on." And she smiled.

Merk got up and went just outside the front door.

"I'll fetch my things from the other room," she said to the two girls. "One minute." Swiftly she left them, and as she entered where Old Hector was, swinging the door almost shut behind her, she said in her normal voice: "Why aren't you lying down? Take a rest. You can help Robert presently." But as the loud words came from her lips she went quickly to him and then in his ear whispered intensely: "Did you tell them that I could eat the forbidden fruit?"

She drew back her face to study his bewildered expression.

"No," he breathed vaguely; then shook his head more firmly.

Swiftly her arms went round his neck and she kissed him. In an instant the drawers of the clothes-chest were noisy. "I don't expect they'll want me very long," she called aloud to him. "But you know how to look after yourselves."

She smiled gaily, her lips forming the words, "So long!" and she was gone.

Old Hector stood like one who does not know what has hit him. Automatically his right hand went up and the fingers rubbed the cheekbone where she had kissed him. He stared stupidly, trying to get a grip on meaning. His legs weakened and he sat down heavily on the bed. What had he said about the fruit? Nothing. It had never been mentioned. The Questioner had not asked a question, had not mentioned it. But now she was going and he had not told her—what he had told the Questioner. She must think he had told nothing.

Mary is Called

His mind darkened. Thought would not form in it. He was done, an old done man, bringing calamity, calamity, calamity. . . . The tragic echoes cried far back in his mind, going down the dark road. . . .

The sounds of voices wakened him where he sat. Getting up, he found his way to the front door and pulled it open. Outside the scene was set. Robert had come from the field, bare-armed, bare-throated. Whatever had been said, the last word had been said. But now upon Mary's face, as she looked at Robert, there came an expression that forms within the silence of a poet's mind. Robert's face whitened and his dark eyes glowed.

The scene was held in that silent cry of love. Merk could not hear enough of it. Mavis's heart seemed to flutter in a way that frightened her. Mary smiled to Robert and her face was very beautiful. "So long," she called, and went away.

Robert strode wildly back to the field. After a little, brown-haired Betsy turned to the door and saw Old Hector. Her face was troubled, the eyebrows gathered as in an irritated effort to recall something. She studied the old man's face with a curiosity from which he stumbled away, going automatically into the kitchen.

"You would like some food?" she asked.

He sat down, put his elbows on the table, and held the weight of his head between his open hands.

She continued to regard him. Then her blue eyes opened very wide, her mouth opened slightly also, and her breath in affright became light as thistledown. Tears were running down the old man's face.

A bushy disordered face, a face seen for a moment in a cave, the moment when the nightmare flashes in the morning light and is instantly forgotten. A tamed but yet grotesque face. She was suddenly afraid to be alone with it; not bodily afraid, but still. . . . She took two steps away on tiptoe. When the body of the old man filled with a great breath, she stopped—and was just about to run, when his face lifted slowly, and slowly turned to her.

"You must forgive me," he said.

The smile caught her breath, for it was not a smile but that which lay drowned ocean-deep in it. She could not stop, could not wait another moment. But the old man got up, saying, "You'll excuse me," and fumbled his way into his own room.

She listened. She observed how still everything had become around her. Swiftly she reached the door and began running for the field.

"Why the hurry?" asked her partner on the scythe.

"I was keeping you back."

But as he presently paused to whet his scythe she took the opportunity to regard his face in a sidelong curious manner.

XV

A TALK IN THE DARK

Betsy had put away the last dish. "I think that's everything."

Robert did not hear her, but Old Hector looked up. She took off Mary's apron and hung it behind the cupboard door. "Good night."

"Good night," answered Old Hector.

Her footsteps could be heard running from the house like quick heart-beats.

Robert went out and came in again. Then he muttered something about the dogs and went out. After a time he came in. There was nothing for him to do inside. The dark was falling.

When next he went out, Old Hector heard him call the dogs and hearkened to his footsteps going round the gable-end. He

A Talk in the Dark

would be off to meet Mary, lest by a miracle she had been allowed home.

It was quite dark when he returned alone. "Are you there?" he called.

"Yes," answered Old Hector. "I forgot the lamp."

"Never mind—I'll find it." But he sat down in his chair and there was silence.

"Have you nothing to say?" asked Robert. "Do you think she will be back soon?"

"Soon or late—she will be back."

"You think so? What makes you think that? . . . Speak up, man."

"It's not easy for me to speak."

"But what makes you think they will let her come back? If you know anything, tell me. Don't——"

"I know nothing certain——"

"Ah," said Robert. "Nothing." His chair scraped on the floor and his throat was harsh. "I suppose you told them everything. But why did you put the blame on Mary?"

"I put blame on no-one. But the questions were too much for me. I cannot stand up to them. I want never to know anything more."

"You're a bit late," said Robert. "But I don't blame you— I blame myself. You thought that knowing would help—and I was fool enough. . . . I'm still fool enough to think that if I knew everything even now I could still help! How we are caught in our own delusions!"

"I did not know—how much he knew."

"And so by denying anything, you might merely land us in deeper trouble. It is made so clear to you!"

"And still—I hope," muttered Old Hector.

"What do you hope?"

"That by telling everything frankly—all will be understood —and forgiven. If we admit we made errors—the past, your past, will be restored. And the boy and myself will go about our business. That still seems likely to me—it seems the only way. And it has torn my heart that—that I had——"

"So you had rather a pleasant examination on the whole. He did reasonably and hopefully by you. And deep in your torn heart you are already the apostle of their ways."

Old Hector was silent.

"It was easy in your case," said Robert, and his voice was smooth as his scythe blade. "But they will take her from the first place to the second. They will not break her there. They will take her to the third place. . . . You do not know what the spectres are? You do not know how they come and sit in your brain. You do not know what it is to feel every barricade you feverishly scrape up against them being smashed down, being flooded down. And then—they start questioning all over again."

Old Hector groaned. "But what have you done?"

"Nothing much. The ordinary simple human being, because he will not give a friend's name, because he has had dealings with some folk, because he is loyal to some faith that's in him or outside him—he is taken away. It does not require to be a great and spectacular thing. It never is. It is always like this, simple, bewildering. You come. Art. The boy behaves after his kind. Mary. Myself. She has been taken. I shall be taken. Each of us will be shredded out and studied. Each of us is nothing. At the best, each of us is a figure which the examiner uses in his sum. And he must get his answer right. Once he gets it right, he can deal with bulk numbers afterwards. You as an individual he can dispose of any time now. For already you are convinced that what *he* said was right and best for us all."

Old Hector did not answer and for a long time they sat in silence in the darkness.

"Would you be prepared to accept what he said and to guide others accordingly?" asked Robert.

"I would," answered Old Hector in a low voice.

A Talk in the Dark

"For peace sake?"

"More than that. I can stand much myself. But pain—suffering—in others. It was always my weakness. And then, whatever happens, however we be held down, we can have our own minds, we can live in our own minds. They cannot take that from us."

"No?" said Robert. "What do you think they are trying to do? Why this concentration on the mind? Not on the body, not on direct physical violence. They'll never lay a hand on Mary—beyond a detaining hand. But should Mary ever come back here—it will not be the Mary you knew."

"Ah no!" said Old Hector.

"No?" said Robert. Then his voice caught a dreadful lightness. "There is a thing called an atom. Scientists, they say, change its nature by knocking something out of its centre. Here the atom is the mind. Its centre is the will. When they knock out that centre, the mind can still work, just as a horse that has been cut can work—in fact the brute works best and most obediently when he has been cut."

Old Hector regarded him with a faint horror.

Robert nodded. "Exactly," he said. "They castrate the mind."

The full tide of darkness came seeping in. Old Hector could find no foothold in it, no grip for the hand, and its infernal wave was threshing his head, stupefying him.

"But why?" he muttered. It was hardly a question and Robert's silence was a mockery of the inner cry.

They sat on in the darkness. An insidious sleep began to attack Old Hector, and inside its shameful darkness his mind struggled with the eternal weakness and shame of man. Questions whipped across his mind like stormy life-lines, but he hardly felt the lash of them and made no effort to lay hold. His own weakness and the shame of it; the selfish stealth by which he would slip away; the soft drowning ease of sleep, of oblivion.

A Talk in the Dark

"I'm feeling sleepy," he muttered.

"I understand," replied Robert quietly. "Let yourself go."

The last thing Old Hector heard was the grunting thrust of his own breath through mouth and nostrils.

He wandered in places where figures came at him. The face of the Questioner, luminous in inexorable purpose, smiling in a concentration that pierced. Another figure, middle-sized, burly and straight, full, not of understanding, of penetration, but of decision and force, a wind about him . . . the terrible one who acts . . . Great walls that slid away. Vast rooms that formed and changed. Merk running, his face over his shoulder. Confusion and crying. Horror. And Axle is standing there by the post, the spike in his hand. So it has come. But Axle does not attack him. Time enough for that. A few things to be found out first. You won't tell? You won't answer? Axle draws closer. No? . . .

Old Hector awoke with a cry and struck out in the dark.

"It's all right," called Robert, who had been shaking him. "I'm only wakening you. You'd better go to bed."

Robert was groping for the lamp when from outside came the distinct sound of a footfall . . . Fingers, searching the face of the door. The door was being pushed cautiously open. A pause, then a low voice: "Anyone in?"

Robert strode into the passage. "Who is it?"

"It's me—Tom. Who's in?"

"Hector and myself."

"That's all right then. I've got Art with me."

There was a slight scuffle. "Now, then," muttered Tom warningly. "You promised!"

Robert lit the lamp.

The men, on their feet, stood looking at this apparition of boyhood, turning dark eyes away from the sting of the light.

XVI

INTO THE DARK

Robert could not stop looking at the boy.

"I saw him," Tom was explaining, "in the darkening. At first I could hardly believe he was real, he ran so fast. But I followed, and inside the cave—the Foxes' Den—you know—in the bluff away to the right, above the birch wood?—I found him there."

From under his brows Art looked up at Robert, then quickly went to Old Hector and gripped him, burying his face.

Robert's brows were drawn in excitement. He was still looking at Art, but already manifestly thinking out his plan. He nodded in decision.

"I may still be in time—to save her the worst. First thing in the morning—we go."

"I thought he would help," said Tom. "And I made him a promise."

Robert wasn't interested, for his mind was still clearly weighing chances. What happened to Art was only of childish consequence.

"He was a brave little chap," said Tom. "I told him that Mary was taken away and would never come back, unless he came with me. It all depended on him what was going to happen to Mary, for she had done wrong in hiding him. So, when he understood that, he came."

"If only I could have gone there to-night!" said Robert.

"So I promised him we would see to it that he wouldn't have to go to school, if we could help it. I promised him that."

"First thing in the morning, Art and myself will be off to the Seat!" cried Robert.

"Will not!" muttered Art into Old Hector's body.

116

Into the Dark

Robert looked upon the boy and smiled.

"Will not go to Seat!" muttered Art wildly. He stamped the floor.

"But you said to me——" began Tom.

"Said I'd come here!" Art hit the floor in a dancing rage.

"Hush!" said Old Hector, putting his hand on his head. Something in the tone of his old friend's voice visibly affected Art. Presently he drew his head back and looked up at the one man who had never failed him; not when Donul his brother ran off on him, not at the time of the smuggling, not after the great fight with Dan Macgruther, not even after his blind betrayal of trust. Never. And now, for the first time in all time, that face was distant from him—trying to smile in the old way—but distant and different and arrayed with others against him. Slowly Art withdrew from Old Hector, and into his face came a touch of that alien considering look, into the stilled tempest of his expression it came, and it accused Old Hector, and in that moment his trust in man was broken, and he was alone and lonely.

As his clear child's eyes passed from one face to the other, in that remarkable interval of the holding of his rage, they were judged and condemned more surely than if the eyes were conscious of what they were doing. And, as if taken from them, there came into his eyes, too, a shadowy incredible simulacrum of age and cunning.

If Robert had not been on his toes Art would certainly have escaped. As it was, Robert just managed to grab him going out the front door. He fought all he could, and any way he could, and the more Robert spoke to him, bending over him on the floor, the more he yelled.

As the yelling died down, the hiccups started.

"He's a bit of a wild cat all right," said Robert cheerfully, as Old Hector took the boy over.

But now Art would have nothing to do with Old Hector. "Leave me alone," he muttered.

Into the Dark

"Very well," said Old Hector. "If it's nothing to you what happens to Mary, if you would not do one small thing for her to save her from terrible pain, we cannot help it. Only I was sure you would do it—once you knew. I banked on you."

Art appeared not even to listen to him, but his face turned slowly, following Robert, who went to the front door. After a time, there was a thudding of wood. Robert was clearly trying to get something to bar the door.

Art's breathing quickened and he hiccuped loudly in distress. Robert came in, "Now I've got you fixed up, young man!" Art would have danced into rage and tears were it not for something cheerful, even friendly, in Robert's voice. The position was frankly declared. Robert had locked him in.

While Art regarded him sidelong, with steady reserve, all three men gazed at the boy. The silence was rent by a terrific hiccup.

Robert laughed aloud.

Art gave a short maddened dance, but got control of himself, and turned from them to the table by the window.

"It's food the lad needs," said Robert and briskly he set about getting some bread and milk. "That'll do you a power of good," he declared, setting the food before Art.

"Don't want it," muttered Art.

"Try it, all the same. When a fellow has been out in the open, he needs food. I always need it myself anyway."

Standing with his back to them, Art refused to touch the food.

Old Hector made a sign not to mind him, and after a little Robert and Tom withdrew into the other room for a private talk.

Old Hector went to Art and said quietly but sensibly, "Eat your food. Times are not easy, but we have to do what we can."

Art remained stubbornly silent.

"They were kind to us and we must not forget our manners, whatever else," continued Old Hector. "If we have brought trouble on them, the least we can do is take our share of it."

Into the Dark

"Don't want to go to the Seat."

"I know," said Old Hector. "I don't want to go myself, but I'll go. It would be a poor spirit that would not do something to help Mary, for she was kind to us. To think, too, that she came from the Clachdrum country. That should be enough for you, or for anyone."

Art poked the bread away. "What will they do to her?"

"Who knows? You are only a small boy and they would do nothing to you. But Mary is big, and because she disobeyed orders by being kind to you and hiding you, who knows what they won't do to her?"

"Will they break her mind?"

"That's what we're frightened of," answered Old Hector. "But if we went at once—first thing in the morning—we might still be in time. So you see——"

"Would they break my mind?"

"What would they break your mind for? You're only a boy. They never break boys' minds."

Art was silent, showing neither belief nor disbelief.

Old Hector looked at him and saw that he was certainly growing. He was already more like a boy of ten or eleven than eight past. The skin was delicate and faintly flushed in the cheeks; the dark hair now came down over the temples; the brown eyes were full of light; his slim body was pliant and well-knit. With a small catch at the heart, Old Hector saw, coming out of this still presence with its impenetrable thought, the vision of the immortal boy.

"Eat the food," said Old Hector, "if only for politeness' sake."

Art began to eat.

As Robert and Tom came in, Old Hector motioned them to take no notice of him. When he had finished, Robert took him to a chair.

"What we want to know," said Robert frankly, "is how you managed to find the cave after Mary woke you in the morning?"

Into the Dark

Art looked at him and looked away, slowly. The face was quite inscrutable, not deliberately but as if it had not heard or was otherwise engaged.

"She did waken you, didn't she?"

Art looked down and with a finger-nail tested the thin scab that covered a long scratch on his knee.

Robert and Tom tried him in several ways, but they both were defeated by Art's silence.

"Why we want to know," said Old Hector, "is because we want to help Mary."

Art looked at him. "Didn't she tell you?"

There was a moment's pause. "No. But then she never rightly got the chance, because they came for her and took her away."

Art looked at him and looked away.

They could make nothing of him. They were not even certain whether he was being cunning now or merely stupidly wilful. The blank crystalline innocence of his eyes infuriated Robert at one point and he got up and went to the dresser.

"If you won't tell us what happened," said Old Hector, "how can we know what to do to help Mary? I can understand why you won't tell. It's a thing you wouldn't do. And we would never have asked you to tell, never—if Mary had not been taken away. But she did not know she would be taken away when she asked you not to tell. Now everything is different. She has been taken. And the only way you can help her is by telling us. Wouldn't she think you were clever if you helped her now!"

Robert, who was leaning back against the dresser, saw the troubling of Art's face, the shivering of the crystalline look. Old Hector's gentle voice was the voice of the deadly Questioner. The boy was being broken.

"It was clever of you to find the cave," said Old Hector. "Many a boy would have missed it who had only been told the way. Did you find it the first shot?"

Into the Dark

"I did," muttered Art.

"Good for you! We thought you were having a long talk with Mary the night before. I expect the two of you planned a good few things together. She was kind, was Mary." His tone was reminiscent.

Art began to show signs of distress.

"It must have been dark when you started out——" Tom began, but Old Hector interrupted him.

"That's nothing to Art," he said negligently. "When he was little he did not care much for the dark, like the rest of us, but it's different now. Once he was wakened in the morning he wasn't frightened to go. Were you, Art?"

Tears filled Art's eyes. He pulled his upper lip stiff over his teeth, but the tears rolled down. Suddenly he got up and Old Hector caught him.

"I did not tell," muttered Art, weeping against Old Hector.

"Not a word did you tell us," answered Old Hector. "You can rest assured of that." Old Hector patted him on the back as he wept pitifully. "All you would like to do is help us if you could. Isn't that it?"

"It—it is," said Art.

"And you'll go with Robert in the morning—if he wants you to go?"

"I—I will," said Art.

"That's the lad I knew," said Old Hector. "I'm proud of you now."

But a change had come over Robert. Three times he strode the kitchen then slumped down into his chair.

"I don't know what to do," he said.

The two men looked at him, and even Art's last sniffs ceased.

"Oh, I don't know," cried Robert. "It was clearly her doing, her doing, though she denied it to us." He got up again. "She'll have denied it to them, too. By telling, we may only sink her deeper." He leaned back against the dresser, his eyes smouldering.

Art turned slowly round and looked at him.

"I don't know what to do." He groaned, got into his chair, and took his head in his hands. "I may lose her altogether, for ever."

They all stared at him as he muttered these fatal words. There was silence in the kitchen, the silence of that eternity in which Robert would be without Mary. Tom could not bear it, and his voice cried out something. In that moment, Old Hector knew why Tom's voice had always been vaguely familiar. It was the voice that had spoken with Robert outside the thicket of raspberry canes.

"Have you nothing to say?" Robert cried.

Old Hector lifted his head. "We'll do what you want."

"You would have to do that anyway!" shouted Robert. "All this nonsense doesn't matter! Doesn't matter a pulped apple!" The chair gave a sharp crack under the stress of his body.

At these words Old Hector fell into deep thought. He was so weary that the thought became very fine. Neither Robert's voice nor Tom's did he hear. Presently he lifted his head and looked at Robert. "I know we are nothing," he said. "We have shown we will do what you want, and we would do it with good grace. But, like you, I'm thinking that maybe you should not go to the Seat with Art to-morrow."

Robert stared at him. "Why not?"

"The boy could go back to his cave for a day and we can wait to see what happens."

"We can wait for ever! It's not us I'm thinking of."

"I know that," answered Old Hector.

"Well?"

"Do you think—it will make any difference to—to the questioning of Mary, whether you go or not?"

Robert groaned. "Do you think I haven't been thinking of that?"

Into the Dark

"There's another thing," said Old Hector. He looked steadily at Robert. "It was a thing she did to me for a moment in the room in there, before she went. I was tired, for they took it out of me. And my wits wander or I would have thought of it before now. For myself, fruit is a thing I would sooner forget. Maybe——"

"What fruit?" It was little more than a husky whisper from Robert. And suddenly, like the terrible thing that had been entirely forgotten, the note of doom could be heard preparing itself to strike.

"The fruit—you had said to me—that Mary had found out how to eat the forbidden fruit."

"Yes?" whispered Robert, living in his eyes.

"She came into the room through there where I was. She was wanting some clothes. She spoke to me in a loud voice, telling me to lie down. Then in a moment she was at my ear, asking me under her breath if I had spoken of the fruit—to them at the Seat."

"Had you?"

"No," answered Old Hector.

Robert, who had been leaning forward, leaned back and blew a slow hissing breath at the ceiling. "My God," he said, "I must have been frightened to think of it." Then, with extreme animation, he was looking at Old Hector again. "What did you answer her?"

"I said No. It was all I had time to say."

"What did she say?"

"Nothing. She smiled. She—she put her arms round my neck—and was gone." He unconsciously rubbed his cheek-bone, in a lost confused way, as if the memory had only now come back in full.

Robert's glowing eyes remained on him with the utmost penetration.

To Art the kitchen became a big empty place in which Robert walked. Now and then his words were thrown into the

air. Old Hector lifted a word or two sometimes. Tom, who had
been shocked by Old Hector's knowledge, also added his word.
But all the words were like birds in the air, excited birds that
could not land. When Robert stood still, however, all the cries
died away, and the words came to rest on him as on a dark
tree. The upward gleam of his eyes gave space to the tree and
invisible branches.

Robert's chin fell to his breast. He sat down. There was
silence for a long time.

"You are right," he said at last. "Whatever she intends
saying or doing, we cannot help her now. It is beyond us. We
are committed."

"Well," said Tom defiantly, "what if we are? The boy can
go back to the cave. We can banish this meeting from our
minds. It is only an incident among many. Then we can wait
to see what happens."

And so it was finally agreed. Old Hector dragged himself
to bed. Robert, now quiet and friendly, made a shakedown
for Art.

"You'll mind to waken me in time?" asked Art.

And suddenly Robert knew that the boy had put the same
question to Mary when the two of them had conspired together. He tucked the boy in with gentle hands. "You can
rely on me now," he said.

Art needed a fair amount of wakening, and at first he could
make nothing of Robert's whispering voice. But soon he was
dressed. "The dawn is only an hour or so away," Robert told
him.

At the front door, Tom was waiting.

Robert watched the two figures disappearing into the dark,
then softly shut the door.

XVII

WAITING

In the cornfield Robert worked steadily and Old Hector kept up with him. All day long Robert hardly spoke, yet never did he turn to whet his scythe but his eyes lifted to the path that came down by the cottage from the direction of the Seat.

Towards midday Mavis appeared alone. Robert's eyes took on a hard glint and Old Hector had to work fast to keep up with him. When Mavis came towards them, Robert's face was a mask. No, they had seen nothing of Art. He asked her no question and, turning away, continued his labour.

Mavis called Betsy and they went off to the cottage to prepare the midday meal.

The meal over and the work begun again, Robert muttered, "I wonder what's keeping her hanging about now?"

"She's waiting for Tom," answered Old Hector.

Robert threw him a look.

"Remember where you are," suggested Old Hector.

Well on in the afternoon Tom appeared and Mavis went to meet him. They stood talking together for a long time. Then they began walking towards the cottage. They went up past the cottage. Robert's scythe got the ground blindly and, with drawn brows, he examined its edge.

"It's all right," murmured Old Hector. "He's not going to the Seat."

And sure enough the two figures stood on the crest of the rise above the cottage for some time, and then Tom took the path to the orchards.

As the darkness fell he returned, coming quietly in at the door.

Waiting

"Why didn't Merk turn up to-day?" Robert asked him at once.

"That's what I wanted to see you about. I had a long talk with Art. I had a talk with Mavis, as you saw. I'll tell you what I think has happened." Tom went to the outside door to make sure he had closed it properly. Their eyes were waiting for him as he came back. "Some time early this morning, Mary broke down and confessed—how much I don't know."

A painful sound came from Robert's throat.

"But what appears to be clear is that she suggested Art may have gone to the old Region you were in before you were sent here. Merk has gone there—to find out."

Robert looked at Tom. He could not understand him.

"It's difficult," said Tom. "Art told me that during the night he slept here, Mary was with him for a long time. He asked her many questions. She told him that once long ago you lived in another Region, and that there everything was fine and happy, with all the friends you knew, but that then the *Change* had come, and you were cleared off into this place, after hard times. She had not told him, of course, to try to find that other Region. Naturally she would not tell him that. There would be no point in it. But I'll question him more closely to-night."

"What exactly did Mavis tell you?" asked Robert, with terrible restraint.

"She said that Mary had broken down early this morning; but Mavis didn't know much, and what she did know she knew she shouldn't tell me. She's in a queer state. Mary told of the night Art spent here. So far, her story would agree with yours, Hector. Then it was taken out of her what she had said to Art about that other Region. That's really all I know. But it's clear she must have led them to believe the boy may have gone there. There just is one thing more." Tom's expression narrowed. "We have no idea here of the rumours that are spreading about the boy. All over. It's become terribly important for them that they find the boy."

Robert kept silent.

"It's entering the region of high policy," said Tom. "We may expect at any moment that the full Hunt will have the tracking of Art in hand."

"The Hunt!" repeated Robert, without moving.

"We are in it now to the eyes," concluded Tom.

"What's the Hunt?" asked Old Hector.

At sound of the word in another's mouth, Tom glanced about him, in the instinctive act of one who might receive a hidden blow even there in the kitchen.

"It's a word we don't throw about," he replied.

"Does it mean," asked Old Hector, "that they'll find the boy?"

"Certain, I should say," answered Tom with dry restraint.

"It means, I suppose," said Robert, still staring at Tom, "that Hector and myself will be taken at any moment."

"That's what I wanted to suggest—you should be prepared for it." The inner tension in Tom now eased. "They may have me up, too, of course," he added, "because of my contacts with the infected area." The wry smile affected no more than his lips.

Robert turned to Old Hector. "Can you face it?"

"I'll do my best," answered Old Hector.

Robert studied him. "Or do you think we should give Art up now? If we don't—you can imagine the consequences—when it is found out."

"I can," said Old Hector. "I can imagine the consequences to you and to Mary."

"And to yourself."

"If it rested only with me and Art," replied Old Hector, speaking fatally, "I know what I should do. And I should do it though you forbade me. I should give Art and myself up now, this night."

Waiting

"Who does it rest with, then?"

"With Mary," answered Old Hector.

"How do you make that out?" Robert's voice was cruelly searching.

"Because it is now clear that Mary has not told the whole truth. She has told them only so much of the truth. If it is enough to make them believe that it is the whole truth, then whatever strange design she may have—it will be her design. I would break that design if I went with Art now, and she would pay double." After a short pause, he added simply, "I hope I'll be able to bear most things, but I doubt if I could bear the reproach of her eyes." He sat down.

Mary's suffering eyes must have come before Robert, for he turned abruptly away. "What in the name of God is she up to?" he cried wildly.

"God knows," answered Tom, trying to relieve the painful tension with a bitter humour, "and He doesn't tell."

Into the silence rose Old Hector's voice quietly: "Does He know?"

They turned and looked at him.

Tom's humour came through his nostrils. "You have a way of putting your finger on it," he said, with a satire that was not usual to him. "For that is what must be worrying the Administration. God has a way, they say, of waking up and finding things out suddenly. That is why the Hunt, we can take it, will be swift and ruthless. For the curious thing about God is that He does not seem to hear about anything until it has become a legend."

The room seemed to fill with dark swirls, but Old Hector did not appear to be aware of them, and sat staring before him in a vague way.

"Well—I suppose," began Tom slowly, "I had better be thinking of going. It will soon be dark."

He stood still. The moment of supreme decision had come. If Art was going to be taken, it had to be now.

Waiting

Neither Robert nor Tom could move. The silence reached Old Hector and, as if realising that Tom had said he was going, he got up. "Good night," he said.

Tom hesitated an instant. "Good night," he answered, and began to move away. Old Hector went with him to the door. Robert did not speak.

XVIII

INTERVAL: THE LEGEND OF ART

Art grew into a legend very rapidly. An orchard worker who had gone out early one morning in order to have some baskets ready for the pickers had caught a glimpse of him. It was not quite light and at first he had got a shock, for he didn't know what dark thing it could be, slipping by tree-trunks like a shadow on pale legs. When he reached the top of the orchard he was just in time to see the figure disappearing round a bend in the path. He never doubted his own senses but felt that others might, and not until the following day had he mentioned it to a fellow worker, who had thereupon looked at him in a curious fashion.

The story went round and the man was chaffed, but when news of an actual missing boy became known the man grew important. When asked by Merk how old he thought the boy was, the man answered: About twelve. Now Art was known to be under nine. But he maintained that no boy he ever knew could run as Art had run unless he was twelve—and a marvel at that, though of course in the dawn-light it was difficult to be positive. The man was relieved to find that Merk, far from treating his estimate of age sceptically, was rendered thoughtful by it. This added to the mystery.

Then one morning a picker who had left an orange tree whole overnight found a small branch broken in the morning.

Interval: The Legend of Art

The fruit that had grown on the branch was gone. It required a good leap for a small boy to grip that branch. The size of the leap grew in the telling.

Next an orange was found well up the steep slope behind an orchard. Soon someone heard from someone who had been speaking to the man who found an apple core elsewhere. A piece of orange skin in a spot that was inclined to move about with the story caught a richer glow than if it had been attached to any fruit, for now the incredible, the utterly staggering notion had to be entertained, namely, that the boy *must actually eat the fruit and yet not be poisoned*.

Watches were set on the orchards voluntarily, so intense became the desire to get a glimpse of the mysterious boy.

When three young men, who had stayed out all night, gave chase under the stars to a small figure that dodged them among the trees and then suddenly vanished, the interest became more intense than ever, for now it was certain that the boy came to life in the night and slept in the day. This was in itself so disturbing an inversion of the divine order that even minds not given to excessive gabble could be heard to creak in an effort at realisation. Then there emerged—whence or from what single mind was never clear—the notion that the boy's behaviour and the poison fruit were interconnected. The boy must be able to digest poison! . . . It must be the poison! There's no getting away from logic. In the mind no longer susceptible to myth, logic takes myth's place.

And just as with myth, so with logic there is no final certainty. For what was their poison was clearly Art's meat. That the forbidden fruit was a poison became now only relatively true. It could not be accepted as a law, at least not scientifically. The Seat's law and the scientific law regarding poison in the fruit no longer coincided. Unthinkable!

So let Art be caught at once in order to have the whole disturbing business cleared up. Obviously now not a difficult job, for all that had to be done was to set watches through the night. Groups of four were stationed at points both in the orchards and on the paths of entrance or escape.

And then the most extraordinary story of all arrived in this country on the Near side of the Seat. For beyond the valley crests, beyond the Seat, lay the Far country, which, together with the Near country, made the vast Region which the Seat administered.

The story was this. In the first glimmer of morning above an orchard in the Far country, Art was seen, but this time not alone. He had with him a great hound. No sooner was he seen than he began to run away with the speed of the hound. The original narrator of the story said that Art had a thong tied to the beast's neck. Gripping this thong, Art went on his toes with the hound's speed. It was a speed that made the narrator so dizzy to think about that he stuttered in trying to find apt words to describe it. They disappeared so quickly that their movement was an arrow-swift glimmer through the morning twilight. They were here, they were there, they were no-where.

In the next Region, which began beyond the Far country, the story of Art took on quite a different form. In the first place, the name Art was surely a most unusual name. Art? It certainly was an odd name. Among the learned or academic, two schools of logic were quickly formed.

The first school said that Art was merely a name used to connote the activities of certain individuals in an earthly existence. These individuals had always been a source of trouble to those who had desired permanence in established thought and institution. These Art folk had had a certain stinging or poisonous power. By attacking an elder of the institution they could frequently make him seethe or even dance with rage and anger. Fortunately there were never at any given time a great number of them, so that when they could no longer be ignored they could be starved. Generally speaking, however, they

Interval: The Legend of Art

exhibited such a persistence in hanging on to life that many thought they must be able to live on their own poison.

There were, however, among the elders themselves, men of cunning, who professed to be tolerant. They found quite a subtle way of extracting his poison from the Art man or artist, for they discovered that he was susceptible to flattery and loved to be paid enormous prices for his work. Why not therefore use him—to decorate their institutions?

In the latest age on Earth this was apparently done on a considerable scale. The artist was even given a place in society, not a fundamental place because his activities, being uneconomic, were not of a fundamental kind; but so long as he agreed to accept the new thought and to decorate its institutions he was given flattery and sums of money, sometimes even quite huge sums of money. This worked very well, for by virtue of the artist's inner activity—a very obscure matter altogether—he could not help making, as it was phrased, a song and dance about the new institutions. Now the people liked nothing better than a song and dance, so the artist's activities thus had great advertising value. The technical term for this value was propaganda, and thus it became logically clear that all art not only partook of the nature of, but was in itself, propaganda.

Accordingly it was quite clear that the story concerning Art was a flash-back in the mind of some new arrival, by original nature individualistic or primitive (the same thing). It was a momentary carry-over from the earthly imperfect upon which Art had battened. No more than that. And if further proof were needed, it could be found, at least evidentially, in the story itself which was concerned, it would be noted, with a refractory boy called Art who lived on poison. In brief, the whole story was a primitive personification.

The second school had quite a different approach to the story. They advanced the theory that Art was an obvious—and even a known—contraction of Arthur. Now Arthur was the

Interval: The Legend of Art

original Chief of the Round Table. He was of Celtic stock. As the Celts had always been pushed back by predatory savage tribes into the bens and glens, into the west coast of every country, it was quite natural that some reflection of the Arthurian legend should appear in the Thirteenth Region. For thirteen was an unlucky number and, true to type, the Celts of the bens and glens had naturally landed on the Thirteenth Region (as Art and Old Hector had done). Further, the conditions of life in the bens and glens and on the adjacent seacoasts had always been of such an austere nature as not to permit of riotous living.

Accordingly when the predatory tribes who had driven them into their fastnesses returned at a later date to take from them what little they had in order to give it to flocks of grey sheep, the folk found that there was practically nothing left to live on but their own legends. They thus continued to die out quickly in a legendary atmosphere. So what was more natural than that such a story as was now under discussion should be ferried across? The one remarkable feature in it was that Arthur or Art should now assume not the appearance of a knight in armour but of a bare-legged boy, for this showed clearly that in the core of the legend there had always existed a youthful hope. In short, the story was no more than the personification of a legendary hope.

The theories of the Eleventh Region were less obvious, but still capable of being presented pictorially to the mind. As the distance from the living Art receded, however, there was a corresponding increase in mathematical presentation.

In the Fifth Region it was no longer necessary to take Art into consideration at all. Just as electrons, protons, atoms, electricity in any shape, or other unobservable or inferential matters, were jettisoned by a quantum mechanics that yet gave mathematically a complete description of the pattern of events, so Art, Old Hector, and the woman Mary were regarded as so many superstitious aids to a man-sized understanding which, in its more primitive stages, could only think in pictures.

By the time the First Region would have its version, the legend would be complete. Then—God would hear of it.

XIX

PROSPECT OF TORTURE

The whole day following the departure of Tom and Art for the cave passed like a day in a suspended nightmare. But Merk did not come. Mavis did not come. Even Tom did not come, though it was part of his allotted patrol duty to make daily contact with Robert. The milkers, however, came as usual, two young women and one man on their light cart or float, and as they had known Robert and Mary over a long period they at once began to ask about Art. They had all the latest stories about him and gabbled away in voices more excited than hushed.

Robert moved about to round up the cattle. Old Hector went into the house. The milkers glanced at one another. When they had heaved the cans of milk onto the float, they turned for a last look on this uncanny place. It was earthly still in the evening shadows.

The darkness fell. Mary did not come.

Robert could not sit. His silence was a high explosive, waiting for a spark. Old Hector went early to bed and slept deep.

Next day the harvest went on. Again neither Merk nor Mavis appeared. Tom failed to turn up. The darkness spread its smothering hand.

Mary did not come.

"They think I don't know what they're doing!" cried Robert in the lamplit kitchen. "I know all right! I know!"

Prospect of Torture

His laughter quietened Old Hector, who sat very still.

"They think they'll break me this way! They think I won't be able to bear it any longer! I know their game!"

Old Hector, who saw that Robert was very near breaking point, said quietly, "It looks as if that was their game indeed."

For some reason, this agreement released Robert. A flood of words came from him, and then he sat down, the inner tension eased, more like himself. "I wonder why Tom didn't turn up?" he said almost calmly.

"He was maybe sent to search somewhere else. He knows the Ridges better than anyone. And we heard the stories about Art appearing here and there."

"Do you think he's doing that?"

"I think it's very likely. And in that case—he'll soon be caught."

"Will he, begod!" cried Robert in one of his wild erratic changes of mood. "Not if we gathered enough food to keep him inside the cave!"

Old Hector remained silent—until Robert started for the door.

"Wait!" called Old Hector in a restrained voice. "This house will be watched. Day and night. That's certain."

"Of course!" said Robert. "Do you think I didn't know? Aren't you and I doing everything in our power to find the boy? The sooner he's found, the sooner the whole mess will be cleaned up—the sooner Mary will be back. What's Art to me? Nothing. Do you think they don't know that?"

Old Hector regarded the glowing terrible satire in the eyes and dropped his head. Robert went out.

When, after a time, Old Hector thought he heard a scream in the distance he became uneasy. Then he distinctly heard voices. Silence . . . a battering with wood near the barn . . . voices again.

After a long time, Robert came in, the night air on his face.

"They're watching all right," he said evenly. "And I enjoyed that! But Bran is gone. Only Oscar outside." He looked at Old Hector.

Prospect of Torture

"Perhaps Bran is with the boy."

Robert stood listening. Then he smiled strangely. "That's what I thought. But what if they should spot it?"

"He'll go with the dark and come with the dark."

"Will he? . . . When I was beyond the barn I saw a movement and knew at once from Oscar that it must be someone— by the willow bushes. I strolled up—and pounced. I stuck my fingers in him and he squealed. I thought you were Art, I said, and dropped him. I felt savage. So I went and got a length of wood and wondered whether I couldn't bar the barn door. We decided it might be better to leave it open, like a trap." He laughed silently. "He's still down by the willows. There seems to be a notion about that the boy sees better in the dark than in the day!"

Plainly action did Robert good. Suddenly he took a whirl about the kitchen. "All right! They can do no more to Mary now than they have done. They cannot do any more to her. Very well! They'll have to find out what they'll find out without any help from me!" He paused and in a desperate earthly voice said: "I could do with a drink."

Old Hector looked at him.

"Could you do with a drink?" asked Robert, probing him.

"I think a small drop," replied Old Hector thoughtfully, "would do me no harm."

"Are you beginning to feel rebellious at last?"

"No," answered Old Hector. "I have not felt rebellious for longer than I can remember. But sometimes a feeling comes on me and I take my own way." He paused, then continued in a thoughtful tone: "I was only wondering what a drop of drink from the grain of Paradise might be like."

"Smuggling in Paradise!" Human laughter was released in Robert, and fantasy, and the wild thoughts of a poet.

It was late when they got to bed, but the wildest thoughts were set at naught the following morning when Merk appeared and took Old Hector away.

Prospect of Torture

As they walked together towards the Seat, Merk questioned Old Hector who replied calmly but with an absent air. Then he began to question Merk.

"Have you found no trace of Art at all?"

"Plenty of traces, but so far no boy."

"That's a pity," said Old Hector.

"Why?" asked Merk.

"I was not thinking of you so much," replied Old Hector. "I am distressed that the boy and myself should have been the means of bringing trouble upon others."

"You mean Robert and Mary?"

"I do."

"How is Robert taking it?"

Old Hector remained silent.

"Why don't you answer?" asked Merk.

"Surely," said Old Hector, "I do not need to answer that. What's the boy to him? But Mary is something—and their pleasant lives together."

"Do you mean Robert would do all he could to find the boy?"

Old Hector paused and looked at Merk with a directness he had never hitherto used; then silently he went on. The obviousness of the answer seemed beyond speech to Old Hector. His manner, however, remained patient. "I can only think," he said in a little while, "as we used to think."

Merk became slightly excited.

But Old Hector grew absent in spirit and replied to Merk in an automatic way—which, to Merk, was the revealing way. Nothing, however, was revealed beyond a strengthening of what had already been said.

In the halls of the Seat Old Hector's calm was such that not even the ghost of a smile troubled his features. He looked absent and weary, but composed. For inwardly he was divided. If he answered the Questioner, the truth would be torn out of him. If he did not answer, then he must have something to hide. Whatever he did he would be broken and would break the others.

Prospect of Torture

In prospect, the questioning was a torture more terrible than any other kind of torture. For torture one can bear to the human limit, but when its end is not the suffering of torture but the degradation of the spirit in treachery, then is born a vileness that no eternity can wash out.

The weakness was kept from his knees by the dim fatal feeling that the time had arrived for him to go his own way. That in itself would not have helped much, for a point comes when, in the calm of desperation, a man believes he can endure to the end. But in Old Hector's mind there was something more, vaguely as yet but there, unformed but possible. And this something, awful to contemplate, he might yet invoke before he was broken. This was what brought upon him the calm of his outward attitude.

Merk took him here and there, but Old Hector lived within himself, husbanding his strength.

Finally Merk ushered him into the Atomic Psychology room.

There was a class in progress, taken by the Questioner, who paid no attention to them, so they remained standing at a little distance.

The Questioner was demonstrating a figure that sat in a hard chair, gripping the wooden arms, leaning forward, with glowing black eyes. He was a young man, with the air of a hunted revolutionary or a half-demented musician. Old Hector had not yet sat in that chair.

There were about a dozen in the class, two of them girls in their early twenties. The Questioner, in his detached way, was demonstrating how to put the figure at its ease, but Old Hector, knowing the deadly process, could hardly listen.

As he stood there, however, he became aware of a few things between Merk's whispering and the voices that spoke. And one of these things helped greatly to distract his attention from the figure in the chair. For a time, indeed, he could not take his eyes off the near girl though he could see but half of her face. She had been a sniper and with her own rifle had shot dead one hundred and seventy-two of the enemy and wounded one. This whispered information, to Old Hector, partook of the nature of apocalypse. It was so utterly beyond his conception of womanhood that it weakened him, and the dread he had anticipated began already to claw at his vitals. Already! He passed his palm over his forehead.

Then he saw her full face. It was open and of a virginal innocence. It was alive and energetic, boyish and confident. Indecent men would be abashed by its health.

Merk, after a penetrating look at the old man, brought a chair and Old Hector was glad to sit down. He closed his eyes. The door opened unceremoniously and two men came in. The class stood up. The Questioner dismissed them. As Old Hector lifted his head, the girl glanced at him in passing. Behind her came the face of Axle.

Merk stood uncertain, as if striving to divine the proper conduct of the moment. He had the alertness of one standing to attention. But the Questioner did not even look at him.

One of the two men was the Vice-Head of whom Old Hector had once caught a glimpse in the hall, and the other was not unlike him in build but broader and of a darker and even more forceful cast of features. Manifestly, by the way in which he was received by the Questioner, he was a comparative stranger from some other Region who obviously held high rank.

XX

THE NATURE OF FREEDOM

Greetings swiftly over, the great ones launched themselves on talk with abounding zeal.

"... Absolutely imperative. For that is what was never properly grasped," declared the Newcomer. "If only we had realised the power of the method. . . ." He shrugged, gave a quick laugh, and moved restlessly on his feet, alive with energy.

"If you had?" prompted the Vice, clearly for the pleasure of hearing what he knew would come.

"If we had, there would have been no war. We never realised that we had already nearly perfected a weapon infinitely more potent than war. It was not that war was tragic, it was silly. It was worse—it was old-fashioned. Incredible!"

"Using the psychology that should have gone with bows and arrows," suggested the Questioner with his quiet smile.

"Worse!" said the Newcomer. "Because we had already developed the psychology that had complete power within its grasp and could have made tanks and submarines as antiquated as the great reptiles. War was not a mere psychological reversion to bows and arrows; it was a physical reversion to the dinosaur order of prehistoric reptiles, almost literal!"

The Vice chuckled. "And you had gone so far, too!"

"Exactly! But we were haunted somehow by this idiotic need for war. We were impatient. We were possibly vainglorious. In short, we were all too human—and yet we weren't! Perhaps the method was so new that we ourselves simply never realised the absolute power that derives from propaganda and a secret police."

The Questioner nodded. "And your secret police were perhaps still——"

"A trifle crude," agreed the Newcomer. "But they were getting on. Refinement was being introduced to their methods. The trouble was that perhaps too many of them were just bullies, instead of psychologists. But we were getting the real psychologist to deal with the more important cases and the results were astounding. And so far as general propaganda went, through the radio and the press, we were on dead right lines. In a word, we had the most powerful organisation the earth has ever known—one that nothing conceivable could have overcome—and yet we delivered it over to be broken by the prehistoric reptiles!"

They enjoyed the enormity of the joke.

"But what about areas or nations where your methods had not yet been tried out?" asked the Vice. "Could you have overcome them?"

"In exactly the same way," said the Newcomer. "In fact we had already such a network of our method over all the earth that we felt we could bank on it. If only we had been a little more patient! But no—we had to parade our reptiles! For the truth was so obvious—that every nation was seeking order, an order in which their only possible salvation as social communities lay. And we had almost perfected the means of achieving it! Earth folk, being what they are, order can be achieved only by the few at the top. Earth folk instinctively realise that. They have always made, and still make, gods of their leaders. In war that is essential. In peace time, should they no longer do it, they crumble. You cannot have obedience without belief, and without obedience you perish. That's the historic law—everywhere. We were merely advanced enough to give it body and form—and to create the machinery that would ensure its permanence."

"But if it is objected that you cannot build from the top down, but only from the bottom up?" suggested the Questioner, the smile in his eyes.

"The objection is perfectly valid," said the Newcomer. "Those at the top build from the bottom up. In fact they must be particularly careful to begin at the bottom."

They laughed, with that quick movement of legs that made the Vice and the Newcomer look like army generals in a hurry.

"And how do you think things are going to shape on earth now?" asked the Questioner.

"Obviously, as I have suggested."

"No more war?"

The Nature of Freedom

"Certainly. There may, of course, be barbaric skirmishes here and there, but never again total war. We have taught the future leaders too much for that. No leader of any great area or nation will ever again turn to war. He will not try to gratify motive in that old-fashioned way. Out of violence comes violence. Reptiles crunch each other up. What distinguishes man from the reptile is his mind or brain. To be truly and scientifically effective, you must work on that. In short, the methods will be psychological, with just enough force behind it to make it completely persuasive. Not a force you parade. A hidden, invisible force, appearing every now and then mysteriously—to apprehend a doubter, to withdraw him temporarily from society, and to show him the error of his ways. When your method is perfect he will realise that however much what he had wanted to do might gratify his own desires, it would have been destructive to society. The parallel is the father dealing with a recalcitrant child. The wise father convinces the child. The unwise merely thrashes him."

"But what about those nations who cry Freedom?" asked the Questioner.

"Freedom!" echoed the Newcomer. "Merely a meaningless sound carried over from the reptile age. How long is it since science proved on earth that there was no such thing for any act, physical or mental? Everything is pre-determined. Science depends on that. All its laws are based on the inevitability that *this* will follow from *that*. In given conditions petrol will explode and tanks be driven with absolute certainty. There *never* is an exception."

"They thought of it more, perhaps, as a mental attribute; the freedom of the soul," suggested the Questioner.

"No biologist on earth believes either in the soul or its freedom, and the best biologists live now in what we call the Freedom nations or groups. They point out that the basic conception of the term freedom is idiotic, for it implies no more than a capacity for idiotic caprice. It could mean no more than that a great scientist would have the 'freedom' to deny what he had proved, a musician to deny his harmony, an artist his colours, a farmer the laws of natural growth, and so on. When men make such denials they are recognised to be idiots and shut up in a lunatic asylum. I stress that, merely to make my point, which is that the system of order we introduced will most certainly be brought to perfection first in the so-called Freedom nations or groups. Before I came away they were already in fact using our methods more skilfully."

"How more skilfully?" asked the Questioner whose curiosity in such matters was insatiable.

"Because with apparently greater concealment from the masses," answered the Newcomer with an ironic flash. "They have learned their lesson extremely well. They will make it clear that the Plan is being planned from the bottom up—in freedom! . . . However, time goes on. About this case of the boy—what do you propose doing next?"

"We are expecting him to be caught any minute. The whole affair is without any precedent." The Vice knitted his brows. "The Hunt is satisfied he is not now in this Region." He turned to the Questioner.

"I am not quite finished with the witnesses yet. But what has been established is that the boy is capable of acting on his own and that he lives on the fruit. By to-morrow or next day I'll be able to give definitely the whole psychological picture of the cottage." The Questioner paused. "I can only naturally at the best get a pointer towards the finding of the boy."

"Quite," said the Newcomer. "I appreciate your difficulties. And I can assure you I have done my best to make it certain he is not in my Region. But—a day or two?—it may be too late. You have a *Power* here that we had not to contend—to deal with—on earth."

"That is so," said the Vice, troubled.

"Do you mind if I give you my suggestions?"

"Please do."

The Nature of Freedom

"I gather that a legend may come to His ears and wake Him up from His meditations. In that case we must be prepared with a complete circumstantial story. I think that you and I"— the Newcomer looked at the Vice—"should get down to that immediately. Meantime we must quicken our efforts to get hold of the boy. It may all seem in a way trifling enough, but it's the snowball that starts the avalanche. Taking all the talk already going around, the wonder, the curiosity—the affair could become grave."

"I agree," said the Vice. "And once He——" He hesitated.

"Is He capable of upsetting——?"

"Absolutely," said the Vice. "It's a delicate matter. Not that He would mean——" He looked around, and saw Merk standing to attention and Old Hector sitting on his chair like a weary peasant, his head down. He frowned.

"It's all right," said the Questioner. "That's the old man who arrived with the boy." There was a noise at a side door. "And this," he added, "will be the woman."

XXI

MARY AND THE QUESTIONER

Old Hector lifted his head and saw Mary at the door, staring at the three standing men.

She was like a woman who had been washed and bleached, her face thinner, her hair heavier so that it stood away from her face in a suggestion of affright. She had come through her ordeal, its experience still about her, to the pale shell of her former being. She was not the Mary Old Hector had known. Robert's terrible prophecy stood alive before the old man's vision.

Her pallor showed no inner stress. She looked cleansed, and

Mary and the Questioner

empty, and alive on the surface of her face. Her thoughts were skin deep. She regarded the three men not in fear, but with an alertness that showed respect and readiness to answer. She was puzzled a little as to what the great could want with her, but she was not afraid.

"Come in," said the Questioner. She approached on light feet, her dark eyes wide upon them.

"This is Mary," explained the Questioner to the Newcomer without taking his eyes off her.

She looked at the Newcomer, but the Questioner drew her attention back upon himself. And now as his eyes rested on her there was a curious knowingness in their expression.

The pause was held in a tension which everyone in the room experienced—except perhaps Mary, who merely showed her faint puzzlement. The pause lengthened. Then the Questioner said to her quietly, "We have someone here you know," and with a slight gesture, while he watched her closely, he directed her attention to Old Hector.

Her brows went up and something happened to the pupils of her eyes. She was plainly disturbed, as if seeing something like a spectre from a far place. Then she remembered. "Oh yes," she said brightly, and smiled with the quick shallow smile so characteristic of those in the Green Isle.

Old Hector had lumbered to his feet, his face charged with feeling. He had the air of one who was ashamed and beaten, of one who had betrayed her.

"Perhaps you would like to have a talk with him," suggested the Questioner.

"Yes," she said. But equally lightly, to an opposite suggestion, she might have answered No. The Questioner turned to the two men and offered to accompany them to a suitable room for their talk. All three went out by a side door. Merk hesitated a moment, then he followed them.

"I am sorry," muttered the old man, "that this should have come upon you."

Mary and the Questioner

She looked at him strangely. "It is good," she said lightly. "I hope to go home to-morrow. How is the harvest doing?"

"Fine. Robert is very busy."

"He must be. Did you manage all right for food?"

"Yes, we managed well enough."

"That's good. I am glad I came here, for now my mind is free again. It will be pleasant to get back to the old life." A slight fret came to her brows. "It is dreadful when the mind goes wrong. I have had an awful time worrying about the trouble I brought upon Robert. It was so wrong. But I'll soon put that right. I know now." She smiled quickly. And then she went on to ask him question after question about the harvest and the harvesters and the milkers. She was like one looking forward to a pleasantness of living that, interrupted by nightmare, would now in true waking hours be found again.

He answered her calmly. There was no more he could do.

Then, suddenly remembering, "And the boy, Art—did you see him again?" she asked.

He looked into her contracting pupils. "No," he answered.

"Ah," she said. "He must have gone away. I had told him of the Region we used to be in. How extraordinary of him to disappear like that! But he was a funny boy." Her brows fretted faintly again. "I was telling Mavis this morning that I was beginning to doubt, the last day or two, whether such a boy had ever existed." She looked at him directly. "I suppose he really did?"

The old man looked down at his hands. The interview was becoming painful. "Yes," he muttered.

"Have you ever had the experience of not being sure whether something happened? You know what I mean. It's like . . ." Her voice took on the gabbling note which he had never quite got used to on the Green Isle. The words had no depth of actual experience. They had the extraordinary effect of being a reminiscence which evoked no feeling. She was an echo woman.

Mary and the Questioner

Merk came silently through a side door towards them. She looked at him expectantly.

"Mavis will be along in a minute," he said.

"Will I go?"

"If you like—she's just coming."

"Thank you, I'll go." She was obviously pleased at the prospect of Mavis's immediate company. "I may see you again," she said lightly to Old Hector and, turning, went quickly out at the door, closing it behind her.

Old Hector sat down heavily. "I'm not so young as I was," he remarked apologetically with that ghost of a smile which so fascinated Merk.

"You think she's changed?"

"I think she's more like her old self," answered Old Hector.

"That's one fascinating thing about you people—the words you use never seem quite to fit what they are presumably meant to express." Merk was being conversational. "There's a discrepancy somewhere, and the listener can never be quite certain where it is. Do you understand what I mean?"

"I don't understand much," answered Old Hector. "I'm only an old man and I'm a little tired."

"And I wonder," murmured Merk, "even if you quite mean that!" He smiled companionably at his own joke. "Tell me——" But just then a door opened and the Questioner came in. Merk went to meet him.

They spoke in quiet voices.

"Satisfied?" The Questioner looked at him.

"Yes," said Merk.

"Not the slightest trace . . . ?"

Merk shook his head.

The Questioner nodded. "I think it was final—for her. I'll have a talk with the old man."

"Will I go?"

"Yes."

As Merk withdrew, the Questioner approached Old Hector.

Mary and the Questioner

"Well, you have come back to see us again." His face was fair and smooth and quite friendly. "I think if we went into a smaller room . . . come."

Old Hector followed him through one of the many side doors into so small a chamber that the walls stood closely on guard about him and the ceiling above. This affected him in a moment, for the natural genius of his evasiveness needed, like sun and wind, the expanse of a moor. Here his eye could not find a horizon nor his thought a hidden strath. The room fitted about his spirit like a clamp, holding it for the Questioner to look at. Often had he himself looked on the melting brown eyes of a rabbit in a snare, the beaked defiance of a hawk in a trap. But he had at once killed the rabbit or destroyed the hawk.

"As you may have gathered," said the Questioner, in his easy, flawless manner, "this business about Art is causing considerable trouble. At first it was natural and even interesting, as a boy's escapade. We were a little amused. But now—it's a very different matter. A boy running about with a lighted torch in a barn of straw. When the barn goes on fire, people get burned putting it out. Mary——" he paused—"she has helped. Robert—*will help*. All those concerned—*will help*. And as to what may happen to the boy himself, amid the burning straw —you see what I mean?"

The chair on which the Questioner sat was a few inches higher than Old Hector's. There was no window in the room and the daylight came in a concealed manner from the roof. When Old Hector looked slightly upward at the Questioner he felt the light on his eyeballs in a slight strain. The pale walls stood closer.

Old Hector lowered his eyes and nodded. "I see," he said fatally.

"I am aware that you would not willingly bring disaster upon anyone. Let me put it to you like this: What, on earth, did you think was perhaps man's greatest crime?"

Mary and the Questioner

"Cruelty," answered Old Hector almost automatically, for once, long ago, little Art had put the same question to him and he had replied with that same word.

The Questioner considered him for a little time. "If cruelty results because someone is hiding Art, who would you say is to blame for it: the boy Art or the one who is hiding him?"

"The boy is young. One can hardly blame him."

"I agree. If you knew, therefore, where the boy was, you would be guilty of cruelty in hiding him?"

"I would," said Old Hector.

"Truly," said the Questioner solemnly. "In your tradition, I find a great reverence for the truth. You could not betray that. To betray that would be to brand you a liar, not a liar in little earthly things, but in the immortal ways of the spirit. Your spirit itself would have for its very heart, cruelty and lies. And not only your spirit. The great immortal Spirit itself— you would be denying that, you would be casting cruelty and lies upon it. At the end of your days, that would be your tribute to the central inspiration that man has dreamed of as the Eternal Spirit. After your fashion, on earth, whatever the errors and the sins, you know you were a good man and a kind man and a true man. It would surely be a horror if at the end you betrayed what your spirit knew was the truth. Here we ask for no more than the truth. Only the truth. The simple truth. Given that, the harmony of goodness is restored for all."

The Questioner spoke slowly, and his voice had the intonation, delicately simplified, of such ministers of the gospel as Old Hector had listened to all his days. Often in those days he had been lifted into the region of immortal truth, and his spirit had known a sweet and abiding peace, a strengthening that brought calm and gave beauty to simple things.

"You do not answer?" said the Questioner.

"I know," murmured Old Hector.

"I am not accusing you. I am simply showing you—the meaning, knowing you will do your best to help me. Now it is possible that some little thing may have happened, some small thing may have been said, that you may have forgotten, that you did not think was of value, and that yet may be very valuable to us. I should like therefore to go over again very carefully everything that happened at the cottage. You must answer me frankly; give the answer without thinking. Will you do that?"

Old Hector took a moment. The room closed in. The light grew stronger, and central in it were the Questioner's eyes. "I'll try," he said.

"Why do you hesitate?"

Old Hector shut out the walls of the room and strove to draw the enduring wall of his skull down over his spirit.

"Have you anything to hide?"

"I am before you," answered Old Hector. His head drooped, his hands fell apart. The weary gesture resigned the book of his mind to inspection.

XXII

THE FINAL REQUEST

There was silence for a little time, while the Questioner looked at him, the clear greenish-grey eyes travelling over every lineament of the old man.

"You have no idea where Art is?"

"No."

"Has Robert any idea?"

"No."

"You are quite sure of that?"

"I am."

"Think again. Think carefully. Because if you are telling the truth, then someone else has told a lie, and we shall have

The Final Request

to question her once more. Last night the woman Mary made her full confession."

Old Hector remained silent.

"You saw Mary?"

"I did."

"She is now free," said the Questioner. "But if you persist in saying that you—and Robert—know nothing of Art . . . then we shall have to hold her. We shall also have to get hold of Robert. There was an evening when Robert and Tom and yourself—were together."

Silence.

"You see what is coming?" asked the Questioner.

Old Hector stirred. "What can I do?" he asked pitifully.

"Just tell the simple truth," replied the Questioner in a sympathetic but firm voice. "I know the loyalty you have to your friends. That loyalty was bred in your bone. I understand it. But it can take you now to desperate ends. It can betray you —and them. And you all will suffer. And your suffering will have no meaning. Except this meaning—that it will have helped to destroy the Spirit."

Old Hector was silent.

"You are an old man," said the Questioner. "The boy is but a natural boy. The woman Mary—when she saw the boy, there came upon her a feeling of the old motherhood. She has confessed it. If you had known her life—and how her only child had been destroyed on earth—you would understand it. That has been the hidden root of the matter. That's why she was moved to hide the child, moved to rebellion. She understands it now. She is sorry. She told us the places where Art had gone."

"And did you look there?"

"We are looking."

"Perhaps, then, you will find him," said Old Hector, and his face lifted hopefully, and his eyes met the Questioner's eyes, and those eyes gazed so deeply into his that the walls and the ceiling came still nearer and wavered.

The Final Request

Old Hector removed his eyes with great difficulty. "I am weary," he muttered.

"You are stubborn," said the Questioner quietly. "You want the woman Mary to suffer still more."

"Ah no," muttered Old Hector. "Not that."

"Have you seen the boy Art—since Mary came here?" The words now were thin and level as a knife-blade.

"No," groaned Old Hector.

The knife came from other angles, but with the same response, until the Questioner said, "It is remarkable that you should so persist in lying."

"You are making me do it," cried Old Hector, his voice thick with anguish.

"So you admit—you saw him?"

"You are making me do it," repeated Old Hector, but now in a low hopeless stupid voice. His body sagged. "The light hurts me. It hurts my eyes." His body lay over, as if about to fall into a hypnotic sleep.

But the Questioner clearly did not want to use hypnosis yet. Hypnosis was too inextricably interwoven with suggestion. Besides, it implied defeat on the conscious level. And this the old man suddenly made clear in an unexpected manner.

"You are making me do it," he repeated for the third time, but now his voice was scarcely audible.

"Making you do what?"

Old Hector roused himself and said in a loud voice, as if tearing horrible adhesions away, "You will make me say anything. You will make me tell lies. You will make me tell lies because—because they will help." Whereupon he sagged.

The Questioner looked at him with extreme concentration. Then he drew back to simple tones and a new beginning. He didn't want to make Hector say any such thing, he affirmed. That would be to defeat truth. . . . "So let us go back to the cottage. Now take the night that Robert——"

"I can say no more," muttered Old Hector.

The Final Request

"But surely you can tell me what happened—unless you have something to hide?"

Old Hector was silent.

The Questioner said he wanted to reconstruct the scene in the cottage, to find out what Robert and Tom and Old Hector had been talking about. In this way, something that had escaped the old man's mind as unimportant might in fact be the small thing that would reveal much. It would help him, too, to understand the attitude of Robert. Otherwise—Robert—would have to come.

At the end of a quarter of an hour, the Questioner was still uncertain and Old Hector weaker.

Either the old man had something to hide—or fear, primitive fear, made him both wary and stupid.

There was no reason in this wariness or stupidity. That was its immense difficulty. It was primitive—mythological—and to get reason's truth out of it was like hunting the needle in a morass.

Whether the old man intuitively knew this and was acting up to it with extraordinary cunning, or whether the cross-examining was actually beating him back into the meaningless mental morass, could not be made absolutely certain; some final element in the old man, some ultimate twist of the serpent, eluded all rational pursuit.

It was a fascinating uncertainty. The chances were clearly a hundred to one that the old man was hiding something. It might mean nothing much. An odd primordial knot hardly worth the immense labour of untying. Again, it might just be the hundredth chance—of nothing. But—it might be the whole truth about Art.

Extremely fascinating. But now it was going to mean a much more subtle approach. And the old man was tiring desperately. He was at the point, where, assailed by suggestion from every direction, confession would of itself be desired, would break upon the mind like salvation, even though it meant death.

The Final Request

There is a pitch beyond which no burden, no pressure, can be borne. Once the dam is burst, confession comes in a stream, complete and absolute, destroying every barrier, washing away every obstruction. It is freedom, freedom, and the body and the mind wallow in it.

But the burden has to be made heavier little by little, the pressure increased by slow degrees. Time has to take a hand, the incomparable torture of time, of dread expectancy. Weakness seeks oblivion; and these two must be kept apart. Weakness must be kept awake; oblivion forever lie on the other side of confession. Delicate work.

The Questioner got going.

Half an hour later, Old Hector collapsed upon himself in a stupid swoon. Yet he did not fall off his chair. He groaned. Like an old beast that had been hit on the head, he groaned, and slowly shook his head.

The Questioner's eyes, watching the old man, narrowed. It was truly remarkable—the fight left in that aged body. Clearly, here was the case of the primitive mind with its parallel in the lower forms of animal life. Break it into bits, and each bit wriggles.

For the first time, the lust of his quest got into the Questioner's eyes. His breathing became a trifle more rapid. For interest now lay in some new suggestion of an indefinable region where the old man might have achieved a primitive integration, a certain living wisdom. The old man's weakness, his only personal lust, was a manifest hatred of cruelty. But that again was unfortunately balanced by an equal capacity to take punishment.

The Questioner decided to pursue the hunt into this primordial region. His lust grew on him. The cruel stroke on the mind could be used. Grunts and extraordinary cries became the speech of the jungle. Old Hector, like the wounded beast, floundered. Cried Yes and then cried No, meaninglessly. Relentlessly the Questioner pursued. Until at last the old man

could bear no more, and, crashing round, like some old stag
of his native forest, raised his stricken head and stood at bay.

The Questioner felt a small shiver from that challenge. The
whole primordial world stood still, this world, and all the universe of men and time.

And upon this silence, holding the Questioner by the eyes,
Old Hector spoke deep out of his throat:

"I want to see God."

XXIII

THE CAVE IS SURROUNDED

"They have now got all the hounds watched in at least
three Regions," said Tom in an undertone.

"Have they?" said Robert.

"Yes. So keep on shutting your hounds up at night. The Hunt
is thorough beyond anything we could imagine. It's terrifying."

"How does Art manage—without your Luath?"

"Pure mystery. When the hound didn't turn up—what did
he think? What did he do?" Tom shook his head. "But it can't
be long now."

"And what's going to happen when he is caught?"

"Don't joke about it. It brings the sweat out on me."

"You've been eating too much fruit," said Robert.

Tom looked slowly around. "Be quiet, for God's sake. See
that milker watching us."

"Yes. He's one of the Hunt."

Tom brought his eyes slowly onto Robert's face. Robert
laughed as if they had cracked a joke.

"No, he didn't tell me. But he tried to draw me last night—
by making a joke about one of Art's marvellous disappearances.
He did it extremely well."

"How?" said Tom, wetting his lips.

The Cave is Surrounded

"He looked at me in a way that implied he was in secret sympathy with Art. I was very nearly taken in."

"Look here—I think I'll push off. They'll be wondering what we have to talk about."

"Wouldn't he like to know?" said Robert.

Tom saw the desperation beneath the mockery. Robert was not thinking of Art. Mary was due home this evening.

"It will be dark before I get back." Tom paused. "It might be to-morrow night before Mary comes. Mavis was not quite certain."

"You said that before."

They looked at each other. "Good night, Robert."

"Good night, Tom."

On that quiet note they parted, and for a little time Tom was sustained by its strength.

But soon the utter hopelessness of their position became clear again. And as Tom walked by the birch wood, where the small birds were singing, a great love of the trees and the stream and the singing and the open land came upon him. The breaking down of the mind that loved this, the banishment to the Industrial Peak, the dark sunless terrors. . . .

For it had been made plain what would happen to anyone who even did not at once report the most doubtful glimpse of Art.

To one who had shielded him, who had brought him the forbidden fruit, whose very hound the boy had used. . . .

The chest of itself stove in, and a cold dew came to the forehead.

That they could not have foreseen this! The madness that could have thought for a moment that Art would not be caught! The dumbness that could not hear the boy telling the Questioner everything! In the Questioner's persuasive hands, what a piece of childish clay!

A sound fell on Tom's hearing. It might have been a lash from the way he stood and waited for the next stroke.

The Cave is Surrounded

The sound came again—a distant choked cry—from beyond the small green crest in front—in the direction of the cave.

Warily Tom turned his head and looked back at the wood. The shadows were thickening, but nothing moved within the realm of his sight. He looked at the crest and wetted his mouth; then swiftly he was climbing, flattening himself as he came to the crest and shoving his head slowly up.

Four men were closing in on the cave, four shadowy men of the Hunt.

They must have seen Art. They must have tracked him.

Art was trapped.

As the men drew nearer one another, remorselessly closing in on the small black hole of the cave, Tom lay over and looked down and around. Though his face was ghastly, his eyes were very wary. It was every man for himself now. This was the way they would bring Art back. If Art saw him, he would at once make for him, crying his name.

Tom slid down the grassy slope and, short of running (for eyes could be everywhere), strode up his homeward path. If he went quickly enough he could come to a ridge from the other side of which he might look back.

He thought he heard cries and increased his pace. When at last he lay flat on the other side of the ridge, his breath was whistling. And he was just in time to catch a vanishing glimpse of bunched bodies against the darkness of the wood. Too dark to separate that ominous grouping, too distant to distinguish a small being in its midst. But it told its story to Tom with certainty.

By the time he had reached the first orchards on his own side of the Region, the hour of twilight had deepened to the verge of night.

His mouth was now drier than ever. That was one thing about the new range of emotions which the fruit had engendered. They were sharp and powerful. They were various and exquisite. They were the singing in the bird; the eternity in life.

By their glistening beauty, he would be caught one night!

Mary—it was Mary who had found out how to make it possible to eat the natural fruit. It was Mary who had found the herbs and made the herb jelly that neutralised the effect from eating the processed fruit. It was Mary's miracle out of the old Highland earth life. It was Mary's creation. Swallow the herb jelly and the fruit thereafter became a natural food as of old. They might have kept the secret for ever!

Now, the break-down of Mary. Mary changed.

Dare they allow Mary to come back, now that she had that secret? They could not knock *that* out of her mind. Perhaps she wasn't coming after all—or perhaps she was coming as a trap? Could they ever allow Robert and Mary to live together again? Never! And deep in him Robert must know it—so deep that he dare not yet confess it openly to himself.

As Tom groaned a subdued voice called to him.

He went towards the four men who stood within the shelter of the orchard.

"Any news?" asked Willie Morrison eagerly.

"None," answered Tom.

They were excited. They gabbled. Art had been seen—in this very orchard. "He fled with the speed of the wind—up this way. The four Trackers were put onto him. They're after him. Up in the Ridges."

"When was that?" asked Tom.

"After midday!" "In broad daylight!" "He's getting bold!" "He's getting desperate!" They laughed in their chattering excitement. It was all like something they did not quite believe in. Like some of the myths about the poison fruit.

"You look as if you didn't believe it?" said Willie.

"To tell the truth," said Tom with a smile, "I sometimes wonder if I do believe it!"

They laughed outright at this, for sometimes they had

The Cave is Surrounded

doubts about it themselves. So many queer fellows said they had seen the boy.

"We'll all believe in Art's existence when he's caught," said Tom. "So the sooner the better!"

They laughed again, then suddenly remembered they should be silent.

"All the others in position?" whispered Tom.

"Yes," they whispered back.

"Hush!" said Tom, and moved away.

He knew where each section took up its watch, and now felt comparatively safe as he came by some apple trees, much larger than the normal trees because they grew out of a slight depression. They provided shade, too, in the heat of the day, for their branches were wide and their foliage thick.

But there was one thing about these trees that Tom knew and the others did not: their fruit was particularly delicious.

In helping to station the watches, he had taken care that this small depression was outside the direct observation of any one section. And correctly, of course, because it was the approaches that mattered. With the approaches watched, no-one could penetrate here without being seen . . . as he himself had been seen.

But once here, there was the fruit. And, by the old Earth, he was going to have his fill of fruit, despite all the Trackers and Hunters of Paradise, for this might well be his last fill.

All the same, he was taking no chances. He spoke softly, saying, "Hullo, there!" so that any inconceivable watcher might answer.

Even while he raised his open hand towards the laden bough, he kept his head level, looking slowly around him.

A slight rustling sound, as of a restless bird, arrested his hand a foot above his head.

An apple was placed in his hand.

XXIV

DRUGS

"Quick!" called Merk. "Give me a hand."

Axle dropped his comb and leapt to assist. The old man was heavier than one would have thought. But they got him laid out on his bunk. Merk studied the whiskered face and, bending an ear, listened to his breathing. Then he nodded and began to take off the old man's boots.

"That was an odd way to pass out," said Axle.

"Not really." Merk smiled. "A matter, perhaps, of bad timing, but he had to get it when he asked for a drink. He wouldn't eat."

"Drugged?"

"Merely a soporific. He was exhausted beyond the point where he might have slept well."

Axle knew that Merk could not resist the temptation to tease him. It was his peculiar conception of humour. Apparently, however, there was little hidden danger in it, nothing much beyond Merk's love to play with concealments. And Axle also knew that in his love of anything lay a man's weakness.

"Have you got what you wanted at last, then?" asked Axle, reading Merk's repressed excitement.

"We have got more than we wanted," replied Merk, as he placed the old man's boots under his bunk.

"You're lucky."

Merk looked at him and looked around. There was no-one within hearing. "You wouldn't believe it," he said.

"I would believe anything—short of your analysis," replied Axle.

"I'll give you a guess. What did the old man ask for?"

"Ask for? . . . ask for?" repeated Axle.

Drugs

Merk's smiling, half-mocking eyes held him.

"How could I know what he asked for?"

"But—you were so sure you knew the mind of the peasant?" Merk reminded him. "It contains so few desires—and them so simple."

"It's not very amusing—this child's guessing game."

"All the same, you can't guess. Rather afraid to risk your reputation by any sort of guess?"

Merk was good-humoured and friendly. Axle could see that, while he racked his brain for a possible answer.

"Probably he asked to be sent back from Paradise to his old plot of impoverished earth," he said ironically.

Merk shook his head. "Quite the opposite. He asked to see God."

Axle's face gathered in a curious narrowing way. "I might have told you as much," he said at last, his face opening in a soundless laugh.

"Only you didn't. Seems obvious enough now, when you take the irrational, mythological, into account."

"Superstition, you mean," said Axle.

"Superstition?" repeated Merk, and the word hung crucified on the silent air.

A warmth slowly stung Axle's face. "I forget sometimes," he muttered.

"We all do," answered Merk quietly. Then his eyes began to lighten again. "The Questioner did anyway. He's in a bit of a sweat now. It actually has never happened to him before."

"Do you mean he has had to—to take notice of it? To report it?"

"Yes. It's the one thing that must be reported."

Axle whistled softly; then nodded, lips tight. This certainly was terrific! He moved restlessly. So did Merk. They sat on Axle's bed.

"But surely they'll be able to make him withdraw it?" said Axle.

Drugs

"They'll try. But the Questioner is not too hopeful. I can see that. He's working out a technique for to-morrow."

"Hasn't he already tried?"

"In every way. Actually he was more subtle, more profoundly penetrative, than I could have believed was possible. You could say nothing would have stood up against what he said, what he offered, so naturally, so simply, so—so complete."

"And the old man refused?"

"He just didn't answer. He sat like a boulder in a stream. When he stopped staring at nothing, he closed his eyes."

"I know," said Axle. His face closed again. "You can't deal with that—by talking."

"You always forget," said Merk.

Axle looked at him—and warmth touched his face, but a dour warmth this time. "It could be done," he muttered, "all the same."

"God," said Merk, "may appear at any moment now. The old man could tell God—what you had done to him. You cannot hide the old man from God."

"Can't you?" muttered Axle.

Merk's expression was simple and piercing. "No," he said.

"As you like," said Axle, with reserve. "In that case, the old man will be able to tell God what has already happened?"

"Yes. But all that has happened is—that he has been questioned about certain matters in the interest of the common good. He has helped to hide Art, to contaminate the woman Mary and her husband. And he has lied. No force has been used against him."

"What then does he want to see God about?"

"To confess his sins, we suspect."

"Well?"

"Not only that."

"What more?"

"There must always be something more. But what?"

"Is that what they're afraid of?"

Drugs

"What?"

Axle moved impatiently. "This seems to me all so much spider web weaving."

"In that case I shouldn't advise you to discuss it with any of the Chiefs—unless with the Chief of the Hunt, and his mood is not too amiable at the moment."

"The more I study, the more I see that it's the Hunt side of the Administration that needs keying up."

"I thought you might come to that conclusion," said Merk, getting off the bed.

"What do you mean?" asked Axle sharply.

"To-morrow," said Merk, quietly ignoring the question, "they will send for the Questioner from the Eleventh Region. He has had no less than three similar requests to see God—and was successful in getting them all withdrawn in time." He paused. "But we're not hopeful. His methods have been studied."

"But——"

"There is a feeling," continued Merk, "that we have got to-morrow yet. Maybe two—even four—days. But not much longer."

"A feeling?"

"That which comes before. The emanation from the beat in the heart of life. The psychic barometer in the tower."

"Good G——"

"Not so loud. The tympanum in the ear of excitement is finer than any gossamer. And it is now drawn pretty taut. I say as much in your own interest. Watch your step. At least—for the next few days—watch your mouth."

Axle scratched himself.

Merk nodded. "That's the way it gets you first. It crawls over you. I'll be here early in the morning. If you happen to waken—have a look at him." He nodded towards Old Hector, who lay on his bed as on a bier.

"But why—why not put him in a room by himself, where

you could be sure, where you could treat him, without everyone seeing——"

Merk shook his head. "Everything must be normal. He
won't waken before six o'clock. The first thing he will ask for
will be a drink. I'll give him one."

"I—see," said Axle.

"We have one or two interesting drugs," Merk admitted.
"One, in particular, that will heighten life and make Robert's
croft and cattle seem infinitely more desirable than ever
before. It will be made clear that Art will not be touched nor
Robert apprehended. Against this perfect optimism, the confession of sins will seem a desperate and gloomy affair. Something to hide the head from."

"Ah," said Axle.

"For we know his weakness. He would suffer anything—
rather than injure another. So—no more questioning, no in-
jury, no retribution. Only freedom in the open, friendliness,
with the cattle eating, the birds singing . . . *and* the mood
induced by the drug."

"That should certainly do it."

"If only," smiled Merk, "you had not been so often wrong."

XXV

THE GREY FEELING OF BETRAYAL

Tom affected the indifference of a very wary man as he
crossed the Ridges and came by the birch wood. When
he looked around without moving his head much, he
whistled idly but softly, for his news burned in him.

From the edge of the corrie, he saw the milkers had arrived.
The field on the other side of the burn was cut. The last of the
sheaves had just been stooked. Robert was walking with his

The Grey Feeling of Betrayal

two hounds towards the house. Betsy appeared at the front door and waved.

It was a peaceful, pleasant scene. Tom glanced idly about him and went on, but more slowly. To avoid the milkers he crossed over towards the harvest field. A good crop. He lingered, making it clear that he did not wish to trouble the house at meal time. From a little distance he saluted the nearest milker cheerfully.

When the meal was over and the workers appeared, he went towards the house. Robert saw him and came indifferently to meet him. Where was Mary? Tom wondered. Then he saw Robert's face.

In the same moment his eyes lifted to the slope behind the cottage and he paused. Robert turned round. Walking down the slope came Mary and Mavis.

Mary saw them, waved, and broke into a little run. Her face was as Old Hector had seen it in the Atomic Psychology room. It advanced like a white flag. A thin smile ran over its pallor like a surface wind. Her eyes were black, her hair heavy.

"Robert!" She gaily shook hands with her husband. She gaily shook hands with Tom. With Betsy. She looked about her, pleased as any schoolgirl. "The field is cut!" she cried. "The cattle!"

Robert continued to stare at her, unable to move. Tom turned away. Mavis came and spoke to him. Tom smiled to cover the sickly beating of his heart.

Mary cried, "Merk!"

Tom saw Merk appear from the direction of the willows. Mary went quickly forward and shook hands with him.

"Robert," she called, "here's Merk." In the light-heartedness of this pleasant moment all were welcome.

The harvesters smiled at Mary's pleasure in being back. The milkers looked on. Mary greeted them all. Then she caught Robert lightly by the arm. "Let's go in and have a good meal, all of us. Come on."

The Grey Feeling of Betrayal

It was the mood the harvesters and milkers understood. They laughed at her gay chattering. But the meal was over and they backed away, thanking her, still watching and laughing.

Robert, turning his head, looked into Merk's face.

Tom's heart stood still, while he chatted to Mavis. By the ancient Earth, surely Robert knew better than to glare like that. Tom felt the cold shiver on his back.

"You'll be glad to have her home," said Merk.

"Had you been in my place, you would not smile so readily," replied Robert.

Mary lifted her head quickly and looked into Robert's face. A faint puzzling came to her expression. Then she laughed, remembering. "It's the same Robert!" She was delighted.

"There they are," murmured Mavis to Tom.

Tom followed her eyes. Down the slope came two men, one like the Ancient of Days, stooping slightly over uncertain feet. It was the wreck of Old Hector.

"Who's that with him?" asked Tom.

"The Questioner," replied Mavis.

"Who?"

Mavis glanced at him. "The Questioner."

"Is it?" said Tom, smiling, checking his tongue before it got to his dry lips.

"Yes. Any word of Art?"

"No. Nothing new."

"I wish they could find him," she said, with unexpected feeling.

"Why?"

"Why?" She raised her eyebrows. "Because it would settle everything. Surely you know that?"

"Of course," nodded Tom. "I wasn't thinking of what I was saying. Look here, I think I'll be going."

"But why? Wouldn't you like to meet——"

"No. They won't want me here, and I feel a bit shy before . . . I'll be going. So long."

The Grey Feeling of Betrayal

"But——"

Tom gave her a smile and turned away. For a moment she watched him with a vague dismay.

Tom went on, every moment expecting a cry of arrestment to stab him in the back. Not once did he throw even a glance behind. Before disappearing over the edge of the corrie, he half-turned his head.

There was no-one about the house. The unholy assize would be going on inside. His legs weakened and he sat down.

But he could not stop his mind trying to picture the appalling nature of the scene inside the house, the quiet deadly words. Mary, the broken Mary, being played off against Robert; Mary eagerly correcting Robert, when Robert denied. And Hector, from whose aged body the lees had been wrung.

Robert losing control. Robert boiling over.

Mary looking at him, with her childish witless face. . . .

Tom got up, feeling his face turn grey.

The grey feeling went with him. In the deep dusk he whispered with the watchers on the edge of the orchard. He sat under the large apple trees until the dark hid him. But he forgot the fruit, for his stomach was full of the fruit of betrayal. Here Art had placed the apple in his hand; had swung down from the branch into his arms, delighted with his surprise, in utter faith.

This grey feeling was the feeling Judas knew. At last he went into his house. His sister looked up at him and continued to look. But he did not meet her eyes.

"Anyone called?" he asked.

"No," she answered. "Anything happened?"

"A lot." He sat down and, about to take off his boots, stopped and stared before him. In a few laconic words, he told her what had happened.

She waited.

"Everything will be known," he said. "They'll be here—any minute."

The Grey Feeling of Betrayal

"Why?"

"To search the place. To put us through it."

"Well?"

"Well? What's the good of saying Well? Any fool can say Well?" He got up in a grey wrath. "It's the only way out. Not only for us, but for everyone."

"Don't shout," she said.

"Who is shouting?" But his tone lowered and he looked over his shoulder. "Could the boy have heard me?"

"No."

"It's the only way," he said in a defeated voice. "If we give him up now—before they come—then—it would help everyone. He's bound to be caught anyway."

All at once she flew to her cupboards and became wildly busy.

"What are you doing?"

"The herbs. The fruit," she muttered.

He staggered and sat down.

She made two trips outside. He heard the soft thud of woodblocks being moved in the near shed. Burying the immortal fruit under the firewood. He went to the front door, opened it a few inches and listened for footsteps that might come in the night.

"All right," she called.

He closed the door and came in.

"Well?" she asked. "Will I bring him in to the light?"

His tongue came between his lips. "No," he said, "I'll go out." The grey feeling of betrayal was a slime in his mouth.

He went to the dark outhouse where the two hounds slept. They came around his legs as he shut the door behind him. "Art!" called Tom softly. There was no answer. He groped. The hidden bunk was empty . . . The boy was gone!

Back in the house, his wild face accused his sister.

She nodded thoughtfully. "He may have gone to Peggy Morrison's."

He stared at her. Good God! she could not have told of the fruit—to others!

"Are you mad?" he croaked.

But she wasn't listening to him.

"I'll slip round and see Peggy," she said. "You wait here." She was gone before he could stop her.

Peggy's brother, Willie, was one of the four men of the watch to whom he had spoken a little while ago on the upper edge of the orchard!

XXVI

THE CONFERENCE

The twelve men sitting round the conference table were silent. The door behind the vacant tall-backed chair opened, and a small man briskly entered and sat down. He looked swiftly but directly at each face.

"Well?" he said, addressing the Chief of the Hunt.

"I have to confess that the boy Art has not yet been found."

"Why?"

"For two reasons: one, our organisation is insufficient and therefore inefficient, and two, the public have taken a hand in defeating its efforts."

"First, the organisation."

"To be completely efficient it would have to interpenetrate the population, as it did for a short time during the period of the *Change*. Only now we should have definite representatives of our organisation living in every community. Which would mean that one or more ordinary working members of a community (the number being governed by its size) would be our secret agents. As such, they would be unknown to the rest of the community. The known agent can be avoided or misinformed. With the unknown agent, that could not happen. All our agents, from the Coastwatcher to the Innkeeper, are known. Secondly——"

"You would lay stress on the insufficiency of the organisation rather than on its inefficient working, such as it is?"

"Respectfully, I would."

"Secondly, you said?"

"Secondly——" The Chief of the Hunt hesitated, the thread of his discourse having been snapped, but after two painful seconds he proceeded, "Secondly, we should require to have the power of secret arrest and removal for detention and examination. Up until now that has not been needed. When the presence of any person has been required here, that person has always voluntarily obeyed and come. To ensure, however, that any person could be taken instantly, the Hunt would require this extra power."

"Has anyone refused to come in the present case?"

"No, sir. But I am now trying to foresee what could happen and so take away from the Hunt beforehand any excuse for inefficiency. In the present case, had we had the secret agents——"

"I understand. Have you considered the possible effect of this extended organisation on the people?"

"As it would all be in the common interest, the common good, it does not appear to me that its institution could reasonably be called a hardship of the Hunt—for which, at this difficult moment, I happen to be responsible."

"Would you consider it possible that we may have to think further than that? For example, the mere fact that members of the public have hitherto come at once, when asked, may imply, not fear of but a profound belief in the efficacy and power of the Administration. Once destroy that natural belief, and public cohesion begins to disintegrate. True power derives from belief, not from force. You appreciate that?"

"Yes, sir. Only——" He paused.

The Head smiled; a pale wintry humour, not without its

gleam. "Only—we mustn't blame you when things go wrong? Very well. Meantime you will perhaps think again of the lines along which your organisation must be extended. It may be that a new type of propaganda is needed in order more closely to align the people with ourselves, rather than to separate them from us by a use of concealed force. It would still achieve the same end—it must do that, of course—but it would last. You might think it over?"

"Yes, sir."

"Now for the hand the public has taken."

"It is very difficult to be definite here. The Questioner will no doubt be able to explain it much better than I can. What is quite certain is that there has been, if not open obstruction, at least concealment. Otherwise the boy Art would have been apprehended long before this. It is absurd to magnify his running powers. After all, he was only about nine when he arrived, and after making all allowances for increase in his physical powers, there is a limit to credulity."

"For instance?"

"The other morning he was seen in the orchard beyond the Ridges, near Bigtrees. There is no doubt he was seen. We have his description. He was followed, going in the direction of the Ridges, but lost sight of. Four of my men, our best Trackers, were near the spot and at once took up the chase. They surrounded a portion of the Ridges, and closed in on a small cave, the last possible spot where he could have concealed himself. That he had lived in that cave was abundantly clear. But he was not there. That night and the following day, the whole area was combed. Yet no-one saw him. And that, in my view, was utterly impossible."

"How was it clear that he had lived in the cave?"

"By the number of apple cores, orange skins, and grape stalks."

"Do you find a temper among the people that might, even for the fun of it, conceal him?"

The Conference

"On the contrary. There can be no doubt that the great majority are all agog to catch him. They want to see him. But here and there—there must be an individual—of a different temper. How to get at him, without some such extended organisation as I have suggested, I, frankly, at the moment do not know."

"Can you extend any organisation in a moment?"

The Chief of the Hunt was silent.

"Can you?" inquired the Head.

"We are doing our utmost."

"Utmost what?"

"Our utmost to find the boy. We have pressed everybody into service we could. No-one has stood back. Short of getting access to every house, to search it, I cannot guarantee the result."

"Has any house refused you?"

"No, sir."

"Are you implying by all this that some of those who profess to help you may not in fact be doing so?"

"I am."

"Without any specific evidence?"

"By overwhelming inference."

"But no evidence?"

"No complete evidence. One of the Trackers said he did not like the way a woman in Bigtrees smiled at him. I mention that," added the Chief a trifle awkwardly, "as an instance of the nature of the difficulty."

The Head concentrated in silence on the face of the Chief of the Hunt. The conference table became very still. The silence, however, was broken by a small buzzing. The Head lifted a speaking tube. "Yes?"

He listened for a long time, without any expression.

Suddenly he said into the tube, "The boy has *not* got away."

After listening, he said again, "He has *not* got away. You understand?" His voice was the cut left by the whip.

He listened again. Then he said, "This is final. I shall accept no excuses," and replaced the speaking tube.

Then he looked at the Chief of the Hunt. "If I thought you had arranged this, I would compliment you." The gleam of his humour was now icy. "It would appear that the boy Art was seen in Bigtrees, an hour ago. Your men would have caught him but for the interference of some women. They blocked the men's way and the men hesitated. The men argued. They said they would report the women. They demanded the boy. The women refused. They at last pushed the women to one side. The women objected. I gather there was a small riot. By the time the men got into the house, the boy was gone."

XXVII

ON THE RUN

"Hector! Hector!" called Art, racing down like the wind. Before the old man could turn round Art had him by the hand and was pulling him along. "This way! This way!"

The old man ran with remarkable speed. They doubled a bluff, slid down a bank, and went splash into the burn.

"This way! This way!" called Art, and, dashing through a thin white screen of water, which curved downward from a ledge of rock, he hauled the old man after him into a shallow cavern. "That was a near thing!" He gulped his excitement and turned round to greet his old friend.

But it was not his old friend. It was not Old Hector.

Art's mouth opened, his eyes opened, and fear tripped over a gasp.

The old man smiled and squeezed the water out of his beard. "You were in a hurry," he said.

On the Run

"Who are you?" stuttered Art.

"Why? Who did you think I was?"

"I thought—you were Old Hector."

"Well—anyone can make a mistake. But why were you in such a hurry?"

Art stared into the old man's eyes. "They're after me. You won't give me up? You won't?"

"Why should I?"

Art suddenly gripped him by the arm. Through the wavering screen of water they saw a man slide down the bank. Art turned his face to the rock and made the old man do the same. They heard cries, urgent angry cries. They stood as still as the screened rock. The voices died away toward the wood lower down.

"I was awful frightened for a minute," said Art, "that you were one of them."

"Who are they?"

Art looked around him, forgetting he was so confined. "The Hunt," he whispered.

The old man did not seem to understand. "Who are you?"

"I am Art—and they're after me."

The old man nodded slowly.

"Are you new here?" asked Art.

"I am just arrived."

"Did you sleep at the Inn last night?"

"No."

"Didn't you? Then you're in for it!" He nodded with solemn eagerness. "You'll catch it—if they get you! You'll have to hide."

"You're good at hiding."

"I'm not bad now," Art admitted. "But you've got to be quick and go like the wind." Then he added, for he had not had time so far to remember it, "You ran well."

"I'm used to it."

"Are you?" Art looked at him and his eyes widened. "Are you from Clachdrum?"

On the Run

"Why? Do you remember me?"

"Are you the man who started the boys' race—for boys under nine—that time I won?"

"You ran that time and no mistake."

"Och that was nothing," said Art. "I could fairly astonish them now."

"You astonished more than them."

Art laughed. "I knew you at once," he said. "Anyone would know you came from Clachdrum whatever."

"How that?"

"By your voice," said Art, "if nothing else." And he withdrew his eyes politely from the whiskers.

There was a soft friendly laugh and Art shyly dug a bare heel in the thin layer of shingle.

"Did I run well yon time at the race?" he asked.

"It was the way you didn't give in and beat the other fellow that took everyone's fancy. You showed great staying power."

"Did I?"

"You certainly did."

"Ach," said Art, "I didn't think so much of it. But a fellow mustn't give in, mustn't he not?"

"Not in a good race."

"The race that is set before you," murmured Art, and then he gave an upward glance. "That's what the minister used to say in the church—'the race that is set before you'." He smiled with a certain embarrassment. "Do you know," he added confidentially, "when he used to say that, I always thought of *my* race. Was that wrong of me?" And he gave his companion another glance.

"Why would it be? And what other race could the minister mean anyway?"

"I often wondered," said Art. "And there's another thing. It's a joke. You'll say to a fellow: 'It's a fine day for the race.' And he'll say: 'What race?' And you say: 'The human race.' That fairly takes him in."

On the Run

"It would," agreed his new friend, laughing.

"Is that a good one?"

"Fair to middling."

"That's what Old Hector always says."

"Were you expecting him when you saw me?"

"No, I wasn't. But many a time long ago he appeared and saved me in the nick of time. And I suddenly thought you were him. And I—I forgot."

The old man looked at him, at the cloud that so suddenly troubled the clear bright features. "What did you forget?"

"I forgot—that he was changed."

The man slowly looked around. It was very damp. A mist of drops, and trickles everywhere. "Do you think we could find a drier spot?"

"No," said Art sombrely. "You cannot move from here until it's dark."

"But that will be hours yet."

"I know that," said Art. "That's nothing."

"Very well. If you don't mind, I don't. Only, I would like to hear your story from the beginning, for it might help me."

"You'll need all the help you can get in this place," said Art.

"Why, don't you like it?"

"I do not," said Art. "And you won't like it either, if I know anything."

"Suppose you begin at the beginning," suggested the bearded stranger. "In that way, the time will soon go in. You must have a good story to tell."

"Fair to middling," said Art indifferently, but already two tiny points of light were in his eyes.

Sometimes Art overshot the story in his speed, but a question was enough to bring him back. Moreover, he was never done asking questions himself right in the thick of his story. And sometimes one of his questions, before it was quite cleared up, became the length of a small story itself. Such a question, for example, as, "Do you think it is wrong to eat the fruit?"

On the Run

"Why should it be wrong? Don't they all eat the fruit?"

Art laughed. It was enough to make anyone laugh. "It's little you know!"

"Tell me."

Art looked at him. "Did anyone see you eating the fruit?"

"No—I don't think so."

"I thought so. You're lucky. And if you take my tip you won't tell them when you go to the Seat."

"Why?"

"It's little you know," repeated Art, politely restraining too obvious a mocking laughter. After all, he had been through a lot. But in the same moment he turned serious and confidential. Indeed the stranger seemed fascinated by the way thought and feeling wrote themselves on that young face in the one living script.

"You see," and Art lowered his voice, "it was after Old Hector had been to the Seat and I had escaped from it. He came and found me. And I had fruit. And I gave it to him. And he ate it just as before. But this time—oh, what pain he had! He had the pain here. He doubled up and he rolled over. I got frightened. I thought he was going to die. A fellow might easily get frightened when he sees someone dying, mightn't he?"

"Easily."

"I used," said Art, in a still lower voice, "to get frightened of the dark. Was—was that—do you think that was——"

"Surely not. Many old men are frightened of the dark."

"Were you ever frightened of it?"

"I don't mind it so much now. Are you getting over your fear yourself?"

"Och, I don't mind it so much now. Though sometimes—just, you know—the littlest bit—sometimes, you know, when you're all alone and you hear a queer sound. One night—up in the cave—I got the worst fright ever I had. It was the night Bran came to me."

On the Run

"Who is Bran?"

"Robert's hound. Oh, he's a great dog. He goes like the wind. I don't know if he's faster than Tom's Luath. And Tom's Luath is wise. I should say he's the wisest dog in the four brown quarters of the world. Do you know, when I had a grip on him and off he went——" Art, demonstrating the start, got the full screen of water down his neck. So he drew back very quickly, listening, for he had quite forgotten where he was.

Then he looked at the stranger, with desperate misgiving. Had he been telling on Robert and Tom? He could not speak.

"You gave no-one away," said the stranger, smiling. "You only mentioned two hounds."

Art gazed up into the stranger's face with wonder and trust. Even the very look of it made him feel safe. "I know you wouldn't tell," he said. "But the awful thing is they can take it out of you."

"Where?"

"At the Seat. It's awful—up there. Mary—they took Mary away. They'll break her mind. Old Hector—told me."

"Don't get upset. Everything will come right."

"It's little you know," said Art sombrely.

"Why did they take Mary to the Seat?"

"Because—because she had been good to me and to Old Hector. You won't tell I told you?"

In this way Art's story got many turns and twists, but skilfully the stranger brought him back to the point where he had broken from his main narrative, and then Art went ahead again.

They were still talking when the shadows fell and Art thought they soon might be able to make a move.

"The worst," he said, "is when you go out first. You must watch then. But if you stick by me, you'll be safe."

"I'll do my best."

"What about—the Inn?"

"I'm sticking by you."

178

"The whole night?"

"We'll think out a plan for a good place to sleep."

"I know one or two," said Art hopefully. "Are you feeling the hunger on you?"

"I might consider one bunch of grapes, six apples, and an orange or two."

Art nodded. It was a moderate estimate of a meal. If he couldn't add to it he would be surprised. The darkness thickened.

Art pushed his head slowly through the tumbling stream; then, the water bouncing off his nose, turned back for a last word of caution.

"Remember," he said, "they'll be watching for me everywhere, in every orchard, on every path."

"But how will we manage in that case?"

"Because they always watch," said Art, "in the same place. Come on."

XXVIII

THE CONFERENCE GOES ON

Eleven men sat round the conference table facing the Head. The Questioner had the empty chair of the Chief of the Hunt on his right hand.

"I may have pushed the man Hector too far," admitted the Questioner at last.

The Head regarded him closely. "A grave mistake?"

"Yes. But, in the circumstances, very difficult to foresee."

"Though not impossible?"

"That is difficult. It is clear now that he had already made up his mind to ask for an Audience before he came to me."

"But if you had not pushed him too far?"

"You cannot, in examination, get at what is deliberately concealed without pushing to the limit. Immediately the

The Conference Goes On

examination began, the request for the Audience was inevitable."

"Knowing his case, couldn't you have foreseen that?"

"No, sir."

"Why?"

"For two reasons. A: a newcomer does not know he has this power of request. B: there was every reason why the old man should not want an Audience."

"Why not?"

"Because to him an Audience must mean a confession of sins, not only since he has arrived here, but also during his whole life on earth. His particular religious tradition makes the thought of such an Audience and such a confession the most terrible the mind can hold."

"He must have been driven, then, to terrible straits before he would demand it?"

"Yes."

"Who drove him?"

"I admit I helped—as an instrument in the process."

"The process?"

"I agree it is not a good word. The process—and the instrument, I think—would have worked as satisfactorily as they have always done, were it not for complications beyond them. I refer to the complications which started with Hector and Art not staying at an Inn and have now arrived at the present difficulty."

"But you knew of the complications?"

"I tried my best to resolve them."

"And failed?"

"Yes."

There was a short silence.

"You have not seen the boy Art?"

"No, sir."

"Have you any idea why he became refractory?"

"As a boy, his conduct could have been only a reaction from

fear. Therefore what he saw since he landed on the Green Isle must have aroused fear. This, of course, is not unusual in any boy. To a boy—if I may go on? It needs words."

The Head nodded.

"To a boy a strange crowd is ominous. Not because he believes it will do him deliberate harm, but because it is strange, because it moves in a way meaningless and incoherent. The human familiarity, the life-warmth, to which he has been accustomed, is absent in the strange crowd. He experiences the nightmare sensation of being lost and turns blindly to flee."

"Do not all boys, then, experience this?"

"In some measure, yes. But the vast bulk of boys come from a city or industrial life where they have got used to crowds and to incoherence. The later phase of life on earth has tended to destroy the wholeness of the child mind at a very early stage. The intensive pursuit of what is called education has also tended to disintegrate the young mind. Where the young mind undergoes disintegration, its capacity for coherence and action are impaired. It can thus quickly be made amenable to those who can gather the parts together and suggest a saving line of action."

"In what way does the boy Art differ?"

"In that he was still the complete boy. The country community he came out of was to him a complete and familiar community. Old Hector—and this is what some of us were slow to grasp—was his natural friend. The boy's simplicity was found again in the old man's—and the old man's was the simplicity refined out of experience. Added to that was the background of what they call Nature. Which means that the subconscious responses had a natural field of action. Which further means that their acts must occasionally have the appearance of a high degree of irrationality. The resolution of this irrationality can be very difficult. An intimate knowledge of their early life is a first essential."

The Conference Goes On

"Is all this an indirect criticism of the life here?"

The Questioner, almost startled, looked at the Head. "No. It is an attempt—however inadequate—at a piece of analysis. So to analyse is my job."

"Assuming you were to make the same analysis in an Audience, *what questions would you anticipate?*"

The Questioner remained silent.

"You cannot answer?"

"I was trying to think it out."

"When I am alone in that Audience, shall I be given time to think it out?"

The Questioner did not reply.

"Reverting to the man Hector," said the Head. "Have you thought out the line he will take in the Audience?"

"I have tried."

"Well?"

"He will plead for the boy Art, and his pleading will take the form of trying to excuse the boy. He will confess how he himself aided the boy, how he lied when he was questioned by me, but how the boy himself meant no harm. That will be his simple story. On it, everything will hang."

"Everything?"

The Questioner nodded.

The Head looked at him. "Everything will be told?"

"With a certain—I was going to say vindictiveness, but the man Hector will simply try to get his own back," said the Questioner. "He will not accuse us. He will say he is stupid. He will say he does not understand. But he will tell what he does not understand—because there is something in his nature that mistrusts us. Beneath the wrong he has done—he subconsciously feels there lies in us a deeper wrong. It is towards that he will grope. And it is for enlightenment there that he will ask. No power can stop him now. This is one of those extremely rare cases where the knot persists, despite physical or mental pressure, suggestion, drug or sleeplessness. I would not say it could not be untied. But now certainly it would be at a cost—which might appear large in an Audience."

"What is this deeper wrong?"

"An illusion of his subconscious. For there has been no wrong."

The Head stared at the Questioner.

"How did the illusion arise?" asked the Head.

"Because of a defect in his intelligence, due in a certain measure to ignorance, and in a larger measure to the persistence of the simple primitive. This difficulty was always experienced when a primitive pattern of culture came in contact with a higher or more evolved pattern. It is nothing new."

"Towards what was all your questioning directed?"

"It was directed towards integrating the old man into a higher pattern. This was done in as simple a way as possible, and twice the old man saw the light. But twice he fell again because of the tribal concern for the boy Art. Had Art not escaped in the first instance, there would have been no trouble."

"How did this legend of Art spread among the people?"

"Very naturally. It represents a lapse into a previous or lower state. An interesting form of atavism. We have seen that it gives rise to rumours and stories and lies. In its next step down, it affects loyalties. A step below that, and force will be tentatively tried, riot will follow. We are merely watching the process of the descent into the primeval abyss."

"At long last we seem to be talking intelligently," said the Head.

The Questioner's expression warmed. "Had I thought you meant that such might be the questions in an Audience——"

"What other kind of questions would you anticipate?"

But before the Questioner could reply an extraordinary thing happened. It was not that the whole Seat shook. Rather the air and their bodies silently quivered so that faces wavered as if seen through a film of running water. A mental rather than a physical earthquake.

"The psychic barometer," observed the Head, almost calmly. "It has been going up all day."

They all involuntarily listened. Then the Head turned to the Questioner.

"Our time is short," he said. "Proceed."

XXIX

THE BATTLE-CRY

Robert lit the lamp. As he drew the blind he looked for a moment on the darkling world, and had the very odd sensation that this was the end of the same day. This was yesterday and it was to-morrow. This day always happened and would happen. The same day.

The same Old Hector sat in his chair before the flame that glimmered, and had glimmered, and would. The yellow flicker of time, of life, on the hearth that never moved. The dream of the old. The hearkening of the still ear.

Mary's needles went in and out, knitting together the beginning and the end. Thought had died in her face, feeling lay in the long sleep, and all that could move on the far fields of the mind were more shadowy than the figures of a vague memory, more vague than the shadows of a sad poem.

Robert lifted his shoulders and jerked them back, and jerked back his head, and glanced about him, and glanced at his chair. His chair was waiting for him.

Mary gave him a sidelong look. He caught that look and held it. But it did not livingly see him, though it considered his eyes very fully for a moment. It considered other parts of his face. But it seemed the face hardly interested her. It was like something she might have come upon in the grass and gazed at, while continuing to be taken up with her own scarcely conscious thought.

Her eyes, travelling over his face, set a delicate itch upon it, and when he caught himself rubbing his cheeks, a shallow but sharp exasperation blew inward over his mind, ruffling it. He turned to Old Hector abruptly.

"You look very lively to-night."

"What's that?" The old head turned round, startled. Then it smiled. "I was just thinking."

"You shouldn't excite yourself," suggested Robert with heavily playful sarcasm.

"It was exciting enough all the same," replied Old Hector.

"Then let's hear it."

"I was wondering," said the old man, "just how I would begin."

"Begin what?"

"To tell Him."

"You still think they will send for you?"

"I do."

"In that case, you shouldn't be short of subject-matter," said Robert, shifting on his chair. He looked at Mary, but her face was now over her needles and her pale hands.

Old Hector also looked at her, then he looked back at the fire.

"No, you shouldn't be tongue-tied," said Robert, in sudden black exasperation. "Mary, here, gives a good enough example of what the Seat can do——"

As he choked on his words for shame, she considered him, and smiled.

Robert got up and began walking the floor. This had become a habit with him in the baffled years.

"You should certainly tell about me," said Mary, in the light eager tones of a stage-struck woman.

"And what would he tell about you?" Robert stopped to ask, smiling brutally.

The Battle-Cry

"He could tell how I was cured." She looked at her husband. "You always liked walking about." She nodded, pleased. "I remembered that—when I was at the Seat." She smiled, remembering. "I thought it so funny, when I remembered it, that I laughed. I couldn't stop laughing. It was the funniest thing. Robert will be walking about, I thought to myself!" She began to laugh.

"Oh, stop it!" growled Robert.

Her laughter increased. "That's—that's"—she could hardly get it out—"that's what he said, the man with the terrible eyes. 'Stop it!' he said." She rocked with her airy laughter.

Old Hector looked at her.

She was delighted to hold his look. "Wasn't it funny?"

"I'm sure it was," said Old Hector politely.

"But you don't laugh!" she cried.

Old Hector gave his attention to the fire.

She sighed, and on the last tremor of her laughter said to herself lightly, deliciously, "Robert walking about!"

The chair protested loudly at the way Robert launched himself upon it.

Her eyes opened. "Please do keep walking about," she said. There was that faint puzzlement over her expression. "Sometimes I wonder what has happened to you both. You are so—so different. And heavy." Her puzzlement gathered in a pale if momentary solemnity and she murmured, "Even the chair finds you heavy."

Robert got off the chair as if it had stung him.

"That's better," she said, nodding, and pleasantly took up her knitting again. She glanced towards Old Hector with the easy look of a woman who would tell him an endless story in every detail. "I told you about the imps that used to come and sit on my pillow, didn't I?"

"You did," murmured Old Hector.

"There was one curious little fellow. I know I was terribly frightened of him at the time, though I cannot remember now why I was frightened. I have tried to feel frightened again but I can't. It's as if—as if—I hadn't the something to feel frightened with. And I know that's right, because Mavis told me. Mavis is a very nice girl. One day we were trying to remember how to feel frightened. It was the funniest thing. Try as we would we couldn't do it. Then I said something about Tom and what he had said about Ridges in the night and a dark cave. And all at once—quick as quick—she got a little of it. She got frightened. She did. She gasped. The most extraordinary thing. And do you know what she did then? You'll never guess?"

"No, ma'am."

"She got up," said Mary, "and walked about."

Old Hector's smile grew slightly strained.

"Shut up!"

They turned to Robert. He was stiff on the middle of the floor, listening to the night.

Far away, they heard the ghost of a cry. It was like a cry on the wind, but there was no wind.

"They're after him," muttered Robert.

"Who?" said Mary.

He ignored her, listening with all his powers.

Then suddenly the cry was nearer, but still far away.

"They're making this way," said Robert, his voice grim, his mouth hardening.

Old Hector got slowly to his feet.

Now there were two or three distant voices, keeping in touch. By the rasp in the throat they were hot on the hunt.

And now, in an instant, just beyond the window, were quiet voices coming up from the willows, from the path behind the house, voices running, fanning out.

Art was being driven into an ambush!

The night came alive with voices, and always—here, there—was one voice, raised in a sudden yelp above the others, the voice of the man who had caught the latest glimpse of the quarry.

The Battle-Cry

Robert went to the outer door, and very quietly pulled it open. It was a starlit night.

The tumult of the hunt was coming this way, swiftly.

Robert gripped the door edge. Under his arm Mary ducked and flew into the night.

She had a clear twenty yards' start of him, before Robert got his legs to move.

Old Hector stood alone.

There was a rushing of feet, the scurry of a storm, and high above the tumult rose Art's voice as in an ancient battle-cry: "Hector! Hector!"

Old Hector could hear him going down, going under, could hear the high thin crying of his voice being broken under the press of the hunting bodies.

The night itself heard, and shivered like broken glass in all the far windows of space. The high thin piping of immortal youth was snapped and broken, and the dark choking tumult swirled in and around.

Old Hector shivered where he stood.

But now, at a little distance, a hoarse voice arose: "Have you got Hector?"

And from somewhere near the willows a voice triumphantly replied: "We have got Hector!"

Old Hector still stood two paces beyond the door—if he did stand beyond the door, if he stood anywhere.

He tried to look at himself but his body seemed insubstantial enough in the night, and of its own accord it went back into the doorway. It could not see itself there very well. It hearkened for a little while to the jubilant sounds, already moving away.

Then it went into the kitchen, and in the lamplight there it was. But no-one came for Hector.

The brain—the brain goes wrong. It goes dull. The surge of blood in the aged body began to recede. Recognising in a fathomless moment the unreality both of life and of death the old man sat down.

XXX

ART IS LED CAPTIVE

The capture of Art created an enormous sensation in the town. The news of his capture flew from mouth to mouth, up main thoroughfares and down side streets, long before the procession itself appeared, so that anyone might have been excused for believing in its magical transmission.

Actually, the method of its transmission was simple enough. No sooner were Art and his elderly friend caught than some of the younger watchers from the town set off on their toes to bring the astounding news.

"Art is caught! They're bringing him in!"

The very speed with which they ran set others running.

The legendary boy was not only real, he was caught, he was being brought into the town, being brought now! They were on the way with him! He was coming!

Even the sceptics, who had had doubts, shook their heads. "Well, well!" And, not to be last, shouted the news with a laugh.

Laughter, indeed, was the keynote of the whole excitement. Laughter and an intense curiosity.

The streets filled. The throngs surged towards the main square, where the town buildings were. Lights and more lights appeared. Windows were unblinded. Officials laid down speaking tubes and hurried to their official quarters.

Such a vast commotion at such an hour was without precedent in the history of the Region's principal town, second in importance only to the City on the Rock.

And the more the throngs were seen, and their size realized, the more excitement grew among those who composed them.

Art is Led Captive

The night became a fantastic gala night, with flowing rivers of human beings, calling and laughing in shrill humour. As the square began to fill up, the chattering became the surge of long shallow seas breaking on skerries, of tropical forests coming alive with parrakeet and swinging monkey. The voices of school children pierced the din, for they had their own particular reasons for catching a glimpse of the fabled boy. A boy—like one of themselves. The boy Art, whom they had whispered about in corners.

Captured—and now coming!

But slipping, too, from one elderly mouth to another went the name Hector. Art's friend, Old Hector. For the mistake had arisen naturally enough. When Art, trapped, and so near the cottage, had called in his desperation on his earthly friend, had called "Hector! Hector!"—for, at the end of the day, whom else had he to call on?—the Hunt had taken it for granted that he was shouting to the old fellow whom they had flushed with him and had also been pursuing. Moreover, the relationship between Art and Old Hector was well known. The story of how they had eaten the fruit and not slept at the Inn had become universal.

There was just one further matter that did not so readily lend itself to shouting about. It was known that Old Hector had put forward the dread request to see God. This was something that hushed the older folk, that quickened their eye-glances, that slowly swelled the chest to suffocation. Art, after all, was an earth-tied boy, but this request for an Audience, following so much wrong-doing and rebellion, this was the blind daring that choked belief.

As the square heard the procession coming in the distance, it grew restless and its chatter whirled like spindrift. The Master of the Burgh and its Chamberlain could not force their way to the Town House. This was utterly without precedent, by day or night. The people, with automatic obedience, tried to get out of their way, but couldn't, for as voices were raised

Art is Led Captive

and orders shouted, those far on the outside merely pressed the harder to see what was happening. Waves of movement went over the people, as waves go over the sea, without displacing the main body. Thus both Burghmaster and Chamberlain remained stuck like ordinary immortals.

But before the procession, headed by the Chief of the Hunt, whose name was Manmar, the people did make an immense effort to clear a passage. They had seen Manmar sufficiently rarely to appreciate his unthinkable importance. Behind him was the Seat, and all the ultimate and final resources of the Seat. Here was the Rock and all the ages.

Yet curiosity was strong, and when, three paces behind Manmar, the old man with the beard was seen and, walking by his side, the boy Art, his young features glancing under swinging light and shadow, his head up, the momentary silence broke through a whisper to a cry, to a roar, and the crowd fell in upon the rear of the procession, crushing out many of the Hunt, who were angered at thus being denied their glorious hour. It was said that blows were exchanged, and indeed this obscurer part of the episode was afterwards used by the Head in his analysis of the processes that lead back to the abyss.

Certainly there could be no doubt that the tail had been subject to continuous attrition, for when the procession did finally reach the middle of the square it was composed only of Manmar, the two captives, and four stalwart Hunters.

But when it stood there islanded in the bright light, the people—according to their height, position on steps, at windows, with the whole water fountain a vast growth of pendent schoolboys—got a better view. When Art lifted his head to look around, it was seen that here was in truth no more than a schoolboy, thirteen at the very outside. Yet one could see, looking at him, something strange in him, strange and wild and fearless, extraordinary, something fabulous.

And then, something that seemed really fabulous did happen. When Art beheld that sea of faces, that immense alien

Art is Led Captive

crowd, and found himself no longer walking, but standing there in its midst, so profound a mistrust of it came upon him that he turned to his bearded friend and took his hand.

This so simple yet so unexpected an act drove the crowd, in an incomprehensible moment, beyond itself.

"Art!" they cried. "Art! Art!" as if he had in fact lifted his hand and laid hold on some obscure part of their hearts.

The cheers and the laughter rose to a mighty surge.

Manmar extended his hand outward and up.

The crowd, pushed mightily from behind, particularly by those who had not seen, surged in. Manmar shouted sternly. But the sea could not be stopped.

It was a dangerous moment, an ugly moment, but Manmar, who had been politely dismissed the Head's Conference in order to prove himself, and knew so well that he was on his final trial, did not lose his wits. Whatever else happened the boy Art must be held. Turning swiftly, he caught Art and lifted him up.

Then the crowd saw the strangest thing that had yet happened, the strangest that had ever happened in the streets of the second town of the Thirteenth Region, and perhaps in all the Green Isle.

For Art had one terrible weakness: in the moment of danger he fought.

And Manmar was at a great disadvantage, for his arms had to be used entirely for holding the lower part of the wildly struggling body, so that when Art thrust at Manmar's face— which was his only way to get leverage in order to break loose —his fingers went into Manmar's eyes and slid up his nostrils. When Manmar blindly crushed Art's abdomen, Art wildly hit out at Manmar's face, and the skelps he delivered upon it and the shouts of his rage were equally heard because of the silence which had come upon the multitude.

It was when the roar, the roar that starts deep in the male throat and high up in the female chords, began to swell that the next utterly astonishing thing happened.

Art is Led Captive

For Hector, as the crowd thought him, lifted his bearded face on which the light shone, and lifted his open hand straight above his head, palm outward, in the manner of apostolic benediction, and in a great voice that reverberated about the square, cried: "Peace!"

It was the sheer volume of the voice that astounded everyone, and in the volume of a great voice there is authority.

Even Art stopped, in order to look down at his friend, who had that night proved himself a good runner, if not quite good enough.

The roar died away—in intense expectancy of what would happen next.

"What more do you want with us?" asked the bearded man gravely of Manmar.

Manmar lowered Art, who at once went and stood by his friend.

"I want you in the Town House," answered Manmar, eyeing the face out of his deep ill-humour.

"Very well. Go," answered the voice calmly.

A passage was opened up and they went slowly along it, the people falling back with struggling difficulty. The Burghmaster and the Chamberlain were freed as Manmar reached them.

"A secure room in which to bolt them up," ordered Manmar crisply.

The Burghmaster, though a somewhat burly man, showed by his active manner how profoundly he recognised an authority so immeasurably greater than his own. Taking the lead, he conducted Manmar to a small inner chamber whose door he flung open.

Very carefully, Manmar inspected that chamber. The narrow windows were high up. There was, in truth, no possible way of escape except through the entrance door.

"This will do," he said, and when the two captives had been shoved inside, he himself shut the door and turned the key.

"Now," he said, turning to the Burghmaster, "I should like to use your speaking tube."

"Certainly, sir," said the Burghmaster with swift respect; "come along to my room."

"And you," said Manmar to the Chamberlain, "would you mind staying here until I come back?"

"Surely, sir."

Manmar walked away with the Burghmaster, while the Chamberlain, a smallish man, gazed after that tall dark figure of iron in a way he had not dared to do in his presence.

XXXI

IN THE SWITCH-ROOM

Restless, excited, Merk did not know what to do with himself while the conference went on in the Head's room where his master, the Questioner, was in attendance. The news of the night, the news of what was to descend upon them, was charged with such fascinating possibilities that he drifted in the direction of the Switch-room.

Moreover, Axle was in control of the Switch-room for part of the night, with the sniping-girl as his assistant, and there was something more than interesting in the fact that Axle had dubbed her Sweet Innocence. His normal wit, or lack of wit, had clearly got a slight fillip! For Merk to enter the Switch-room now would hardly be to Axle's liking—a cheerful point in itself!

Merk smiled as he hesitated by the door—and heard Sweet Innocence expressing a desire to meet the man who had sniped her on earth.

"Why?" asked Axle's voice.

"Because he was that split second quicker than me. And that split second—it is a—a *fascinating* time."

In the Switch-Room

"Does the thought of him fascinate you?"

"You are soft," she answered, as if she had poked Axle with a forefinger.

"How? That one should fascinate another is not unknown. At least, so I am told."

"That may be so. I do not know. But if it is—it is different."

"Different from what?"

"From you," said Sweet Innocence.

As Merk entered, she turned to him with a smile, which spread wide her generous mouth, then she leaned back against the wall. Something tickled her nose, and, as she raised her hand, her elbow made a knob click. At once the Questioner's voice said:

"With all respect, I do not see that. Or rather, if I may be permitted to say so, I see confusion of thought. After all, the parallelism is fairly complete. First, in early Earth history you had the individual hunting his own food. This hunt required continuous concentration, endless physical effort, and was accompanied by continuous danger. There was no development, no progress of any kind, until the hunters began to settle in agricultural communities. In other words, development, or the creation of a higher culture pattern, depended entirely on the change from an individual to a corporate way of life. No-one doubts this, whether he comes from an autocracy or a democracy. He cannot doubt it because it is fact."

"No-one doubts it," said the Head's voice.

Axle's face had shown wild consternation and, cautioning Sweet Innocence with a silent forefinger, he began to tiptoe with infinite care towards her elbow in order to click the knob back and sever the connection, when Merk stopped him with a soundless "Hush!"

The Questioner's voice continued: "The change, then, is the change from the individual pattern to the corporate pattern. If that is fundamental, if that is axiomatic, then whatever the structure we rear it must be on that foundation."

"Well?"

In the Switch-Room

"I regret," said the Questioner, "that so many words are necessary. But I have found that unless we build on self-evident truths, on axioms, discussion becomes confused and issues irrelevant. My attitude to any One Who might question me on such matters would be: Is this axiom true; is it still valid? The onus of its possible denial, its refutation, I should cast upon Him. If He cannot refute it, then our whole argument stands, and what we have done is in consonance with it, and therefore is rational and sound."

"And if He does refute it?"

"Then the whole scheme of things is meaningless, science is a delusion, and brains were given to us in mockery."

With a greedy excitement, Merk drank in the Questioner's words. Nothing in all time had ever excited him as did the Questioner's flawless style of reasoning. He knew it as *universal reason*, and the more he imbibed of it at any one time, the more exquisitely intoxicated he became.

Now as the Questioner proceeded from primitive times to the modern age where a creation of wealth *"from corporate effort* permitted the few—and only the few—to indulge again in individual hunting, now called individual freedom", Merk looked at the stolidly staring Axle and could have pierced him in triumph. Could not the dull fellow see what was coming, the inevitable progression of the exquisite dialectic, the marvellous marshalling of the utterly incontrovertible, from . . . "from individual love, and castles, and heroes, and fairy princes, and dragons. The stuff of the hunter's wood; the irrational; the jungle. Perfectly understandable for that primitive age, but on earth to-day to sing the individual hunter, the individualist, is not only a clear piece of atavism, but the worst kind of atavism—that which is weakly romanticised, idealised. It is not a genuine going back to a lower culture pattern, which would be understandable, though it would mean annihilation. It is the weak wish—without any possible fulfilment. It is a sickness that inevitably breeds war—but now meaningless war.

In the Switch-Room

So the effort was made to achieve, in the modern world, the fully corporate state. This effort was hated, naturally, by the individualists—and so we saw the alignment in war of the corporate states against the individualist or 'freedom' states, of objective purpose against inherent disruption."

"How then did 'freedom' win?" asked the Head.

"'Freedom' did not win—or at least it did not win until it had organised itself in a highly corporate way. While in process of organising itself it was, in fact, very nearly swept away. In that earthly affair, as a psychologist, I merely observe. And I observe that though each side fights for its own label, what both sides are getting at is clearly the same thing in final result—namely, an efficiently organised State, with each individual integrated into the whole, giving his labour and receiving his benefits, secure in health and sickness at all times. All individualists together make up the State. They are the State. What label you give to this condition of affairs is of no consequence. The axiom remains. The individual capitalist, like the individual hunter, moves into a higher culture pattern, the pattern of the corporate state. And so we have development now—just as we had it long ago, when the hunters achieved the agricultural community."

"All this seems very familiar."

"I know. And I regret if I appear sententious. It is unfortunate, but unless I can make clear how that fundamental economic matter is held by me, I could not go on to the next stage, which is our real argument, and the excuse—I mean, the reason—for all we have done."

"Go on—though time runs short."

"We now simply have to construct our parallel in the realm of mind to what happened on earth in the realm of economics. Just as we saw a corporate social state being achieved, with its individuals part of it, and the whole representing a great human advance, so we now have to consider the creation and evolution *of a corporate mind*."

In the Switch-Room

At this perfect climax to the first part of the Questioner's thesis, the desire in Merk to let Axle have a sharp thrust became almost unbearable. Yet he dare not open his mouth, for if he did his words would be heard in the Conference room, and then! ...

In his mind's eye he saw the room vividly. The figure of the Head, dark, pale, not much taller than Merk himself, with a capacity at times for dynamic stillness that was terrific. There was no need for concentration of purpose in him. He *was* concentration of purpose. No-one looked at his eyes long, and his tall-backed chair had the extraordinary effect of concentrating their power.

A rectangular room, with the light coming from the windows behind the Head's back and showing up the faces of the Regional leaders, solemn still faces, their hands on the table before them.

And now the Questioner was in the "group" field. The desire among men to gather in the group. To live and work in the group. To die for the group. To die for it was, in fact, their highest glory. The Party. The Fatherland. The State. Man by his innate nature had always been driven to find that higher integration. Even the ultimate solitary, like the saint, the mystic—what, in the end, was *his* desire on earth but to achieve the beatitude of the Universal Mind, to lose himself in That to become one with It?

Merk glanced at Sweet Innocence. He could have laughed aloud. She was hardly listening. For she did not need to listen. This was the kind of argument she had always heard. That she did not try to understand it with her head did not matter. She was caught in its dream—and was probably thinking of something else!

And the Questioner's voice went on: "In the human body each cell is an individual, each organ fulfils its function, yet the whole vast complex is under the control of *one mind*. So here on the Green Isle we have been proceeding to the creation

In the Switch-Room

of an interregional mind. *And this is creation.* It is not—as it was before the *Change*—a case of individuals plucking fruit off a tree and spending or putting-in eternity in a changeless way. That hopeless stagnation was cast off. We are on the march again. We are on the march to the interregional and so to the Universal Mind. We have planned our fruit, our system, our lives, in accordance with the Universal Plan. We have formulated our Green Isle Order. On this we found. There will be throwbacks, dangers, difficulties. But against so august a scheme as this, what, for example, may possibly have happened to an irresponsible earth-tied boy, with his rather symptomatic name of Art, is a matter——"

There was a buzz and Axle jumped. Swiftly Merk was at Sweet Innocence's elbow, closing the connection to the Conference room.

"Chief Manmar?" said Axle into the tube. "Yes, sir. I'll put you through at once." Axle switched to the Conference room. "Manmar wishes to speak to you, sir."

Then the three in the Switch-room stood in complete silence.

"He's excited," whispered Axle, though now there was no need to whisper.

"Who?" whispered Sweet Innocence.

"Do you think it would be the Head?" inquired Axle sarcastically.

"Don't be childish, Axle," she answered.

"Has Manmar caught Art?" asked Merk.

"His voice sounded important enough," Axle replied, his eyes on the board. "They're finished!" But the buzzer went.

"Yes, sir?" said Axle.

"Speak to the main gate," said the Head. "Tell them to have everything in readiness to let Manmar and those with him through. We remain in session till they come."

"Very good, sir."

XXXII

ROBERT AND MARY

Mary had fought Robert like a wild cat. But the shouting and the cheers when Art was caught on the slope by the cottage drowned the sounds she made, the thin screaming sounds, as she struggled to get loose.

Robert, deciding her mind had given way, became obsessed by an anguished desire to shield her, to hide her, from the rushing, merciless feet, from the exultant tumult. He gripped her strongly, pinning her arms, and when the scream thickened he worked a hand up and smothered her mouth. That she was so unexpectedly strong helped him, for it made him put forth all his own strength, and when it still seemed she might wriggle free, his strength became ruthless, until at last, defeated at every side, she lay panting.

As Art raised his cry for Hector, she made a last desperate effort, and then collapsed.

But Robert was taking no chances, for he knew the cunning that can lie behind the deranged mind, and not until the Hunt was well up the slope on the way to the town did he ease his grip and finally release her.

She lay unmoving, her face buried in the grass.

"Come, Mary," he said calmly.

He heard the dry spasmodic sobs, dimly saw the shoulders jerk. A coldness came upon his face and even his own mind seemed withdrawn from him and distant.

"Come, Mary—we'll go home." His voice was cool with sorrow. "Come, now."

He gave her a little while, then bent down and lifted her up.

She swayed, but when his arm went round her to support

200

her, she pushed it away, not wildly, but with what seemed to him a dreadful finality. Then slowly she began walking back to the cottage. No word was spoken between them, and he ushered her in at the door.

Old Hector was sitting before the fire, his body leaning forward, like someone who had been left there ages ago.

Mid-floor, she stood and gazed at him. Slowly he turned round, and he looked older than a figure in a cave, his body shrunken and his face ravaged by time which had left him behind.

Slowly he arose and like one speaking out of a legend, his voice gentle with the rhythm that lives on of itself, he said, "You have got back."

She turned away.

Robert quietly closed the door and stood looking at her.

For a little while no-one stirred, then Mary, with a weary dragging movement, came to her chair.

Robert could not take his eyes off her, and his breathing stopped.

"Sit down," she said quietly to the old man.

Old Hector stared at her, and as he stared he saw that she had changed and that here before them at last stood Mary the living woman.

The moment of surprise passed into pure revelation. It was as if from Mary's still presence, as she paused by her chair, there in the kitchen before them, a missing keyword was spoken on the silent air, and the incalculable and broken bits of a story came together and were made plain as a story told to a child.

The supreme cunning with which she had deceived the inquisitors at the Seat, the torture she had borne, the deceits and shifts, the incredible acting, the undefeatable core of the woman, Old Hector understood now.

Here at last was Woman, who for the warmth of life and for the love that sprang out of life and made life, would fight

Robert and Mary

till the stars went down in their courses and rose no more. Here in her weary presence was the child who had been destroyed on earth. All the children who had been destroyed on earth lay quiet in the pallor of her skin and lay asleep deep in the wells of her eyes.

Always he had been haunted by an unreality in the beings who inhabited the Green Isle. They were like shells from which the core had been removed, bright shells washed up by the deeps onto a shore.

In this woman only had life, as he had known life, striven to be born again. She had affected Robert and together they had struggled in the net. Now for Mary the net was broken, the struggle was over and here, washed of all emotion, spent, defeated, like a woman at the end of a tragic drama, she stood before them, gripping the back of her chair. Her lids drooped as she gazed at the chair. Then she sat down.

As old Hector got slowly into his seat he was invaded by that fatal calm of which the great tragic dramatists of his world had told, from the Greeks onwards.

In the silence, he looked across at her woman's face, on which no expression lay, only a great weariness. "So they have got him at last."

"Yes," she answered.

"They were bound to get him," he said. "What is one against so many?"

"So many," she answered.

"Yes," he said, and the fatal acceptance had now its own strange ease. "They are too many."

"Too many," she answered.

"We can do no more than we can do. And you did your best."

"I tried," she answered.

"Great was the trial you made. I did what I could myself but it was little. You did what I did not think was possible

202

to living being." His voice eased yet more, and the rhythm caught at the legend that still, perhaps, lived somewhere.

"Did you know?" she asked in her fatal calm.

"No," he answered. "When I saw you in the room at the Seat, then I thought you were indeed broken. Not by a movement nor yet by a sign did you tell me and I was sorely troubled. But I thought to myself that you would go your own road and I would go mine, for when the testing time comes it is all we can do, leaving our trust to find what it may at the end of the day."

"I could not give you a sign, because I knew they were watching me."

"It was greatly you behaved," he answered, "and it comforts me. It comforts me now. For indeed I was wondering what I could say to Him. For what could I have to say to Him? Better that my old head was covered up and wrapped away and forgotten. But now I know."

"What do you know?" she asked.

"I do not know," he answered, "but I will ask Him. I will ask Him what it was in you that made you do it—and made you keep the secret even when you returned, lest, by telling it, you involve us and restrict your own action. For what you did was not for yourself. It was done for us all and for yourself. What moved you to the doing seems lost in this place. If it is lost for good and is no longer at the heart of all things, from eternity to eternity—then at least He will tell me."

Robert came forward.

"Mary," he said.

She looked up into his face. "Ah, no, Robert, not now. Don't break me."

He bent down and gently caught her in his arms. "Mary, my own love."

"Ah, no, Robert."

Then her arms were round his neck and she was clinging to him and he lifted her up. Her eyes, which had been dry

Robert and Mary

so long, flooded with tears and they went away together into Old Hector's room and the old man was left alone.

His meditation now was like an arid ground that had been rained upon. It was softer and there was growth in it. For what are the tears of love but rain?

What, indeed? And what growth can there be anywhere in all the brown quarters of the universe unless so rained upon?

"Charity" was the word used in the Bible. But he had heard it expounded that the word in the original tongue could also be translated "love".

He was getting near it now. Or, as the little fellow would say, he was getting hot!

The old man smiled.

Growth. Increase. The flower. The fruit.

No creation without *that*. Never had there been any creation without *that*.

Never had anything been created, beautiful and shining beyond man's dream, unless love had been at the core. It was known. For love is the creator; and cruelty is that which destroys. In between is the no-man's land where men in their pride arrange clever things on the arid ground.

If only he could find words——

Mary came in on quick feet and, stooping, kissed him on the cheek. Her own cheeks were wet.

"You must be famishing with hunger," she cried, and hurried to the cupboard.

But there she paused and turned her shining eyes.

"Robert, where——"

"One minute," said Robert, knocking a chair over as he dashed out to the wood shed, where he had buried some of the immortal fruit together with a jar of herb essence.

A poem was already singing in his head.

XXXIII

A CIVIC RECEPTION

From the speaking tube, which had conveyed his triumphant tidings, Manmar turned away, still with the Head's voice in his ears. So rare was the word of approval from that voice, so precious when it came, that Manmar failed to see the waiting Burghmaster and strode off in a warmth of power.

His four Huntsmen were guarding the door against public and officials alike. They stood on the steps of the Town House in full view of the populace in a firm and a tall manner. There Manmar joined them and coolly surveyed the multitude. It had been a long road, through legendary swamp and wood and cave, but here inevitably they had come. Let it be a warning. They could afford now to be, not outwardly triumphant, but inwardly inscrutable.

"The Grand Council," said Manmar in his normal voice, and therefore loud enough to be heard even by the senior magistrate, who was slightly deaf, "remain in session at the Seat. They await us."

The faces of the four Hunters flashed their smile.

The senior magistrate plucked up the courage born of long controversy. "I am the senior magistrate of this town," he began, "and—and——"

"Yes?" said Manmar smoothly.

"And it is my duty to—to see——"

"Do you mean that you would like to enter?"

"I would, sir."

"Certainly," said Manmar, bowing with a soldierly grace and making way.

"I—I am the Burgh Surveyor——"

A Civic Reception

Manmar turned to the senior magistrate. "Perhaps you could do me the favour of arranging this matter?"

"By all means, sir," agreed the senior magistrate at once. But now the Burghmaster had arrived on the scene.

Manmar turned to him. "Ah, Burghmaster, I was just coming specially to consult you."

The small cloud on the Burghmaster's face faded away, and Councillors and officials began to file past under the decisive nods of the senior magistrate.

"Way for the Burghmaster! Way for the Burghmaster!" called the Burghmaster's personal bodyguard, a tall stout man.

As Councillors and officials made way, Manmar said to the Burghmaster, in a pleasant manner: "An important conference is taking place at the Seat which I have to attend. This—ah—singular matter has delayed me, and I should not like to keep"—he paused for a moment—"the *Head of the Grand Council* waiting. I am sure you will understand."

"Perfectly, sir," said the deeply impressed Burghmaster.

"Accordingly," proceeded Manmar, "it would be very convenient if you could provide a conveyance which would take—let me see—four, five, six,—seven—yes, seven persons —one of them not being very heavy—to the Seat immediately."

The Burghmaster wheeled and, as if calling to his bodyguard at a distance, gave the necessary instruction.

"And now, perhaps," said the Burghmaster, "while you await your conveyance you might care to rest and be refreshed?"

"So very good of you," said Manmar in so charming a manner that the Burghmaster with vigour led the way to his Room. Throwing the door open, he bowed the Chief in, then paused on the threshold before the hopeful gentlemen of his Council.

"Perhaps I might take this occasion," began the Burghmaster, "to welcome to our midst Chief Manmar, whose high distinction has become as a legend among us." If no-one cheered it was because they were all visibly overcome. The Burghmaster turned to Manmar. "Before I have the pleasure of offering you some refreshment, sir, may I be permitted the honour of presenting to your Excellency those members of our Council who feel it their duty, by night as by day, to preserve the rights and duties of our ancient burgh?"

Manmar bowed. "I am grateful for the welcome you have given me, and you can understand the considerable pleasure it will afford me to report in due season, not only on the fine vigilance of yourself and your Council—and this has surely been a high, because so unpremeditated, a test of that—but on the helpfulness and great courtesy shown to me, as one representing for the moment a higher authority. Accordingly I should be honoured by the presentations which you have suggested you might care to make."

The presentations then followed.

Whereafter the Burghmaster produced from his low wall cupboard a few bottles containing pre-*Change* wine.

The proceedings became very agreeable, and as they gathered more confidence, the Councillors began to chatter and laugh, and some of them even to get a word with Manmar when the Burghmaster was attending to the seal of the next bottle.

Presently a cry arose from the crowd, a scattering cry. There was the clatter of hoofs on the paved way before the Town House.

"Your conveyance has arrived, sir," said the Burghmaster.

"Ah—very good," said Manmar. "I am sorry, gentlemen, to have to interrupt this most pleasant occasion, but none more than you will understand that duty is duty, and you will forgive me."

The Burghmaster spoke again.

Then the procession to the inner chamber began, headed by Manmar and the Burghmaster.

A Civic Reception

The Chamberlain stood before the door. The Burghmaster formally introduced him to Manmar. "I'm afraid," said Manmar, "you must have missed your wine."

"Not at all, sir," said the Chamberlain.

Manmar turned the key and threw open the door. Every head craned forward for the first glimpse.

"Come along!" called out Manmar in tones so crisp that they contrasted strongly with his recent agreeable ones.

Nothing, however, came along.

"Come out!" cried Manmar, striding at the same moment into the room.

There was, however, no-one in the room.

XXXIV

THE SOUND AND THE SILENCE

Manmar's face as it regarded that empty chamber might have been a study for the other faces, had there been sufficient consciousness left in them to study anything. Then he turned and his voice rose out of its crispness into something much more formidable. "What's this?" and he eyed the Chamberlain.

The Chamberlain was speechless.

Manmar swept their faces, then strode to a wall cupboard and, catching its knob, pulled it open so violently that suction drew a cascade of buff and blue forms fluttering upon him. Beyond shelves and paper, the cupboard was empty. Nothing under the table. No door but the one door. No window of escape.

Manmar wheeled. "What's all this?"

All the city fathers stood arraigned before his terrible eyes.

The Burghmaster slowly turned to the Chamberlain.

The Sound and the Silence

"I don't know," muttered that unfortunate man. "They—they did not come out by the door."

"How then did they get out?" thundered Manmar.

"I—I don't know," stuttered the Chamberlain.

"You don't know! Didn't you watch?"

"Yes, sir."

"Did you leave the door?"

"No, sir—I just only—I just stretched my legs—in the passage. But I never lost sight of the door."

"How could you stretch your legs without turning your back on the door?"

It was difficult. Manmar strode swiftly to him. "Let me smell your breath."

The Chamberlain opened his mouth.

"Breathe out!"

"Ha—a——" breathed the Chamberlain.

"So!" said Manmar.

"It was Councillor—he came with a glass——" the Chamberlain began to explain; and at once his loyal friend, Councillor Macroarie, stepped forward and said that he had certainly come into the corridor with a drink because on so—so auspicious an occasion——

"Sir," interrupted the Burghmaster, getting back some of his wind, "we should soon solve this matter. The front door has been guarded by your men. The back door is so placed and barred that they could not possibly——" Taking a step forward in his confidence, his foot, crunching something, stopped him. Bending, he lifted on his palm the broken shells of two nuts.

But what kind of nuts? Certainly not the nuts that grew on the Green Isle.

"We are wasting time!" shouted Manmar, sweeping the mysterious shells aside. Some of the Councillors staggered from the violence of the gesture.

Then the hunt proceeded, from the barred back door to

the safe in the Chamberlain's office. Indeed the Chamberlain opened some of the small drawers in his filing cabinet. But there was no trace of Art.

And, more mysterious still, there was no trace of the bearded stranger. For whereas Art might have conceivably slipped between and around, like an eel in a bouldered stream, the bearded man of the great voice could hardly have been so unnoticeably nimble.

As Manmar saw the waste-paper basket being shaken up, he could not but have his worst suspicions aroused.

He called them together and spoke to them. He composed his voice to an iron calm. His eyes were the tips of spears. He asked them in so many simple words if they thought he was a fool or what. His restraint was so terrible that they stood in the one flock.

Thus, it seemed to him, in the horrid fantasy of that moment, might they stand forever, with their pale faces and echo minds.

Then he opened his own mind, and it was as if the drawers flew out and the cupboards toppled and the round black rulers flashed about hitting them indiscriminately. Amid this pandemonium, seeing the senior magistrate struggling for words, the Burghmaster cleared his throat and at once the floor—or was it the future?—dipped sheer from under him.

Whereupon Manmar took the civil law upon himself.

His forcefulness was not only without precedent in the town's annals, he grasped as it were the whole Town House in his fist and shook it.

The crowd outside grew silent. Then from this mouth to that went the whisper, "Art has escaped!"

It was the incredible thing that has perfect aptness, the impossible joke that so rarely fulfils itself for man's wonder and delight.

Manmar appeared before them and raised his arm. A woman, who had been leaning over a distant balcony and had

The Sound and the Silence

just caught the whisper about Art's escape, laughed before straightening herself. The laugh spread among those beneath her. Like a wind that had struck the far side of a forest, the sound advanced. When Manmar shouted, his shout was lost in the gathering storm. As the storm reached its height, the opening and closing of Manmar's mouth and the swinging of his arms gathered an irresistibly comic aspect, all the greater for the element of dread. The horses reared. The Burghmaster's bodyguard hung on.

By the swelling mad anger in Manmar's face it could readily be seen how this town was going to pay. Meantime it would be surrounded, surrounded and dredged.

The Burghmaster stood before him. "You are wanted on the speaking tube, sir."

"What?" shouted Manmar, glaring at the Burghmaster.

"The speaking tube," repeated the Burghmaster with some reserve.

But no—this was too much.

"In my Room," added the Burghmaster.

Manmar paused at the door of the Burghmaster's Room. The speaking tube appeared so simple and quiescent a contrivance, so innocuous. What could he say to them at the Seat?

This was the question whose answer was being awaited in the Conference room, and awaited with an ever-increasing impatience. The Switch-room and the main gate had been in fruitless touch more than once. The psychic barometer in the tower was approaching its highest point.

Even Sweet Innocence could look through Axle's face with a certain calm wonder, recollecting in this tranquillity the split second that has a fascination.

Then the buzz came and Axle swiftly put Manmar through.

"Manmar?" said the Head.

"Yes, sir."

"Well?"

The Sound and the Silence

"The—the boy Art—has—for the moment—escaped."

"Will you repeat that?"

Manmar repeated it. Then, as shortly as he could, he explained what had happened.

No voice came from the other end.

Manmar explained further, directly accusing the Chamberlain of complicity and the whole Council of deliberate collusion.

No voice replied.

Manmar looked at the dead speaking tube as at his own life and was about to put it away when its small voice spoke.

"Yes, sir?"

"I repeat—what sound is that?"

"It's me, sir—Manmar—speaking to you."

"I am more interested in the sound behind you."

And Manmar became aware that the cheering of the crowd was a roar in the room.

But that roar faded as now something else drew near, in silence, in a terrible, slowly-mounting quickening of tension.

The members of the Town Council began to gape at one another.

Merk, Axle, and Sweet Innocence stared at their switches as if truly fascinated.

The Head, though looking before him, saw none of the members of his Council who were still around the table.

No-one thought of speaking.

Then it came, the small still sound, far within the ear, of a deep bell struck in a distant tower.

Some women in Bigtrees hearkened silently to its overtones.

Luath crept to Tom's feet.

Leaves rustled over the orchards, whispering in a low dancing measure together.

The birds awoke, and many of them sang.

The Sound and the Silence

Mary stopped in the middle of her great story.

Old Hector bowed his head.

God had arrived at the western Peak of the Seven Peaks that crowned the City on the Rock.

XXXV

THE FLYING CORRIDORS

The activity within the hierarchy of the Thirteenth (assisted by the hierarchy of the other Regions) became such that it hummed with the intensity of the dynamo wheel. The very air about the Peaks was drawn so fine and taut that rumour could leap a whole league on it at one bounce.

At first, amid the high ones, there were comings and goings of dizzy speed and purpose. The City populace, vastly swollen from all over the Green Isle, stood and stared in uneasy wonder. When any were moved to the dim relief of a jest—for strange long-buried things had begun haunting them—they had but to turn and look at the Seventh Peak to find hanging in the sky above it the invisible stroke.

Perceptibly, however, the goings-on became reduced in speed, circumscribed in motion, until at last, from the outside, the official world of the Administrative Peak was as a hive that, after the nuptial flight, draws inward upon itself to a fecund centre of superb intensity.

Axle kept guard over his mouth. Merk increased his silent speed by going on his toes. Sweet Innocence had the innocent solemnity of one whose profoundest smile has come home to roost. As she guarded her door, the cool accuracy of her salute might well have been the sublimation of a blown kiss.

The Flying Corridors

As the hour of the first Audience drew nigh, there emanated the secret intelligence that the Head was to take with him, as his sole support, the Questioner.

At that, Merk stood still as a spinning top.

When the messenger appeared, requesting his own presence in an inner room, Merk wobbled, but only for a moment. The door was swung back, and Sweet Innocence saluted him as he passed through.

The Questioner, who was regarding his own appearance in a mirror, for he had just put on the appropriate coat, received Merk alone.

"Is it all right," asked the Questioner, "behind?"

"Perfect, sir," said Merk. "You would think it was made for you."

"Who knows?" said the Questioner, with the subtle smile that Merk had so often practised. Then he regarded Merk's apparel. "Try this," he said, picking up a second coat. "For you must accompany me—not into the Audience, but so that you may be near, should I require more material evidence than it is possible to carry in one head."

Merk tried on the coat.

"It fits you also behind," said the Questioner.

Any kind of reply was beyond Merk. Never had he known the Questioner more quietly confident. He was like one about to enter a realm where his abilities would for the first time be called upon to transcend the repetitions of everyday. There the trained psychologist would naturally flower; there, in the realm of pure mind.

"I am very glad," murmured Merk.

The Questioner glanced into his eyes. "So am I," he said. "At last we shall be able to give an account of ourselves."

"You will, sir," said Merk.

"That's one thing about the mind," remarked the Questioner, blowing an invisible speck from a lapel, "it is the ultimate, the final realm. Nothing can transcend that to which we have been giving our attention. It is therefore a fair assumption that not many can know more about it. In the last debate, if the last word will not lie with us, at least it should be directed towards us. If it has not been our province to direct action in this place, who knows in what province it may?—if we are evolving towards higher mental integrations. Does that appear clear to you?"

"Nothing," murmured Merk, "could be clearer. Its logic is —is final."

"I am inclined to think so," said the Questioner lightly. "It's a pity, perhaps, that they bungled the business of catching the boy Art. But that, after all, was their affair."

"That's what I always thought," agreed Merk. "I did my best——"

"You see," continued the Questioner, "they do have some conception of the individual as only possessing purely unitary value, the drop in the great ocean, but they have not clearly grasped my conception of the corporate mind, which not only justifies all their simple practical expedients but aspires towards—indeed directly contemplates—the mental Universal, the Whole. Now it is going to be very difficult, it seems to me, for Anyone, emanating, shall we say, from that Whole, to counter a conception which is in consonance with It. So that naturally I anticipate an argument of—well, of some length at least." As he tugged his lapel flat the messenger arrived.

The procession of the one carriage drawn by four bay horses along the main thoroughfares of the City that lapped its Seven Peaks was remarkable for the importance of its silence. The crowd, many deep, were as a continuous crowd in an endless theatre watching the figures of destiny move to their places in the culminating Act.

They arrived. The doors rolled back. They were received in the halls.

The courtesies of the occasion had an impersonality smooth as the well-known movement of deep water. Merk was so overcome by its effortless perfection that even his curiosity paled.

But when presently he found himself alone with the aide who had accompanied the Head, his curiosity returned so strongly that he found it necessary to make a simple excuse to withdraw for a moment.

Unlike the normal throng in his own vast halls, here there was hardly anyone about, and when at last he did bespeak a man, he was told that the water-room was the second on the left.

It is an easy matter to lose one's way in a strange building of such large dimensions, particularly when one overhears the expression "Switch-room".

Merk followed the spell of that word with the excuse ready that he must have lost his way. Thus he moved with an outward air of confidence, keeping the young man just in sight.

The lay-out of the interior was at any given moment more simple, but in a series of moments more complex, than that of Merk's own headquarters. The twist of the corridors, for example, was smooth but also (or so it seemed to Merk) serpentine. And it is not always easy to know whether a serpent's tail is being brought to its mouth or is wriggling away from it at a fast pace, unless one can see the whole serpent. The matter is complicated when there are many corridors.

The young man, moreover, was in a hurry, and though this was a difficulty to Merk it turned out also to be an advantage, for when at last the young man disappeared, the door, which he pushed to after him, did not quite close. By the inch-wide opening Merk stood with the air of one too timid to knock in order to inquire his way.

After listening for a moment, however, he smiled in a knowing, excited manner. Man's nature had elements of sameness wherever encountered! The tube to the Conference Room was not plugged.

When the beat in his ear-drums subsided this is what he heard:

The Flying Corridors

Questioner: I questioned them in every way and there was nothing else.

The Voice: You exhausted all the possible elements?

Questioner: Yes, Sir.

The Voice: Now you have a very important position in the Administration: in many ways, the most important inasmuch as you are the interpreter of the mind of the people. Should you have failed here in some rather obvious fashion, in how far then would you assume the infallibility of one propounding the Higher Integration?

Questioner: In no way, Sir.

The Voice: That, at least, is definite. Accordingly if I should suggest a way in which you may have fallen short, and you yourself agree, then perhaps our discussion of the Corporate Mind might meantime be deferred?

Questioner: I should crave your permission, Sir, to retire.

The Voice: Very good. You realise, I take it, that as the fruit grows on the tree it contains certain vital properties which once upon a time—perhaps a primitive time—were called the knowledge of good and evil. These elements, being at least psychological, are within your realm?

Questioner: Yes, Sir. But—if I may be permitted to say so—I always regarded the psychological elements as being within the mind, not within the fruit.

The Voice: Ah, now I see why you made no allowance for the fruit at all.

Questioner: I do not understand.

The Voice: Not even yet?

Questioner: No, Sir.

The Voice: It never occurred to you, as a possibility, that the old man Hector, and the woman Mary, and Robert her husband, ATE THE FRUIT?

The Flying Corridors

In the silence that followed, the corridors began to spin around Merk, while a stupefying light flooded his mind. Silently through this excruciating light his mind began to yell that of course they must have eaten the fruit! Of course! That the Questioner and himself should never have conceived the possibility! Appalling! appalling! His body so twisted itself that it very nearly tied the knot. The sound of the Head's voice just stopped it in time.

Head: They could not have eaten the fruit, and its use in this new way was decided upon for the following reasons——

The Voice: I shall discuss the fruit with you presently and in every respect. Meantime I am awaiting the reply of your colleague who seems to have grown strangely silent.

Questioner: I beg leave to withdraw, Sir.

The Voice: Granted. And once we have dealt with the realities, perhaps then in some leisured moment we may again take up your theories. Meantime you might think over the contention that at the core of a theory or a plan, *in addition to the highest intention there can abide self-delusion and the last refinement of cruelty.*

At the scraping sound of chair-legs, Merk staggered. The Audience, so far as his master, the Questioner, was concerned, was over! It was over before it had really begun! His master was defeated, was being dismissed!

Merk put his head against the door for support. It swung open and he all but fell in. Staggering in and then out, he turned and fled.

Wildly he fled the corridors, down and up and along the corridors. And as he fled, the corridors themselves fled the other way, the corridors and the arches of the corridors.

He would be late now. He would never find his master whom

The Flying Corridors

God had dismissed. Never would he find his way out to his lost master.

Panic came at his heels. And behind the panic—the gentle clarity, the piercing clarity, the awful clarity, of *The Voice*.

At last, at the end of a corridor, which led to the end of everything, Merk saw a door and the door was slightly open. He pulled up, and looked back over his shoulder, and waited till his gasping eased. Then softly he approached that door.

It was sufficiently ajar to permit his head to enter without touching wood.

But his head had only begun to enter when it was arrested by an incredible vision. A boy sat on a tall stool regarding an apple in his hand. The apple went up to his mouth. The lips drew back and the white teeth bit. As the chunk came away, the face lifted and looked straight at Merk.

It was the boy Art.

Merk experienced a suspension of movement that seemed to last a long time. Then quietly the boy slid off the stool and disappeared backwards, and he had no legs.

So quickly did Merk withdraw his head that the wood hit it a hefty crack. The crack sobered him, for it assured him that at least he still had his own head.

Then something altogether wild—perhaps primitive—got the better of him, and, shoving the door open, he entered.

There was no-one in the room.

As he swept his eyes from a tall but vacant stool there was a flicker of movement. Merk made for it. It came to meet him, as things do in a mirror. It was a living person. It was—Merk himself, without legs.

He fled from that ghost in the mirror, and on nimble feet delivered himself once more to the flying corridors.

XXXVI

KNOWLEDGE, WISDOM, AND MAGIC

It was a divine morning and Art was bubbling over with life. There was nothing for him to out-race but the gentle breeze that went to meet the sun, and as that was too easy to do he took another running jump to himself, and measured its flight by placing one foot in front of the other. It was a pity that no-one could see these record leaps; still, it was as well to have them tucked away in one's legs, because, when the day came, there would be those who would be astonished. The mere thought of it was enough to make a fellow laugh. How their eyes would open in Clachdrum!

So divine a morning that, indeed, it was almost a pity the Hunt had been called off. Not that he was quite sure it had been, though the Starter from Clachdrum had said so. But then, being the Race Starter, he was just the sort of man who would know. And he was a marvel at doing things, the queerest things. If only Art had had one nut left from the cluster that contained the nuts of knowledge, he could have tried the trick of taking a leap with the eyes shut, clean out of one place into another, but he hadn't. They had eaten the last two yon time.

Honestly, people would not believe what could be done until they had seen it. It's a fact. Who was it used to say "It's a fact?" And folk said they didn't believe him when he said that. But maybe he was right enough. It's a fact. Funny to say! It's a fact. Art began to laugh. It's a fact.

Fact—fact—what an idiotic sound! It's a fact.

Art rolled over with his mirth in among some hazel shoots, gave the fright of its life to a small brown wren, and startled two yellow-hammers, three chaffinches and one bluetit.

Still as a tree trunk, he watched their antics as they scolded him. There was something so familiar in the scolding that his eyes glimmered in a woodland look of their own. They kept up the noise just to make sure that he was no more than a new kind of tree trunk. When he had completely deceived them, and then suddenly sat up, they were outraged and said so. He laughed.

What fun it would be to give Old Hector a fright! Perhaps it was time he was moving down.

He went through the birch wood with the quietness of a roe, and if his eyes didn't miss much his ears missed less. From the last birch, he surveyed the land, then slipped down the bank into the burn. The clearness of the water was a perpetual wonder. It was the wonder one got at the end of the jetty where the sand below the deep sea-water is clear as a face in a mirror. He made his toes move in the water. They were his own toes. And though the water was cold it wasn't really cold.

From the lower edge of the corrie, he gazed, lying flat. Yes, they were stirring . . . And there was Robert . . . and now Bran and Oscar . . . coming for the cattle. Art wriggled into a safer spot.

Bran came over the bank and looked at him.

"Hsh!" said Art, waving him off. "Hsh, now!" as if Bran might speak at any moment. Art's earnest miming made the situation perfectly clear and the hound went on.

Art began his favourite stalk down the burn where the banks were shallow. It was his favourite because it was so difficult. But what fun to be able to watch everything going on and not to be seen!

Old Hector!

When he saw the old man, Art had a twinge of pity and pleasure. He looked weary, and it was perfectly clear by the way Mary and Robert stood watching him move off that they were sorry for him.

As indeed they were. For the old man was heavily weighed down by the burden of his approaching Audience. It had engendered in him a terrible loneliness. He could only think of it

Knowledge, Wisdom, and Magic

as a state or condition beyond any the Questioner had been able to evoke, in which his tongue would desert him, his whole being would be exposed, and he would fall through guilt and misery into a hot shame of dissolution. Before those Eyes, what could a man say—what single word that would not be too much? Bow the head only, and—with a grain of charity shown —be wrapped away forever. Would there be that single grain? Then to get it over—to get it over quickly. . . .

Art stalked the old man. It was so easy, he could hardly help laughing. And once Old Hector must have heard him, for he stopped and listened. Then he went on—clearly thinking he had not heard anything in this life! It was really difficult for Art to keep the laugh in.

Like an old done stag going to the forest sanctuary, Old Hector was making for the birch wood.

Art stalked him through the trees until he came within a couple of yards of the sitting body, with its still face, about which the bright morning and the pleasant woodland sounds tumbled in happy ease.

But the old man seemed lost in a sad dream, and Art hesitated lest a sudden shout might make him jump too much It was hardly the moment, perhaps, to frighten a man out of his wits, even if the temptation was very great. So the next best thing to do was. . . .

Art noiselessly appeared at Old Hector's side. "Good morning," he said.

Old Hector's mouth fell open as he stared at this boyish apparition, smiling in the dappled light, with a luscious bunch of purple grapes hanging from the right hand.

"God bless me, boy," he whispered.

Then Art laughed.

It was a sound Old Hector had always liked, because when it was quite natural and a little shy it shook the body like a peal of bells.

Old Hector looked about him with such uneasy concern

Knowledge, Wisdom, and Magic

that Art enjoyed the moment even more, and sat down, swaying in careless happiness, and laid the bunch between them. "I kept them for you," he said. "And you needn't be frightened," he added. "There's no-one near. Just ourselves."

"Well, well," said Old Hector on a last big breath. He shook his head.

"Did I astonish you?"

"You have never done anything else."

"Am I good at it?"

"Too good for an old man like me."

"Am I?"

"You take the breath itself clean from me."

"Ach, that was nothing to what I can do sometimes. I nearly caught a bluetit one morning with my naked hand. Do you think a bluetit is the most beautiful bird in it?"

"About that——" And then Old Hector paused, for out in the pure sunlight, framed by near branches, a grey wagtail hovered. Entranced, they both watched it hang on nothing with incomparable grace. Old Hector slowly nodded, his eyes glimmering in tribute.

As the wagtail fluttered away, Art nodded, too. "I think maybe it's the best."

"Maybe it is," said Old Hector. "Though I will say that the bluetit, with its blue bonnet, takes a lot of beating in its own way."

"Try them," said Art.

The grape smashed in Old Hector's mouth and juice came out at his eyes. He nodded, but could not speak for a moment.

"The best yet?"

"By far and away," replied Old Hector huskily. "Where did you get them?"

"You'd never guess?"

"I would never try."

"In the special orchard on the slope of the Seat," Art confessed.

Knowledge, Wisdom, and Magic

"Where did you sleep last night?"

"I'll give you three guesses."

Old Hector gave three guesses through his growing bewilderment, for indeed only now did he realise that Art should be in captivity.

Art shook his head three times. "No. I slept in the Seat."

"God bless me," whispered Old Hector, "did you escape from that?"

Then Art swayed in his merriment again, his eyes glancing and brighter than any bird's.

Some of this merriment went into the old man. There was an inconsequence about the boy, a bubbling up of life, so vivid, so real, that it was more real than anything else. The sunlight, the fluttering leaves, the slim still trunks of the silver birches, the darting bird, the sound of the tumbling water, the blue sky—the boy drew them into himself as flame draws air.

Never had Old Hector known him like this. For the fear and the hunting should have been wearing him down. He might have tried to laugh—but his eyes should at least have been furtive. He was so young, little more than a child. Yet here he was, a slim immortal boy, into whom a strange virtue had passed, a living grace.

"It's easy to escape," said Art. "The Starter from Clachdrum——"

"Who?"

And then Art told how he had first met the Starter, how he had called "Hector! Hector!" and raced down—down the bank—in through the water—"and then, and then—it wasn't you at all. Wouldn't you call that very unexpected?"

"I would indeed," nodded Old Hector.

"It was," agreed Art. "But I saw at once he wouldn't tell on me. So it was all right. And after that we had the greatest adventures. He's the rarest man you ever met. Oh, he's good! There isn't a thing he can't do—except maybe—I mean, when it comes to the racing——"

Knowledge, Wisdom, and Magic

"But then, he would be an oldish man, and you——"

"Yes," said Art, "and, between ourselves, they wouldn't have caught me yon time, only I didn't like to leave him—you know what I mean?"

"I do indeed."

"But you needn't tell that to him. Because he was awfully clever later on. You wouldn't believe it." Art looked at the old man doubtfully. "Do you remember the nuts from the great cluster that I put in this pocket—remember, at the Hazel Pool?"

Remembering, Old Hector smiled as he used to do long ago many a time.

"They were the nuts of knowledge all right. When I was hard pressed, I always took one. And it helped me at once. Well, I had two left. So there we were prisoners——"

"Where?"

"In the Town House." And in a few words, for he was in a hurry to get to the real marvel, Art told how they had been taken through the great crowds and locked up. "Now remember you used to tell about how Finn MacCoul ate the salmon of wisdom? That was quite right. Because it's no use eating the nuts of knowledge only. It's some use, maybe, but not the whole thing. Do you see?"

"I see," said Old Hector.

Art paused and looked into the distance. "Remember yon time when my brother Donul brought home the salmon and I burnt my finger trying to get the first taste of it in order to get the wisdom?"

"I do," said Old Hector.

"Yon couldn't have been the real salmon."

"Couldn't it?"

"No, because I had a feeling I never really got it—the wisdom, I mean. Sometimes I might let on I had it, but—you know——"

"I know," said Old Hector.

Knowledge, Wisdom, and Magic

Art nodded quickly. "And it couldn't have been the real salmon—do you know why?—because the Starter from Clachdrum got the real one. He has the wisdom."

"Did he tell you that?"

"He did. And it's quite true—because I know. And do you know how?"

"How?"

"Because—because there's another thing." Art's voice dropped a tone in a way both solemn and eager at the same time. "You see, first of all you get the knowledge. Then you get the wisdom. You follow that?"

"I follow."

"Then," said Art, another tone down, "you get something else." And he looked at Old Hector who looked at him.

"What?" asked Old Hector.

"The magic," said Art.

But if he had feared old Hector might smile, he was mistaken. The old man's face took on a profound expression, that was both solemn and bright with light. Slowly he nodded. "You have it all there," he said. He fell into a meditation, and murmured to the deep distance, "I wondered what it was in his face."

"What?" said Art, watching him.

"Magic," murmured Old Hector to himself coming out of his meditation. He nodded, and at once Art felt even more happy.

"Well," said Art, "there we were all locked up. And I only had the two nuts left. And I told him they were the nuts of knowledge and I had my knife. So I wasn't long getting the shells off. Then we ate them, and then he said to me that if I gripped his hand and we shut our eyes then there would be the magic." He gave Old Hector a sidelong glance.

"And was there?"

"There was."

"What was it like?"

"It wasn't like anything," confessed Art. "I just closed my

226

eyes—and when I opened them we weren't in the Town House at all. Do you know where we were? You'll never guess!"

"Where?" said Old Hector, looking at him.

"We were in the Seat."

"Were you indeed?"

"We were. And do you know where we went next?"

"No."

"Into the Industrial Peak."

"Did you though?" said Old Hector calmly. "And what did you see there?"

"Remember the pictures in yon book of the miners working underground?" said Art with animation. "Well, it was like that, only—oh, bigger. There were great boiling pots, each one as big as a room, and caverns, and men stripped to the waist pushing little waggons that ran on shining rails, and lights everywhere, and gloom, and places going away, away into the earth. You wouldn't believe there was such an awful place. It would frighten anyone, wouldn't it?"

"It would indeed. And did anyone speak to you?"

"No. They never even looked at us, as if we weren't in it. I—I didn't like it."

"You wouldn't, I'm sure."

"And then we went to another Peak." Art hesitated. "It's queer, isn't it? how we just went, and there we were."

"Just as in a dream?"

"Yes," said Art eagerly—and then he paused, for he thought he saw the glimmer of a smile in his old friend's eyes.

"Perhaps you were dreaming somewhere," suggested Old Hector.

"No," said Art, though suddenly a wild misgiving had him —and then in an instant he had Old Hector by the shoulder and was shoving him flat to the ground.

Presently seven women appeared, coming from Bigtrees. They looked like seven on a pilgrimage and the talking among them beat seagulls among herring.

Knowledge, Wisdom, and Magic

When they had passed, Art said, "That's Tom's sister Nancy, and Peggy Morrison, and Bets Grant, and Jean Robertson, and the other three are new to me."

"Where can they be going?" wondered Old Hector.

"Wait," said Art. "Wait here." In a moment he was gone.

Old Hector sat until there filed into the wandering blank in his mind the three—and he knew they were the immortal three—knowledge, wisdom, and magic.

He had never thought of magic before like that, the light in the eye, the mystery for which there is no word, the *living* mystery. When knowledge completes itself in wisdom, magic is released—as Art was in his sleep!

Art had to shake him. "Come on!" he cried with low-toned urgency. "They're coming for you. Hurry! I know a place."

"Who's coming?" asked Old Hector.

"The Hunt," said Art. "They're coming for you. Quick!"

Old Hector got slowly to his feet, and, smiling, shook his head sadly.

Art stared at him. "You're not going to give yourself up?"

"My time has come upon me," said Old Hector.

"No!" said Art, and his eyes grew brilliant in distress.

"Take care of yourself." Old Hector smiled upon the boy out of the ancient deep kindness that was native to his eyes. Then he turned away slowly towards the sounds that were already in the wood.

XXXVII

THE CHAMPIONS TAKE A FALL

Lift the top off a hive, poke the ant-heap with a stick. Such was life in the corporate City on the Rock.

For by corporate instinct it got known that there was something wrong at the focal point, the generating centre.

The Champions Take a Fall

The scouts were aware of this, equally with the workers. Something was amiss with the brood chamber.

The conferences with God in the Seventh Peak went on and went on.

The famous Questioner had shot back to his own Peak, staring straight in front of him.

But he was no sooner back than another took his place in the carriage and set out. In no time, however, the carriage had returned—to pick up the next champion.

Brilliant representatives of the most advanced Regions, champions in dialectic, they sallied forth, in turn, to the great encounter, and at least achieved one circumstance in common, namely, that they all returned more quickly than they went.

What had happened? Could they have failed? Was God knocking them over like a row of pins?

The excitement of the populace mounted like waves that smoke in a gale.

There was excitement, too, in the room of the champions in the Administrative Peak, but how different the excitement there!

When the Questioner of the Thirteenth returned defeated, his colleagues buzzed around him. Having drawn from him all that had happened, they were amazed. Clearly they could not believe that he had omitted to ask simple persons like Old Hector and Robert and Mary if they had eaten the fruit. It was so obviously the very first question any of them would have asked that, out of consideration for their distinguished colleague, they almost refrained from shaking their heads. Yet this was the very man whose reputation had been growing so quietly and steadily that the Head himself looked upon him with special favour! What could they make of it?

They had hardly begun to make nothing of it before the champion of the Eleventh rolled back.

What, back already?

"The beehive," muttered the Eleventh champion.

The Champions Take a Fall

Surely not the beehive! Never the beehive!

"Yes, the beehive," he replied angrily. "I was floored with the old beehive." He flung his arms wide in a flailing gesture and collapsed in a chair.

But the beehive as an example of the corporate state—the thing was elementary! Its evolution of a corporate intelligence —known to the meanest mind! To be floored by that!

"I was not floored like that," shouted the fallen champion. "Of course I know that the workers are neuters. I was prepared for the neuters and the drones and the appalling fecundity of the corporate queen. There was no subtlest analogy there but I could parry. What do you take me for?"

But, then . . . !

"It's not that. It's that the whole affair has gone static. There is no lifting of the corporate beehive mind into a universal mind—even a universal beehive mind." He flung his arms again.

But . . . !

"But of course I saw His point. Do you think I would let Him take me for a fool? But I was not going to let Him off with it. No fear! So I looked Him straight in the eye and asked: 'Why then create a thing that reaches a dead end?' "

Ah! . . .

"Do you know what He answered me?" The Eleventh champion leaned forward from his chair, scanning their faces. "I see no one of you would risk making a guess!" He leaned back on his irony. "He answered me: '*Why, indeed?*' "

The silence grew pregnant. Then from it swarmed forth: "The reply was a trick!" "After all, He *had* created the beehive!" "You shouldn't have let Him off with that!" . . .

The champion groaned. "At least I know about beehives," he said. "If you cannot think of anything better than that to say, we may as well pack up. For surely the inference is clear that unless we deliberately want to make a beehive, with neuters and corporate mind all complete, a static nightmare in

The Champions Take a Fall

the evolving Universal, then——" He flailed. "Who made the first accursed beehive is beside the point."

"You do Him an injustice," said the Questioner of the Thirteenth with suave irony. "The inference is that we shall create a beehive here, unless Someone interferes to stop us, as He did not interfere in the bees' beehive."

"Why encumber our thought with unnecessary inference?" asked another. "It is a question of a question, not of an inference. And the question is simply: Why, if we consider the hive a dead-end, do we build one? And our answer must show that we are *not* building one. It is quite simple. He did not say we were building one; all He said was *Why, indeed?*"

"But why did He say it?"

"Why, indeed?" asked yet another in a distracted voice.

When the argument had attained considerable intricacy, the next champion returned with no less than two unresolved points. The first was that the more man concentrated on his administrative power the more he came to believe that this was the only kind of power that existed. The more it was believed that everything was economic the less it was seen that anything was psychic.

The second point derived from the first: Concentrate entirely on the outward, the physical, and clearly the inner, the spiritual, will be forgotten; there then follow certain results, which, on earth at least, were seen to be appalling—that is, of course, if the horrors of war were appalling.

"These were two points which I had specially studied. So I felt on sure ground. Indeed I started by showing that concentration on the inner only might have as unfortunate results as concentration on the outer only. What we were trying to achieve was a balance of all forces, an integration leading to an ever higher integration, and so——"

"What did He answer?"

"He admitted it. He said, *Your theory is excellent.*"

The Questioner of the Thirteenth laughed aloud.

The Champions Take a Fall

There was commotion for a little while. Then the champion, not unruffled, proceeded:

" . . . And so at last I brought the matter to the test. For we must face up to it. I said we were prepared to be judged by our fruits."

"What did He answer?"

"As a matter of fact, He answered, *Which fruit?* but——"

The same Questioner laughed again.

After a little while this argument began to get intricate also, but with the edge of bitterness that had lined the Questioner's laugh.

Their faces were growing pale; yet the more they felt themselves losing ground as each new champion returned, the more avid and even ruthless their faces became. It was quite clear now that, before coming to the Seat, He had shed His meditations and possibly been in actual contact with certain disturbing elements; either that or He had deliberately concentrated on the whole situation, observing by clairvoyance and other august attributes of His omniscience exactly what was taking place—a thing He so rarely did.

However, great hopes were placed on the Master of the Fifth Region. For he was perhaps the Green Isle's most brilliant mathematician. It was he, in truth, who had shown that there was no need to take Art into consideration, any more than electrons or protons, in describing the pattern of events.

Not until the grey light of the morning did he return. The discussion had been of great length and classic proportions, so much so that the Master of the Fifth Region had forgotten himself in the mathematician and would have held the discourse exclusively to its mathematical realm, where it was easy as falling off a logarithm to give a sheaf of formulae for an infinite series of corporate minds.

The appalling trouble about an ordinary silly feeling, about individual psychology generally, was that the miserable illogical stuff was insusceptible of mathematical demonstration. You had only to try to demonstrate it for it itself to say No.

Then, at a culminating point in the discussion that concerned the grafting of the mathematical absolute upon the mechanical absolute, a sentence had been uttered by Him—and the Master of the Fifth had been reduced to a searching silence.

He was still searching and silent when he returned. The others gazed at his abstracted air as he sat in his chair, legs extended, looking unseeingly over his toes.

To himself he muttered the sentence.

Heads were lowered. "What's that?"

And he repeated: "*The psychic barometer dispenses with psychic apprehension.*"

Certain physical movements implied that this was a thought-provoker which stung in the elusive place it was difficult all at once to put a finger on much less to scratch.

Presently a glimmer came to the face of the Master of the Fifth, a faraway look such as occasionally troubles the face of an ordinary idiot, and he murmured softly: "One thing I will say: He fairly knows His mathematics."

XXXVIII

THE MACDONALD AT THE END OF THE DAY

From the middle of the milk-float, Old Hector raised his arm in farewell. Robert and Mary waved strongly. The four Hunters, two in front and two behind, went forward up the slope at a smart walking pace.

The firm politeness, even deference, that had been shown to the old man by the four now troubled him. He would rather

The Macdonald at the End of the Day

have walked, but they said their orders were to take him in a carriage, and as this was not a carriage road, they had done the next best.

Nothing could have been better devised to increase his mood of isolation and loneliness, and to that mood was now added the sadness, nearly the bitterness, of the reflection that Mary and Robert had clearly placed their last hope in him.

But Mary and Robert were forgotten when on the high road to the Main Gate people stopped and stared—and then whispered. And the whisper flew in front and behind, and gathered the people in whirling eddies as a wind gathers scattered leaves.

"It's Old Hector—the man who wants to see God!"

The middle of that milk-float became lonelier than any small rock in any ocean. His head bobbed, for the float had only two wheels, and he felt like one who was being taken to his execution. And not only his own execution, but the execution of other lives and times and places, and the bobbing of his head was the mockery put upon him.

Then, here and there, people began to call his name. "Hector!" they called. "Hector!"

And as, growing bolder, they eddied behind, he could see they were laughing, but not scornfully.

Then a voice from a high window called: "Do your best, Hector!"

At that there was a cheer.

And this was bitterer than any mockery.

The great gate to the forecourt, which he knew so well, was closed, for all the ordinary business of receiving new arrivals was temporarily suspended. The seven dark women from Bigtrees were there. They had been clamouring for admission. There was a fair crowd as well. But the roar that greeted Hector was like the roar of a host. The seven dark women easily fought their way to the milk-float. There was neither fear nor doubt in them. Indeed there was little in them but

234

anger and fight. They stopped the float by sheer weight and climbed onto it and grasped Hector's hands and shook them. What they said lacked neither in clarity nor in force.

To shed the women and get the float through the gates, with Old Hector still enthroned, took the better part of ten minutes.

What with the bobbing and the inner stress and the outer turmoil, there was some dizziness now in the old man's head, the dizziness of one who has gone under for the first time. The looming face of the great building began to waver in ascending ripples. His own legs seemed to waver as he was set down by the door, but these same legs held him upright, and even with a strange buoyancy began to carry him between the wavering pillars. The interior now was a vast sea-green cavern, and the corridors undulated slowly like sea-serpents waiting with their mouths open. In one mouth Axle stood, and in this under-sea of distortion his face had the look of a pike. Merk flowed by another mouth like an eel. Sweet Innocence had the remarkable appearance of a simple but astonished haddock standing on its tail.

Merk came wavering towards him. Old Hector could now hear no sound but the soft choking buzz in his ears. He floated away with Merk through a door that opened upon that room where the high officials and champions were gathered together.

Here the sea-green was faintly irradiated with blue, and while this for some reason brought an extra pallor to the faces, it darkened the bodies, so that the denizens of this inner cave seemed mostly faces. And strange faces they were, solemn as the faces of all fish are solemn, and sharp. Their round eyes never blinked, but were steady even in the moving water. Then the water grew steady, and all that was left were the eyes.

They were the eyes that a pearl diver of an Eastern sea encounters only in his nightmare. Before them the breath bubbles up from him and he can no more rise to the surface.

The Macdonald at the End of the Day

With expressionless menace, they float towards him, and he falls over.

As Old Hector began to sink down, a seat came to meet him. Then a face moved—towards him. It was the face of the Questioner in the guise of a shark. The shark opened its soundless mouth.

In his day, Old Hector had seen brutes like conger eels or dogfish worry a dead cod on the sea's floor. His hands came up and covered his heart, for he knew it was for the heart that these pallid monsters would now fight.

He slid away from his seat and now exactly opposite him, having also slid away from his seat, was the figure of the great mathematician of the Fifth Region and his mouth was twisted to one side like the mouth of a flounder or a lemon sole, and it kept opening and shutting as if repeating a strange sentence to itself, and the whole twist of the face had yet such a twist of puzzled humour that Old Hector wondered, before he passed away, what this innocent fish was doing in so hungry a company.

As he felt himself being hauled to the surface, Old Hector opened his eyes, waved aside the drinking glass, and managed of his own accord to seat himself in the carriage with its four restless bay horses.

The outside gate was flung open, the vast crowd—for it had greatly increased—was pushed back by a contingent of the Hunt, and the carriage drove slowly through.

Surely for any other being, mortal or immortal, this would have been a procession of triumph.

But the rearing of the horses above the breaking waves of faces, the multitudinous acclaiming sounds which uprose and fell far away only to rise again as the near wave broke, the surge of that ocean against the bastions of Peak after Peak, was too much for this simple man, who out of all life confirmed now in this final journey only the dread and utter nature of his own lonely insufficiency. That there were those who could put

The Macdonald at the End of the Day

their trust in him seemed in this moment to make of all humanity something inexpressibly pitiful and sad, vast and forlorn and lost, and the old man bowed his head in sorrow and in shame.

As the spindrift of laughter and of hope whirled faster and higher, deeper sank the old man, and in truth he felt it coming upon him that he was going under for the second time, when the carriage stopped suddenly and jolted him. As his head jerked upward, his eyes stared at the Great Gate before the entrance to the Audience Halls of the Seventh Peak.

His time had come upon him, and, feeling the vague need for a last farewell of all he had known and often loved, he lifted his eyes to the blue of the sunny sky.

But they never reached that azure of pure peace, for sitting astride a gargoyle to starboard of the Great Gate, with bare legs dangling and the left hand gripping the stone hair of the gargoyle's head, was the figure of a boy. The right hand saluted and waved, and the mouth in the vivid face opened, and from it came the battle-cry of Old Hector's clan, for Old Hector was a Macdonald, and his clan had many a time found itself sore beset, but never, as its rallying cry showed, had it lost faith, had it lost hope.

So "Hector! Hector!" cried Art at first, eagerly, and then, when he had drawn the old man's eyes, came the ancient cry: *"The Macdonald at the end of the day!"*

It was a great help to Old Hector, not so much the cry, maybe—though while the blood remains warm it travels its own hidden ways to and from the ancient heart—as the sight of the boy himself.

Old Hector fell away from the vagueness of crowds and the formless roar of corporate sound, and so falling he forgot himself in the vision of the boy. For the boy was real. If, then, for this one boy he could yet do something, the smothering away of himself in shame and dissolution might find its own lonely moment of final peace. Inasmuch as he might do this to Art, he might do it to that which had somehow always seemed right in his heart.

They were quiet in their voices and friendly, those who waited for the messenger to come to take Old Hector to the Audience.

Ah, but then the footsteps came, and they came walking on the heart, and the breath grew thick in his nostrils and a great heaviness beset him.

"You are ready?"

"I am ready," answered Old Hector, and he lifted his head, and if he walked slowly, he walked steadily and with dignity, for at the end of the day he was a Macdonald, and not even a child should depend on him but he would do what he could. More than that no man can do. Never let it be said in the histories of the world that a Macdonald did less.

The shades of his people now went with him, the people of the clan, those who knew what was right and true in all time, his own people everywhere, the sons of men.

The messenger opened the last door.

XXXIX

THE AUDIENCE

Whether from a flow of blood to his head or not, Old Hector experienced a slight darkening of his vision as he entered, and the bearded face of the man who awaited him seemed, in that strange moment, to be the face of someone he had seen long long ago in a tall mirror at the end of a landing in a forgotten house.

The face looked back at him and smiled, and Old Hector went forward and took the extended hand. And then the voice in Gaelic, saying:

The Audience

"How are you?"

And because Old Hector was bewildered by this second strange familiarity, he answered in the same tongue:

"Fine, thank you. I hope you are well yourself?"

"Very well, thank you. And how did you leave them all at home? Please sit down."

Old Hector sat down.

"They cannot complain," he replied politely. "Agnes may be worrying a little, but she always had a lot to do."

His Host nodded. "Perhaps she is a little of the worrying kind," he said, "for affection finds many an odd way of expressing itself."

"Indeed and that's true," replied Old Hector. "I remember trying to tell the boy as much when we came away, but he's young."

"Have you seen him lately?"

"I have," said Old Hector at once, but his face clouded. "He was sitting on a stone head by the Great Gate as I came in."

His Host smiled.

Old Hector swallowed nothing, for his mouth was very dry. He would wake up in a moment, when these politenesses were over, to be taken where he must be taken, for this could hardly be the final place and the last occasion. But apart from that hidden fear, the talk was comforting beyond measure.

"And how have you enjoyed your sojourn on the Green Isle of the Great Deep?"

"It has had its ups and downs maybe," replied Old Hector, trying to smile, "but it is a beautiful place."

"You have been in trouble?"

"I have," confessed Old Hector, "but if so it was myself who was to blame for it. At my age I ought to have had more sense. But—I hadn't. And I am very sorry for that."

"Are you?"

"Yes, indeed. Not that I matter much. But I was thinking of the boy. If he ate the fruit, it was I who encouraged him.

239

The Audience

And when he hid, it was I who would not tell where he was. If only I could deserve that that should be visited upon me." Old Hector bowed his head.

"Is there anything else?"

"Robert and Mary——"

"Yes?"

"I had words to say, but they have gone from me. Once I was pushed far—and then I asked to come. I see now it was a great presumption. But for the boy, and Robert and Mary——"

"Who pushed you too far?"

"It was when the Questioner was trying to get me to tell the truth and I wouldn't tell it. I couldn't," confessed Old Hector remorsefully.

"Why?"

"I don't know. It seemed to me that deeper than my lie and his questioning, there was something hard and cruel. It was all being done for the best, I know, but—I couldn't help it. It was not what I had expected."

"Did you feel there was something forgotten?"

"I did." He lifted his face, and the room gave him the ease of distance. "They have great knowledge, and everything is done to perfection. They are far beyond me, and who am I to talk? I do not understand this new life."

"But what?"

"It is the feeling that—they live in their heads."

"The face is pale—the questioning face—and, without feeling, it bores into you, to lay you bare."

"It does," answered Old Hector quietly. "They take the heart out of you."

"Your heart?"

"I think," answered Old Hector, "I would have given them my heart to save all trouble, had it not been for the boy—and Mary."

They sat in silence for a long time.

The Audience

"That is bad," said the Host thoughtfully. "Nothing could be worse than that."

The silence now fell softly, and its ease came about Old Hector's spirit.

"It is bad," continued the Host, "but we cannot blame them. And we cannot blame them because we leave things to them, you and me. We forget them. We forget that they live in their heads, where the knowledge of power gives to a good intention the edge of a sword."

"The nuts of knowledge," murmured Old Hector dreamily. "But the salmon is beyond us."

"How is it beyond you?"

"Because it is the landlord's," answered Old Hector. "Those in power keep it within their own law."

"The salmon of wisdom?"

"The salmon is caught in their net, and when the salmon is caught in the net of the law, its wisdom, which must be free, escapes through the mesh."

"But cannot wisdom be within the law?"

"It can," answered Old Hector, "but only also if it can be without. And to be within, it must first be without."

"It must be everywhere?"

"Everywhere," answered Old Hector.

"The problem then is how to bring wisdom to knowledge, so that knowledge, instead of getting the sword's edge, which is cruel and sterile, will be given wisdom which is kind and fruitful."

"Knowledge is high in the head as nuts on a tree, but the salmon of wisdom swims deep. It is very difficult," answered Old Hector.

"Yet the way must be found."

The silence was as the silence of a twilight when the birds sing at the end of a day.

"One thing seems clear,"—and the voice was speaking now in that twilight—"the head alone will never find that way. It

241

has tried and always failed. For in the conscious power of the head there is a fascination. It is the instrument of logic, and it has within it the itch to fashion and sharpen and dissect. It dissects and finds out, and it takes the bits it finds and puts them together in an invention, and then it pulls the trigger. Whether with a system, or a plan, or an instrument—that is what the head alone has always done. There was a time when the Questioner had wisdom. He used his head and drew on his wisdom. But the more he used his head only, the paler his wisdom became, until at last the elements of wisdom were no longer so but only the ghostly bits he used for making a pattern with his head. He knew in his head that you suffered, but as the head itself does not suffer, he himself was not affected, for what is affected swims deep with the salmon. He has divorced knowledge from wisdom, the head from the heart, the intellect from the spirit—for man has many words for these two regions—and because of the divorce, the taste of life has gone bitter and its hope sterile. They think it is not bitter with them yet and not sterile, for they still have the fascination of pulling the trigger, yet sterile with them, too, because they have to destroy."

"Why have they to destroy?" asked Old Hector.

"They have to destroy, because wisdom is always beyond logic at any moment. They have to destroy because though, as you say, their plan for running affairs is smooth, and their concept of the corporate mind permits of a logical exposition, yet as you also say, beneath their plan lies that belief in its logic which always grows merciless. So it has always been. And no matter with what force and cunning the plan is imposed there will be those who will rise against it. And bitter and terrible then is that rising."

"How, then, can wisdom and knowledge be brought together in the affairs of men?"

"How were they brought together in the legend?—for your question is as old as the legend you told to the boy Art."

The Audience

Old Hector's eyes glimmered. "The ripe hazel nuts of knowledge fell into the pool and the salmon of wisdom ate them."

"And was made the wiser for the knowledge he ate. It is the natural order. There is no other."

"And the pool——"

"The pool was everyman's pool in the river of life."

"It is a beautiful legend," said Old Hector. "I never saw it like that before."

"You saw it—but you had not yet brought it into your head in order to put words on it."

"All the same, the putting of words on it makes it beautiful."

"There is one thing that has disturbed me gravely. I find that Robert has made no poems since the *Change*. Not one legend of wisdom has he created."

"I can well understand that. He suffers, too."

"It is the proof," said his Host. "For poems, too, can be made in the head out of a pattern of words. But they are not true poems. They have no eternal life in them and so they never become a legend. Art dies."

Old Hector turned his face and looked at his Host, who smiled and said:

"Young Art is the living poem and the eternal legend. Or is it that he is the poem and the legend set to music, the song?"

The silence was as the twilight of the morning when the birds sing from among the shining fruit on the trees in the orchard, and the pool in the river sends up its slow ripple of humour from the deep movement of the salmon.

The voice now changed from sound into picture, from what was heard by the outer ear to what was seen of the inner eye, and fine it was to sit there and watch the moving picture of the Green Isle of the Great Deep as it should be, on the screen of the mind.

The Audience

Only when the voice spoke out of the head was it overlaid on the picture, and then it was heard as a commentary set to music.

For to achieve the blessed intention, something practical had to be done. Things could not be left in the sole hands of the Administrators. In the story of man, that had been tried times without number and always it had failed.

(The revolving Earth, pitted with its tragedies, cried in a far voice from the midst of space: "You cannot leave me to the politicians.")

But politicians, administrators, are needful, are necessary. To fulfil their high function they work with the cunning of the head. But to leave destiny to the head is to leave the trigger to the finger. And after the trigger is pulled, they cry above the desolation—

(and the desolation was terrible to behold):

"We will make a new earth, and share the fruits thereof and the fishes of the deeps."

But what happens?

The fruit is processed and the salmon is canned.

It cannot be left to them; not solely to them. You have to bring in the wise men.

And suddenly it was as if Old Hector awoke out of the reverie induced by the moving scenes and heard his Host talking quietly:

"Among the Administrators there are two or three who have a certain wisdom. There is for example the mathematician of the Fifth. I am much taken with him, for by nature his cunning is directed towards keeping the discussion in the pure realm of the higher mathematics. This realm is to him his true fulfilment and, in the moment of fulfilment there supervenes the oneness of all formulae, the perfection of the pattern, and the spirit rising through the head opens upon the eternal air like a flower. As a Master Administrator, he is unfortunately liable, therefore, to leave all political affairs to his Vice. But as a

244

The Audience

wise man, among the new council of wise men, his opinion of any proposed change would be of value. For he knows the direction."

Old Hector nodded. As the conception of the Council of the wise men grew clear, he was greatly heartened. And particularly was he pleased when he saw that the Council was to have no power. For well he knew that a wise man will give the best he can distil with the finest grace when he gives freely and without reward.

Where administrators seek the counsel of the wise, blessed will be that land.

Most of the present Administrators, then, would be removed, and in their place would come those who had the urge to serve in an administrative capacity and who from time to time would have to consult with the Council of the wise men.

Old Hector could not help nodding. For behind the wise men was this Wisdom that saw. And this Wisdom haunted man. That was its awful potency, its strange and elusive delight. Man might get power in the head and destroy without measure, but the Wisdom would haunt and draw him. The mathematician knew the direction; the saint knew the way. Too long had the head-hunters ruled them without mercy, turning their mathematics in the direction of death and their saintliness to the way of disintegration in the atomic psychology chamber. Too long, O Wisdom!

Knowledge and wisdom——

"And magic," murmured Old Hector, "which is the scent of the flower, the young feet of the runner, and the deep smile in the face."

And these three are all?

"All," nodded Old Hector.

Have you forgotten the Creator?

From staring into the distance, Old Hector turned his head and looked at the face of his Host. And so it came upon him that here indeed was the last place and the final occasion.

The Audience

The Creator? That which creates?

"Love," breathed Old Hector.

The eyes of his Host were deep as the salmon pool that stirs gently on its surface when the fish moves below.

But from the eyes came now to Old Hector a new and terrible intelligence. In silence they spoke to him, saying: *You will be one of the Council of the wise men.*

With a great effort he turned his own eyes away, and in his discomfort he hung his head.

The silence spoke to him again.

"No," he answered in a small voice.

Why not?

"I am not wise enough to be one of the Council. I am ignorant and unfitted for it."

Knowledge of ignorance is the end of so much knowledge and the beginning of wisdom.

"No," muttered Old Hector. "I would only like to do what I could."

His discomfort now became a faint distress.

If the wise refuse, who will be in it at the end of the day?

At that, Old Hector tried to smile. "The honour is too great for me. . . . But you know me," he decided, lifting his head, "and what is of me I will try to give."

Why is distress still on your face?

"If only," murmured Old Hector, and he turned in appeal to his Host. Clear now it was that he would not ask for anything lightly.

Yes?

All the salmon pools of the world glimmered expectantly in the sun.

"If only," said Old Hector, "I could find my wife—she would keep me right."

XL

THE LAST JUMP

It was truly very pleasant to listen to the birch wood singing through its individual birds and to observe the Highland cattle disport themselves in an unusual manner on the other side of the burn.

For altogether it was an unusual day. It was, in fact, a holiday, and all the people everywhere had come forth to see what it would be like.

And quite naturally it was just like what they had wanted it to be, only more so because there were more individuals with different antics than anyone could have anticipated.

The cattle, for example, were not merely surprised at the shouts and the goings-on, but also showed it by kicking up their heels, mooing, and looking at any moment as if they might charge—then, wheeling, they charged their own shadows.

The children who had been let loose from the schools were affected in a similar fashion.

From long disuse, the grown-ups came at all this with groping difficulty. The cows made them cry with a mirth that though thin choked now and then on real laughter.

To a girl like Mavis, of course, the sense of responsibility adhered more strongly. Though confused somewhat by the knowledge, which she never forgot for a moment, that Tom's eye had her under fairly constant observation, she manipulated her four apples with the proper detachment of a school mistress.

The four small children, sitting before her, considered them with a concentration in which there was less detachment.

The Last Jump

"Now," said Mavis, "I take these two apples and add them to these two, and what have we?"

"Four," answered a little boy.

"Quite correct," answered Mavis.

But the mathematician, who was watching this elementary demonstration of the unsearchable meaning of number, shook his head.

"Now," said Mavis, "if I take two away—what's left? You, Shiela."

"Two apples," said Shiela, who liked the idea of apple.

"Very good," said the mathematician aloud.

They all turned and looked at him, and he smiled on them in such a way that they saw he was quite harmless. The urge to attempt the distinction between "four" and "four apples" nearly got the better of him but not quite, and he continued to take the profoundest interest in the lesson.

When at last number was divided equally among the four scholars and they began to consume its mystery, he regarded the rite in so concentrated a manner that Shiela timidly approached him and asked if he would like a bite.

He refused in such a way that Shiela trusted him completely. Thus he was able to continue to observe how she would deal with the whole insoluble problem.

She dealt with it without the slightest difficulty.

Mary was very busy and people watched her with wonder as she moved about, for though every preparation had been made for the Feast of the Fruit, it might easily happen that some children had dodged their dose of herb jelly.

"You're very busy," Old Hector called to her as she climbed up.

"I'm fair run off my feet," she said, and threw herself down, her cheeks in a rosy flush.

"Take you a rest," said Old Hector. "It's pleasant up here."

And it was in truth particularly pleasant by the edge of the birch wood. The fields and the orchards lay quiet under

The Last Jump

wandering and running feet, while here and there distant groups from the Industrial Peak disposed themselves with an air of wonder. What were they talking about?

The town was white, and the Seven Peaks stood against the sky with folded wings.

It was difficult to look at anything very long for a strange turmoil that started in the breast, a turmoil which had no words but only the awful and exciting difficulty of the ineffable, as if it were to be found not to-day but to-morrow, not here but round the invisible corner.

No wonder it set children running and jumping and grown-up people groping after laughter. For running and jumping and laughter engage the attention that is not yet strong enough to look too long.

But then again, like the mathematician's apples, the running and the laughter had something of it as well.

Of them all, Old Hector was the only one who knew a word for it. And that made him think of Art.

"If the little fellow was here now," he said, "it would remind him of the Day of the Games at Clachdrum."

"I wonder where in the Isle he can be?" sighed Mary, with the mixture of concern and resignation women have for children of his age.

"That was the day," continued Old Hector, who had no concern, "that he won the race. Proud he was that night."

"He has done a bit of practising since then," said Robert. They could not help laughing, including Mary.

"He has a new word now," said Old Hector.

"A new word?" repeated Robert, turning his head quickly. For once more he had become a poet.

Old Hector nodded. "He got it from the Starter of the race at Clachdrum. Here, he met him for the first time over there on the green. That was the night Art was caught—you'll remember that night?"

An even rosier colour came to Mary's face.

The Last Jump

"Well, they were caught, as you know, and taken to the town and shut in a room. Do you know how they escaped from that room?"

"No," answered Robert.

"By *magic*," said Old Hector.

After a moment, Robert smiled in a peculiar way, for, of course, the word was very old, and only mathematicians had been able to find anything new in it, and then only because they dealt with imaginary numbers, the square root of minus one, and the dimensions that began where the third ended. All the same, he looked over the fields and the orchards and he saw the groups whose words he could not hear. And he saw the white town and the Seven Peaks whose wings were folded under the blue dome of the sky.

But the word spoken to-morrow he could not yet catch, nor that which was round the invisible corner could he see— but, oh, so very very nearly, that the ghosts of words began to stir in the deep wood.

He paled and his eyes glowed. . . .

He began to see the people round the corner, and they were dancing in eightsomes and sixteensomes, and they were singing, for they couldn't sit still because the happiness in them was so energetic from the poems and the dramas and the leaping spirit, the high laughter that was magic's cry, and the fruit, the golden oranges, the russet apples and the red, tossed and thrown, in arcs and flying patterns, grapes in high relief, fountains falling like a woman's hair, the golden grain, the spirit of the golden grain distilled by wisdom, the peace of talk and the contemplation of most subtle silence, the direction and the way, and all all in the ascending that goes deep and in the outward that penetrates, around the corner made visible, to-morrow and to-morrow and to-day.

"Look!" said Mary, in so low and dramatic a voice that it was one of the ghosts speaking out of the wood.

They looked, and lo! there was Art-of-the-surprises staging

The Last Jump

his master surprise, with an ease that was the greatest he had yet achieved.

For he had hold of the hand of the Starter from Clachdrum, and as they walked together down from the Ridges, he occasionally gave a small skip, for he was inclined to miss his step when the conversation was very interesting, and the extra skip gave him time to turn half round and look up into his companion's face.

Out of the silence that fell upon the watchers, Mary, in a whisper, asked of Old Hector:

"Is it Him?"

And Old Hector answered gravely, "It is."

They could not take their eyes away, much less their bodies, so what had to be would be now.

Art, however, was so various in his interest that when he came to the place where he had been in the habit of taking a running jump to himself he stopped to point out his longest leap.

"Wasn't that a good one?"

"Fair to middling," replied the Starter.

At that challenge, Art spat on his hands.

"I think I could beat it now," he said. "Watch me."

He withdrew a long distance, then, steadying himself, came running like the wind, shot from the mark into the air, and landed without falling backward. It was a wonderful jump.

"Five inches out," he shouted.

"Fully," agreed the Starter.

"You couldn't beat that," said Art.

"Couldn't I?" said the Starter.

"I should like to see you try," challenged Art, laughing sceptically.

"I may astonish you," said the Starter, nodding. Taking a few steps backward from the mark, he steadied himself.

"Mind, if you fall by the back," cried Art, "it will be a foul and won't count."

The Last Jump

The Starter nodded—then, in an instant, he was down on the mark and off—off—off through the air . . . He was gone! There was no Starter! There was no-one! . . . There was nothing.

Struck by a dark wind, with the sun burning itself to a sizzle in the sky, Art was seized by the fear that sends the feet running round in a circle, tethered to the cry in the throat. Then he felt for Old Hector, and he grabbed him, and together they rolled in the agony of the slow recovery, in the terrible pains of the blackness, in the awful choking sickness, fighting the nameless that clawed at them, with the Green Isle drowning like a moon of terror in the gulf of a stormy night.

XLI

THE WAY BACK

The first thing Art saw when he opened his eyes was the face of Mavis, which was above him. But though the bewilderment of the terror was in him to the exclusion of all else, he had not the power to raise his fist to push that face away. Then his whole body took a slow squirming wriggle to itself and his mouth opened so wide that the throat tried to come out of him, not to mention the region below, but all that came out was a dribble of water.

"That's you!" said her voice, but with such a cry of gladness in it that it was like a cry of distress. "He's coming round!" And she turned him on his face and slowly squeezed the light and the water out of him.

By the time this had happened more than once, he was so full of the pains of anger that he would have bit her leg had he been able. So far, however, he couldn't bite his thumb.

Then she began to say things, to cry them to him in an

urgent yet intimate voice, such as, "Art! My own Art! My lovely little boy! O Art my darling!" that though he was smothered by them, there yet was in the smothering a fearful comfort. This so roused him that he tried to tear the comfort and did actually get a weak wallop home somewhere. Whereat she laughed with delight, she laughed and she wept.

As he saw the tears running down her laughing face, he also saw that this was not the face of Mavis, but the face of Morag his sister.

In the given circumstances, one might easily say that nothing could have been more bewildering.

But it could, for nothing less than Art's own word could have described the way in which grass, rock, water, tree, in which all the dreadful and disparate elements, the unknown and menacing, suddenly took on the look of the known and the familiar, and in such a sunny way that the Hazel Pool all but smiled at his surprise. So might a nose, a mouth, an eye, strewn about the grass, come together in a friendly face.

There were other cries, too, for Tom-the-shepherd had been working on Old Hector, and now that ancient warrior, mouth open and gasping, was hanging on to his beard by the right hand, the better to keep the way clear from his mouth.

And that wasn't everything. For Tom and Morag between them had got together the elements of a picnic. It was their first picnic, and much scheming and great secrecy had gone to its making. No shred of evidence had been allowed to escape, except maybe that piece of newspaper which the wind had snatched off their basket and Art had caught, but which they had deemed it unwise to leave the shelter of the Little Glen in order to recover.

The pan for the tea had been on the fire when Art's scream before he went under came down the river.

Behold now Morag coming running with the basket and the steaming pan.

The Way Back

Thus did the two young lovers, who seemed, indeed, by the way they found it unnecessary to look at each other, to be but the merest chance acquaintances, give their picnic in the service of that one under whose spell they had now been for a considerable, if somewhat fugitive, period.

Morag, in fact, was a little beside herself. She sat and stood at the same time. Even Art found out some while back that she was good-looking. Now even Tom was astonished almost. She was more than a wild rose; she was a fire. And she saw to it that silence had no more chance than the snowflake on the river. After all, she was the only woman among them and life was her concern. And life she brought back as far as it could come.

Until at last Art rebelled, for he refused to be removed by her to have his wet clothes taken off him. He did not want to be rubbed down, nor rubbed up. He only wanted to go home. He began to cry.

Whereupon Morag showed how deep and affectionate was her mothering heart, but if she did, Art struggled free and hit her a fair wallop in the process. She took more punishment, laughing. Then Art began his small dance of rage.

"I'm surprised at you," said Tom.

"I don't care s-s-supposing you are," said Art. Which showed the courage that was still in him, for Tom had been his secret hero more than once.

There is no denying the virtue of hot tea and time. But when all the water that could be squeezed out of their clothes, by a process of undressing in parts, had been squeezed, Old Hector got up.

"We'll try and foot it out," he said, "before the cold settles on us."

"Tom will carry Art," said Morag.

"Will not," said Art, who gave his hand to Old Hector, for they had now been in a few battles together.

The Way Back

"Come, then," said Old Hector, and if he staggered a little, it was nothing to wonder at.

But when he had taken no more than six paces, he stopped altogether, and Art stopped, too, and Morag and Tom as well. It was a cock fish of fully twenty pounds and he lay his length on green grass. Behind him the ground uprose in a tuft of grey grass and hazel withies. A bracken frond, which the autumn had touched, curved outward and over his tail. He had the girth which makes length deceptive, so that his proportions had the perfection which becomes legendary. Then there was his colour. It was not, below the blue-black, pure silver. It was silver invaded by gold, as knowledge might be invaded by wisdom. And finally, beyond the mouth, which was closed, lay also on the grass two hazel nuts which had fallen out of a ripe cluster from the bough overhead.

With a secrecy, which even lovers hardly know, Art moved his head slowly and looked up at Old Hector, to catch Old Hector's eyes looking down at him.

"That's as lovely a fish as ever I saw," declared Tom, in the voice of one suddenly inspired. "Good for you, Art boy! Your first and certainly the best that ever came out of the Hazel Pool. And I'll tell you what." He glanced from Art to Old Hector. "Do you think you could manage home alone?"

Old Hector glanced back at him, and Morag was silent for the first time.

"You see," said Tom, "we cannot take the fish home in the daylight, or they would have the law on us, but if Morag and me waited here until it got almost dark, then it would be as easy as falling off a log."

Old Hector nodded in understanding. "What do you think, Art?"

"Where will you bring it to?" Art asked Tom.

"To Hector's barn," answered Tom.

"Will I be there?" asked Art of Old Hector.

The Way Back

"Where else would you be?" asked Old Hector.

And so it was arranged. Old Hector thanked them for their services, and then Art and himself moved off, Art holding to Old Hector's hand.

From the edge of the wood, Morag and Tom watched them slowly climb the slope and pass over the crest. Then Morag's heart misgave her, for woebegone the little fellow had looked.

"We shouldn't have let them go alone. If Art fainted on the way, Old Hector wouldn't have the strength to carry him."

"Nonsense," said Tom. "That's not the first time the old man has been in over the head." He laughed in a light mocking way.

But Morag was not reassured, and nothing would stop her but she must at least go as far as the crest to see how they were faring.

As Tom and Morag lay side by side, looking over the crest, they watched the two adventurers wander on. When a peewit fell away crying down the air, the two stopped to gaze. There was a long curlew's whistle and Art pointed.

Tom laughed. "They're glad to see the birds again."

"Oh, Tom," said Morag, with a catch of her breath, "what if we hadn't been there?"

"It will be a good place wherever we are at any time," answered Tom.

When next they looked at the wanderers, they were resting, but equally clearly they were talking. They got up and went on. Then they stopped, and forgot to sit down, but they kept on talking.

"I wonder," murmured Morag fondly, "what it is they can find to talk about."